A Fox in the Fold

A Runway Dreams Novel

T.K. Ambers

Star Spirit Adventures

Copyright © 2019 T.K. Ambers

All rights reserved. No part of this book may be reproduced, stored, or used in any manner without the prior written permission of the copyright owner, except for the use of brief quotations by the media.

First paperback edition June 2019.

Edited by Kate Seger

Cover designed by GetCovers

Runway Dreams: A Fox in the Fold is a work of fiction. All people, names, places, businesses, events, or incidents are utilized in a fictitious manner. Any resemblance to actual people, alive or deceased, or incidents are strictly coincidental.

Printed in the United States of America in EB Garamond.

Published by Star Spirit Adventures

www.StarSpiritAdventures.com

eBook: 979-8-9878663-3-7

Paperback: 979-8-9878663-4-4

Hardcover: 979-8-9878663-5-1

10 9 8 7 6 5 4 3 2

Books by T.K. Ambers

The Runway Dreams Series:
Runway Dreams: A Pricey Affair
Runway Dreams: A Fox in the Fold
Runway Dreams: Prideful Vengeance

For my family, both blood and adopted.
You know who you are. Without your support,
I wouldn't be who I am today.

A MURDER MYSTERY NOVEL

Runway Dreams

A Fox in the Fold

T.K. AMBERS

Prologue

Many years had passed since they took Neith's brother from the family. She'd been six, and despite her young age, that moment was still fresh in her memory. The smell of her grandfather's pipe tobacco had filled the small room. She could hear her father yelling and her mother pleading. Neith could feel the rough fingers of the officer who restrained her. She tried to break away from the man who held her back, but she was too small. Neith snarled and flailed as hot tears ran down her face. She wanted to go with her brother, but there was no room for a six-year-old girl in her grandfather's life.

Over the years, she begged her parents for more information regarding her grandfather and where he had taken her brother to. He was a worldly businessman, they would say. She didn't understand what that meant. They never spoke of what business he belonged to, and most of the time they changed the topic when she brought it up. The only thing she had learned over the years was that he was a mysterious and powerful man with many unknown allies.

At seventeen, she understood what her place was to be in Egyptian society, but she didn't care. Her life hadn't been easy, and she still had a stale taste in her mouth regarding her grandfather taking her brother and leaving her behind. They'd fled to America for unknown reasons. He gave her brother a better life and left her with the sinking ship that was once their happy little family. She vowed that one day, she would get out, find them, and let her grandfather know how much she hated him for what he'd done.

Sitting in a sterile white room, she waited, slowly circling her thumb around each perfectly manicured nail on her opposite hand. The practice was obsessive but most often came out when she felt impatient. It felt like she'd been sitting on a concrete block for hours. She realized it was her fault alone for sneaking out of school for the third time that month.

While contemplating her situation, the door swung open, and a short, sweaty officer walked in. He eyed her suspiciously, pulling a handkerchief from his pocket and wiping his brow, then shook his head at her and shoved it back into his pocket.

"Why are you here?" he asked with impatience.

"Humph, why don't you tell me? You're the one who brought me in. I'm supposed to be in class," she grumbled. She realized her response would simply aggravate him more.

"Yes, you're supposed to be in class, so why do you seem to have such a problem doing as you should?" he asked.

Narrowing her eyes, she said, "You ask such stupid questions. What do you want me to say?"

He shook his head. "How can you be so disrespectful? You have no other family. I take care of you and make sure you have a home and food. I keep these silly games you play off the record so your future can go unscathed, yet you continue disobeying me. I wish your mother was here, but there is no bringing her back from the dead. I'm sorry we couldn't save her, but these things happen. Illness happens."

A tear ran down Neith's face as she looked up at her uncle. She understood it wasn't his fault, but it still hurt. First, they took her brother, then her father died two years later in a boating accident, and now her mother had passed from illness.

Straightening up, she looked her uncle in the eyes. His face held the sadness she knew so well. His wrinkles and graying hair had grown more prominent over the past few months. He hadn't been the same since her mother's death six months earlier. Neither of them was.

"Listen, I've made a decision regarding our situation." He stepped closer to her and said, "I love you, but we cannot continue with this destructive dance we're doing. I'm sending you away."

Neith's eyes lit up with rage. "What? What do you mean you're sending me away?" she shrieked. Fear settled over her. She never thought her uncle could be capable of such a thing. How could he abandon her?

"Neith!" He slammed his fist down on the table. "You're a smart and gifted young lady, but you're ruining your future. This has not been an easy decision for me." His face softened as he looked at her. "I've been considering this for two months. I know someone who can get you back on track. I don't want to send you away, but you've left me without other options." Her uncle, Akil, rarely showed any form of emotion. A single tear glistened at the corner of one of his eyes, and she could see he was being truthful about the pain he felt over his decision.

Sitting silently, she stared back at him. A knock sounded at the door, and an important-looking man entered. He wore a black suit and shiny black shoes. His dark brown hair was slicked back against his head. A slight smile crossed his lips, and she could see his perfect white teeth shining in the harsh fluorescent light.

"This is your little troublemaker?" His tone was full of amusement. "She doesn't look like much. Her brother at least had a fighter's physique when we recruited him."

Neith's ears perked up.

"Trust me," said her uncle. "Neith's smart, fierce, and stronger than she looks. She can hold her own in a fight. She needs a guiding light to turn her around. I can't do it. If I could, I would've succeeded by now. Believe me when I say you're the last person I wanted to call but the only person I felt I could trust to help her."

"I'm honored." He laughed. "Your father, Faramond, trained me well, but he shouldn't have been so hard on you when you decided to be an officer instead of an agent. There's nothing wrong with that."

Turning away from Akil, the man approached Neith and held his hand out to her. She stared at it blankly.

"I'm Agent Pickett. Go ahead, I won't bite you."

"Hi." She hesitated, but grabbed his hand anyway. The fight had drained out of her and curiosity had set in.

"Do you know who I am?"

"Yes," she replied smugly. "You're Agent Pickett."

"You're a funny one. I can tell we're going to have a blast." He gave her a lopsided grin.

Neith got the feeling that Pickett didn't mean the ha-ha sort of blast. "No, I don't know who you are. Why don't you tell me?"

"Well, young lady, I'm your new daddy." He laughed.

Neith's uncle cringed at the statement but kept quiet.

"That's rich," said Neith. "How do you figure?"

"Well, I may as well be. I'm your handler, darling. You're about to join the United Intelligence Agency. I'll teach you how to fight the good fight."

"Um, aren't I a little young for that?" she asked.

"You're barely a year early, but now and then, we make an exception, and that exception is you. Yay!" he said with enthusiasm. "Anyway, you're no longer Neith Gamal. From here on out, you'll simply be known as F, like the letter. Once you show me what you're made of, I'll give you an alias and a code name. If you fail at your training, you'll, in fact, be F'd, because if we can't fix you, no one can."

"Oh, freakin' sweet. I can't wait," replied Neith. She rolled her eyes at Pickett. "Why F?"

"The F stands for failure, which is what you currently are. Now change that tone, or we're going to have a long, hard journey in front of us. We leave tonight. We're headed to Ireland. You'll be trained in combat, and I will educate you on the UIA. You'll also be tested, and then it will be determined to which division of the UIA you will be assigned. If you're lucky, you'll become a field operative and travel the world."

He continued to grin at her. It was clear he loved his work. Neith's imagination went into overdrive, creating all types of scenarios when she heard the word travel. Maybe this wouldn't be so bad. Perhaps she'd reunite with her brother, and they could fight the so-called good fight, together.

"Sure, what the hell, let's give it a go," she assented and got up from her seat at the cold metal table. Her uncle walked over to her and hugged and kissed her goodbye. Without a word, she followed Pickett out of the room and into her new life as a letter.

Chapter One

It had been the longest night of her life, and all she wanted to do was go home and curl up in Matthew's arms. Bell stared at the clock on the wall, tapping her chewed-up fingernails impatiently on her leg. Her little sister, Bernie, had been speaking to Officer Wells for two hours. How much more could there be to say?

The room was quiet. Matthew sat at Bell's right. He was softly running his fingers through her long strawberry blonde hair. Alex and Bradley sat in the two chairs to her left. Her brother, Alex, was also staring at the clock in a zombie-esque way. Bradley appeared to be napping peacefully in the cold, hard plastic chair. How she wished she could nap, but it wasn't possible at a time like this.

She was worried sick about her sister and the fact that she was basically reliving the horrors of the past ten months while describing every detail of her controlling and torturous marriage to Martin Day. The only consolation was that Bernie was again free to live her life as she saw fit, and Martin would be behind bars for a long time for the murder of their parents, Bradley's kidnapping, and several other heinous crimes from his past. Thank the stars she had recorded Martin's confession, or she and her siblings may not have been so lucky to be alive to tell the tale.

Reaching over, she grabbed Matthew's free hand, and he smiled back at her. "I can't believe my parents are gone," she said, tears glistening at the corners of her eyes.

His expression turned pained. "I wish I could have stopped that from happening. I would give anything if it were possible to fix it for you. I let your whole family down."

"It's not your fault, Matt. None of us knew how to handle this situation. It was never easy, and there's no way of knowing whether any of us could have prevented the outcome. I believe things happen for a reason, whether we understand or not."

"I'm here for you. If you need anything, just ask," he replied.

She gave him a smile, and then, squeezing his hand, she stood and turned to the group as a whole. "I'm going to grab some water. Does anyone want anything?"

"Nah, I'm good," said Matthew.

"I'll take some coffee, please," replied Alex.

"Are you sure you want coffee?" Bell raised one brow. "I'm hoping we'll be leaving here soon and that we can go get some sleep."

"It won't matter. I can drink coffee all evening, and it doesn't seem to hinder my sleep. You know that," he said.

"Fine. I'll be back in a moment." Bell headed around the corner to a vending area which included a coffee pot and a bubbler. Grabbing two cups, she filled the first with coffee and the second with water. She paused for a moment and took a big gulp of water. It felt refreshing as it ran down her dry throat. Setting the cups down, she grabbed an elastic band out of her pocket. She brushed her fingers through her long, wavy hair, and, gathering it all together, twisted it into a loose knot on top of her head. Fastening it in place, she stared at the vending machine. "Who eats this stuff?" she mused aloud. They stocked it with every type of sugar imaginable. Turning to the bubbler, she grabbed her cup and topped it off. Picking up Alex's coffee, she started back toward the waiting area.

Rounding the corner, she slammed directly into another person. The coffee and water went flying and exploded into a million tiny droplets.

"What the hell?" yelped a familiar voice.

"Oh man," said another.

Bell wiped coffee and water out of her eyes, and the two people before her came into focus. Recognizing one of the men, she immediately took a step back. She had run directly into Martin and the officer escorting him.

"I'm so sorry," she said to the officer, who was blotting his face with a napkin. Officer Marx, is it?"

"Yeah, it's Marx. No worries. It's a tight corner, and I've been hit with worse." He gave her an awkward smile.

"I'm not however sorry that I spilled all over you," she hissed, pointing her finger at Martin.

"I'm sure I can arrange a way for you to regret it," he barked.

"Watch yourself," interjected Marx.

"Careful, Martin. You might add more time onto your sentence making threats like that," she replied.

"You tell your sister that this isn't over," he said with a snarl. "You hear me? This isn't over!"

"Enough," snapped Marx. He gave Martin a jerk and pushed him onward.

Bell glared after Martin until he was out of sight. Forgetting about the coffee and water, she walked back into the waiting area, her entire body shaking.

Alex looked up when she walked into the room, his brow wrinkling as he took her in.

"What happened?" he asked. "You're shaking. Are you okay?"

"I had the beverages, and I was turning the corner into the hall when I literally ran into two people. One of them was Martin."

"O.M.G.," said Alex. "Did he say anything?"

"Yeah. He said to tell Bernie that this isn't over."

"God, I hope it's over," said Alex, shaking his head.

"It's over, don't worry," said Matt. "He can't hurt your family anymore. Besides, I'm here with you." He reached out and squeezed her hand. "Come sit down. It shouldn't be much longer. Do you need a sweatshirt? You look like you're freezing."

"No, I'll be okay," she said. "I'm not cold. I need to take a few deep breaths, and I'll be fine."

"Let me know if you change your mind," he said.

He'd barely finished his sentence when Detective Wells appeared with Bernie.

"You're free to go. I think I've got everything I need. Please let me know if you think of any further details. And don't hesitate to reach out if you need anything. He patted Bernie on the shoulder, then turned and left the room.

Bell looked her sister over. She, too, was shaking, but from cold. Her eyes had dark rings around them, and she looked as if she might fall over at any moment. Thankfully, she was no longer bottomless. The station had given her some sweatpants to put on. Bernie walked over and put her arms around Bell. Her cheeks were wet, and the water dripped onto Bell's shoulder. "I'm so tired, Bell. I just want to forget all of this. Let's go to Alex's house and sleep. I can't go back to the bungalow. Not right now. Dad's property makes me feel sick whenever I think about it. The last thing I want is to smell the smoke wafting off the ruins of his home."

Bradley opened his eyes. Seeing Bernie, he got to his feet. "Are we free to go?" he asked with a yawn.

"Yeah. We can go to my house," said Alex. I have enough guest rooms for all of you. We'll sleep better if we're all in one place.

Then, after we've rested, we can discuss our situation and what we want to do next."

Bernie grabbed Bradley's hand and pulled him toward the door. He brought her hand up to his lips and kissed it. "I'm sorry you had to describe everything that happened over again. I'm sure it was difficult."

"It was," she said with a frown. "I'm glad it's over, though I know there'll be trials to deal with down the road."

"Let's not think about that right now. Let's think about what we'll do together in the near future." He grinned. "I think I'd definitely like more kisses and a formal date."

"Oh, you would, would you? Well, I think we can arrange that," said Bernie. She pulled him to a stop in front of the doors to the station. Reaching up, she drew his face to hers and gave him a long, passionate kiss. Pulling away, she looked into his eyes. "How's that for starters?" she whispered.

Smiling back at her, Bradley reached for the door, and they stepped out into the night, walking hand in hand. The sun hadn't yet risen, and the breeze gave her goosebumps, but she felt happy to be leaving the stuffy station. Looking around, she didn't notice any cars on the street or hear anything but a few crickets chirping. The door closed behind them, and as they proceeded down the stairs leading away from the station, a strange sound buzzed past Bernie's ear. She could feel something warm spraying her face and arms. Everything, including the cricket's song, had stilled. Jerking her head in Bradley's direction, she watched in horror as he fell from her side.

A blood-curdling scream ripped through the early morning stillness. Bell's heart wrenched, and a chill ran through her entire body as she realized it had come from her sister, who had passed through the station doors a moment earlier. She bolted for the exit, and her stomach soured and lurched. She was doing everything she could to keep from panicking. She didn't know what she'd find on the other side, but that scream meant one thing. Her sister was in trouble.

"Bell," yelled Matthew. "Wait! You have no idea what's beyond that door!" Alex and Matthew sprinted after her. She hadn't heard a single word coming out of his mouth. Adrenaline propelled her forward.

Arriving at the door, she paused for a moment, then shoved it open. Nothing could have prepared her for what she saw on the other side. Bernie stood frozen on the stairs. There was blood spattered everywhere. Bradley's lifeless body was splayed across the precinct steps, and the blood pooling around him had created a waterfall as it flowed downward.

Stepping through the door, she hurled herself toward the railing as she lost the contents of her stomach. Overcome with dizziness, she slumped to the ground. She tried to focus, but waves of sickness flooded over her. She heard her brother and Matthew talking, but she was unable to decipher any of their words. All she could hear was a buzzing. Bell knew she was moments away from losing consciousness. She took in a long, slow breath and released it slowly.

"Pull it together," she urged herself. With the back of her sleeve, she wiped her face clean. Despite her legs uncontrollably shaking, she pushed herself off the ground and stood with the help of the railing. She realized she had to turn around, but seeing her sister standing there covered in her friend's blood was by far the most horrendous thing she had ever witnessed in her life.

Bracing herself, she turned away from the railing. Bernie was now on the ground next to Bradley, holding his hand. Her body shook violently beneath the guttural wail she was emitting. Alex had his arms wrapped around her and was whispering in her ear. Matthew had disappeared, and Bell felt panicky, not knowing his whereabouts. She froze in place, staring at Bernie and Alex. Her sister's heart-wrenching sobs ringing in her ears.

As if a giant rubber band had snapped, Bell was jerked into action. Her brain and body told her they needed to head for cover in case the shooter was still present.

"Alex, where's Matthew?" she demanded.

"He's inside, getting officers and calling an ambulance."

"We have to get out of here. We can't stay here. Get her away from him! Bernie, can you hear me?" shrieked Bell. Their sister didn't react. The wailing continued. "You cannot stay there. You have to go inside. We don't know if the shooter is still here. Please! The officers will need to get at him. Bernie! Can you hear me?"

Alex stepped forward and crouched over his sister. "Okay, sweetie, we have to go inside." He gave her arm a tug, moving her body slightly. As if on cue, another shot hit the building directly behind them, barely missing Bernie.

"Go inside," he yelled to Bell, who had dropped to the ground by the railing. She counted to three and then hurled herself toward the entrance with full force. Another shot hit the door as she launched herself through. Once inside, she peeked around the corner to keep an eye on her siblings.

Alex threw himself over his little sister. Wrapping his arms around her midsection, he hoisted her into the air with incredible strength. Bell pushed the door open, and Alex dove through. Turning, he kicked the door closed behind them. His arms were still wrapped around Bernie.

"No! Nooo!" screamed Bernie. "I can't leave him! I can't! Take me back! Take me back!" she sobbed.

Bell watched as officers raced down the hall toward the scene. She heard Alex once again speaking to Bernie. He was amazingly patient with her, given their current situation.

"Sweetheart, I can't take you back," he replied. "We need to let the police do their jobs. We can't stay with Bradley." He exhaled. "There's nothing you can do for him. I know you're hurting and upset, but we have to let them do their jobs. It'll be okay, honey. We'll get through this," he said as he exchanged a pained look with Bell. Their helplessness of the situation was apparent. From the look on his face, Bell could tell Alex wasn't certain he was speaking the truth. Would they get through this? Only time would tell.

The screaming and flailing stopped and turned into a slow, monotonous cry. Alex hugged her like a toddler. Mascara and blood ran down her face with every tear. It stained Alex's light blue shirt.

Bell took a seat on the floor next to them and wrapped her arms around Bernie, too. Alex removed one arm from his younger sister and put it around Bell. Resting her head on his shoulder, she cried.

"This shouldn't have happened," said Bell, her voice shaking. "Martin is behind bars. This shouldn't be happening!" she raged.

Alex looked at Bell with wide eyes. "The truth is, we knew he had a partner, and we knew that partner was still out there. We may have poked a bear." A shiver ran down Bell's spine as his words sank in. She had been naïve to think it was over. They all had been.

An ambulance siren sounded in the distance. Bell knew they'd take Bradley away in a few minutes, and they would usher her and her siblings back into a room for yet another round of questions to which they had no real answers.

"This hurts so much," squeaked Bernie. "It's too much. It's just too much. I loved him, and I didn't say it. Now he's gone. I wasted time, and I'll never get that chance again!" she wailed.

Bell's empathy for Bernie made it feel like her own heart was being torn in two. There was nothing she could do to make things right. This loss would likely haunt their memories for life.

Chapter Two

Three weeks had passed since Martin's placement behind bars, and the brutal murder of Bradley Cordine. All three siblings were currently living in Alex's house. No one wanted to go back to the bungalow because of the fire, and neither Alex nor Bell wanted to leave Bernie unattended. Their younger sister had gone mute. The only sounds she made were sobs and screams in the night.

Thinking back to the day of the shooting, Bell's adrenaline spiked. She couldn't get the memories out of her head. She could still see the officers in protective gear with guns rushing past them. She heard more gunshots being fired as she, Bernie, and Alex were pulled away from the entrance and dragged to a safe room by Officer Marx and a couple of his colleagues.

She recalled Officer Wells meeting with them and saying that the shooter had gotten away, but not to worry. They would track them down and bring them to justice. Bell's heart had sunk. Safety wasn't a real thing anymore. They'd be looking over their shoulders until the shooter was behind bars.

She could hear the questions coming from Wells' mouth while he asked them what they had seen or heard. None of them had seen anything. Bernie wouldn't speak, and the only thing Bell recalled was the blood-curdling scream that had come from her sister and the images of Bernie clinging to Bradley, covered in his blood.

She vividly recalled taking Bernie into a locker room after the questioning. Carefully, she had stripped herself and her sister down to their undergarments, then guided her into the showers. She'd washed Bernie's hair and soaped her up to remove all the blood. There had been so much blood. Her sister didn't move. She'd stood there like a scared rabbit, shaking and staring blankly at the wall. Tears mixing with the water from the shower. Blood flowing down the drain. Bell, trying to keep it together for Bernadette's sake, but feeling as though she could shatter into a million pieces at any moment.

The department had given them each a pair of shorts and a shirt and sent them on their way as if nothing had happened, and they had no reason to fear for their lives. Shouldn't they have been in an armored vehicle? A squad car followed them, then two officers checked Alex's home to make sure it was safe. An unmarked vehicle would post up outside to keep an eye on things for a few days, but after that, they were on their own.

Bell was terrified. Despite the fear, she had been glad to go to Alex's house. The police concluded that a sniper had shot Bradley from two buildings away. They had no idea who they were dealing with. Martin wouldn't respond to their questions. They believed the incident was a revenge mission and that Bradley had been the primary target. If the shooter was smart, they'd moved on. While the department would continue to investigate, they didn't perceive any further threat to the Price family. In the following weeks, there were no other attempts on any of their lives.

Coming back to the present moment, she knew she would be dealing with a long and stressful day. It was the day of the funeral, and she prayed she could get Bernadette out of her bedroom. Her sister hadn't left the room since their arrival three weeks prior. Luckily, there was a bathroom in there, or Bell would have been even more concerned.

"Alex, did you take Bernie her breakfast?" called Bell from the sitting room. She'd been curled up on Alex's white leather sofa with a book, but she hadn't read anything. She'd spent a lot of time staring at everything in the room. His living room was pristine. It had oak floors with a large black and white area rug. The white leather sofa had two matching barrel chairs and a chaise. He had white floor-to-ceiling bookcases that made up the walls on alternate sides of the room, one of which had a large bay window built into it. It was Bernie's favorite feature of the house, along with the massive brick fireplace that divided the entry to the sitting room into two access points. They could enjoy the fireplace from either side, which Bell absolutely loved. Alex's favorite item in the room, however, was his coffee table. It was a large black iron mermaid base with a glass tabletop. She mused about how mermaids were his favorite mythical creature. He loved the stories of the sirens of the sea luring in sailors. He liked to joke about how he'd make a great captain because they'd never be able to get to him. Bell smiled to herself. Her brother was a bit extra, but she wouldn't have it any other way. He made life more interesting for all of them.

Alex appeared in the entryway to the sitting room, a cup of coffee in hand.

"Yep, I took her some eggs and half a grapefruit. I can't be certain, but I think she ate it. The empty plate was on the floor outside her bedroom."

"I hope so. She'll need energy to get through today," said Bell.

"Um, yeah. She and I both." He walked into the room and sat down at the opposite end of the couch. He gave Bell a concerned look. "How exactly are we going to get her out of that room? If she misses the funerals, she'll be devastated. Maybe not today, but eventually."

"I've already put a plan into action. Let's hope it works. I called her psychiatrist, Doctor Andra Jones. She's coming over. She'll get Bernie out of there. She said it won't be a problem and to trust her."

"Oh, thank goodness," said Alex. "I thought maybe I'd have to go in there and whack her repeatedly with a pillow until she wakes up and agrees to start living her life again."

"Don't make light, Alex. We've all been through something highly traumatizing. While we were bystanders, Bernie experienced everything firsthand. She needs extra care right now. If we aren't careful, I worry we could lose her."

"Well, of course, Bell. I'm worried too, but enough is enough. We're all hurting. We need to talk to one another to get through this. Keeping it bottled up inside will only prolong the depression and keep her from healing."

"Okay, what do you think we should do?" asked Bell.

"I don't know. You said it yourself last week; we've never seen her act this way. This is unknown territory."

"Which is exactly why I say this needs more sensitivity and understanding."

"Fine," he replied, holding his hands up. "I hope this works and Bernie is able to take a step in the right direction."

"All I'm asking is that you be present when Dr. Jones arrives and that we all work together to get Bernie out of that room. Missing the funeral isn't an option. I don't want to give her any further reasons to place blame on herself."

"She'll go if I have to pick her up and carry her there myself," he stated.

"Alex, what's with the hostility today?"

"Ugh." Alex pointed at her. "You should have figured this out already."

"What? Why should I have figured it out?"

"You're the one who always finds the solutions to hold this family together."

"We've never been in this situation before." She glared at her brother. "It's unfair of you to place the blame on me. I'm not a magician. I can't wave a wand and make Bernie feel better."

"I'm sorry, Bell, but our lives are one big freakin' mess right now. I'm tired of dealing with loss," he lamented. "We need to bury our family and move forward. I can't stay in this place of death any longer."

Bell let out a sigh. She knew her brother was on edge because of the funerals. "Blaming me will solve nothing, so let's take it a moment at a time, and it'll be over before we know it. Is Hector coming to the funeral?"

"He'll be there. He was a huge fan of both Mom and Dad. He took it hard when he heard about their deaths."

"I'm glad he's coming. That's at least one good thing, right?" Bell asked with a half-smile.

"I guess. I haven't seen him since before this whole mess took place, so hopefully he's still interested in pursuing a relationship."

"Why wouldn't he be? You're a great person, Alex. He knows that. Besides, if tragedy makes him walk away from you, you don't want him, okay?"

"If he were to walk away, I couldn't really blame him. I haven't felt like myself when we've spoken. I've been short and unavailable. So, I need Bernie to snap out of it so we can show support and understanding for one another when others don't. I need both of you. I know I might act like I'm fine, but I'm not. Nothing feels fine. Considering our lives over the past few months, I wouldn't blame him if he walked away. No one needs this much drama." The pain on his face was clear. Bell scooted closer and gave him a hug. Sometimes she forgot that her brother was human because he had such a positive outlook, even when life tossed dirt in his face.

"Everything will be okay. Tonight, the healing begins," said Bell.

"I hear what you're saying, but we still don't know who shot Bradley or if they'll come after us."

"Matthew agrees with the detectives. He believes it was an isolated incident and that Bradley was the main target. He's the only person who could possibly identify what Martin's partner looked like, which could have had them scared. With Martin in jail, hopefully, his partner has moved on. There have been no other malicious events to prove otherwise. We can't stop living our lives. The healing begins tonight," she said again, mostly to convince herself.

"The healing begins tonight," Alex repeated quietly.

The majority of the day had been quiet and lazy. Bell and Alex had lounged in the sitting room. With music playing low in the background, Bell read *Little Women* for the umpteen-millionth time, and Alex caught up on his magazine collection.

Bell couldn't believe how many magazines Alex had. She noted each of the following in his collection: *Yoga Magazine, Men's Health, Esquire, GQ, Vogue, O, The Oprah Magazine, Us Weekly, Life & Style Weekly, Men's Journal, Muscle & Fitness,* and *The Family Handyman.*

No one has time to read that many magazines, she thought.

"Why do you have so many, Alex? This is a bit over the top, don't you think?"

He looked at her and gave an exaggerated sigh. "I don't recall where I bought the subscriptions from, so they just keep coming."

"You know, an email or a couple of phone calls to the actual magazines would help you figure that out."

"It's such a pain in the butt, though," he whined.

"Alex, I bet you're paying at least fifty bucks per subscription. When you let them lapse and renew after the discount period, they charge you full price." She frowned. Ever since she'd gone overboard on her spending back in high school, she made sure she wasn't throwing money away, even though she had plenty of it now. "Seriously, you should pick three or four you really like and get rid of the rest. And, once you decide which ones you want, you can negotiate a better price or find them on a discount site. I know you have money, but that's no reason to throw it away."

He rolled his eyes at her. "Fine. I'll look into it this week."

"Make sure you do. That's at least three-hundred and fifty dollars you're tossing out the window right now."

"I know you're right. It's $350 I could be giving to a charity rather than wasting on killing trees."

"Yeah, quit killing trees!" she said, lightly whacking him with her book. "Our planet is in enough trouble without you slaughtering more trees."

"That's me. Tree killer, Alex. I single-handedly keep the magazine companies in business with my outrageous magazine list." He rolled his eyes. "I know you're into saving trees, but just once, you could buy a new book to read."

She looked at him wide-eyed. "What?" she asked incredulously. "You mean other books exist?"

A knock sounded at the front door. Alex made no move to get up. Bell threw her book at him.

"Hey!"

"Serves you right," she said. She redirected her attention to the clock. It was three o'clock on the dot. "That must be Dr. Jones. Don't bother getting up. It's not like this is your house or anything." Alex ignored her, so she headed for the door. Opening it, she saw a tall Amazonian-looking woman with short white-blonde hair. She wore a white pantsuit and black cat-eye sunglasses.

Dr. Jones removed her sunglasses and thrust her hand out in greeting. "Hi, you must be Bell. I'm Doctor Jones, but you can call me Andra."

Bell shook Andra's hand. "Nice to finally meet you," she said. "Do come in. Alex and I have been doing some light reading. Bernie, of course, has been in her room all day, as we've already discussed. You know, I'm surprised we haven't met sooner, considering how many years you've been looking after our family."

"Yes, fifteen years is a long time. Your mother was one of my first clients."

Bell recalled their mother seeing Andra years before. Her mother had been a difficult case, but Andra had helped her significantly. Narcissism had run deep within their mother. The girls had been lucky to escape such a diagnosis.

Bell led Andra into the sitting room. Alex stood and shook her hand.

"Lovely to meet you," he said. "What's the plan for dealing with this situation regarding our sister?"

Andra sat down on one of the barrel chairs as Bell and Alex took their places back on the couch.

"First, I'll go in and do a brief assessment of the situation. After I have a better idea of what we're looking at, I'll work with her to set up a more consistent plan for moving forward with her life. If necessary, I'll give her something to help her get through the next couple of days, but she needs to follow through on the plan we make so that she can be under more consistent observation and care."

"Okay. That sounds like a good plan," said Bell.

"Let's get to it." Andra stood. "In which room is she?"

Bell jumped to her feet and set off toward Bernie's room. She led Andra around the corner and down a long hallway. "She's in the last room on the right." The therapist nodded and proceeded onward. "We'll be in the sitting room when you're done," she added.

"Okay." Andra turned away from Bell and knocked on the door, but Bernie didn't answer. Bell watched as Andra turned the handle and went inside, shutting the door behind her. Bell headed back down the hall to the sitting room.

"I really need Andra to work her magic on this situation," said Alex.

"Have faith, brother. It'll work. Andra has done amazing things for Bernie and our mother in the past. I don't see why this time should be any different."

One-and-a-half hours passed, and finally, Andra and Bernie appeared in the sitting room. Bernie had showered, applied fresh makeup, and dressed in a long black gown with her red hair piled neatly on top of her head. She looked like a completely different person, though her face held no emotion.

Andra stepped forward. "I think you'll find that the evening will go quite smoothly where Bernadette is concerned. I've given her a Xanax, and it's currently helping to calm her anxious and depressive state. I've started her on half a milligram three times per day. You can give her another one before bed. She has enough tablets to get through tomorrow and Wednesday, but after Wednesday, I want her to come into the office before prescribing anything further. She should make an appointment to see her regular therapist, Claire Harper. This is not a long-term solution. It's meant to get her through the next couple of days only. Do you understand?"

"Yes," said Bell. "We understand. If we are able to get her to the funeral home, then you have provided us a great service."

"Okay, if there's nothing else, I'll leave her in your capable hands. Make sure she stays on her pill schedule."

"Thank you, Dr. Jones," said Alex. "Let me walk you to the door." He escorted Andra from the room.

Bell stared at Bernie for a moment. She looked like her sister, but she recognized she still wasn't quite herself. She hoped and prayed that the situation would improve over the following week. Bell couldn't take much more of this zombie-hermit-like behavior. Her biggest fear was that Bernie would never speak again. She'd heard of this happening to others who had suffered trauma, though most were children.

"How are you feeling?" she asked her sister with hesitance.

Bernie didn't answer. She silently walked over to Bell and wrapped her arms around her. Bell hugged her back. She hadn't expected such a loving reaction from her sister. She watched as Alex walked into the room. He stopped and frowned at them.

"Bernie, do you want anything else to eat before we go to the funeral home?" he asked.

Turning toward him, she shook her head no and plopped herself down onto the couch.

"Okay then, I'll go get dressed," said Bell. "We have to leave shortly."

Walking down the hall, she could still hear everything going on in the living room. The house erupted with the sound of Bernie laughing, which caught her even more off guard than the hug. Then, without notice, the laughter turned into the sound of uncontrollable sobbing.

"Oh, honey," she heard Alex say. "I know this is awful. We're all feeling the pain of loss. You need to know that Bell and I are both here for you. You can talk to us. We love you, and we want to be supportive of each other as we get through this. Please talk to us, Bernadette," he pleaded.

The crying stopped, and Bell heard no other sounds from the living room. She could tell Alex was trying to be patient. It was a struggle for him because he was an open book, whereas Bernadette had a tendency to shut down when she didn't know how to deal with something.

"Okay, you speak when you're ready," she heard him say.

Bell changed her clothes and touched up her makeup. Her stomach churned as she stared at herself in the mirror. She wasn't looking forward to the evening, but on some other level, she was. She didn't want to say goodbye because it meant her parents and Bradley were really gone. Leaning forward, she turned on the faucet and sucked some water into her mouth, swallowing back the lump in her throat. They had to close this horrible chapter in their lives and move on. Bradley and their parents would want them to.

Walking back into the room, she took a deep, slow breath, sighing on the release. "Are you ready?" Alex grabbed Bernie by the hand and pulled her to her feet. Without another word, Bell turned away, and they followed her out the door.

The ride to Mason Laney Funeral Home was quiet. Bell sat and observed Bernie the whole way there. She could smell a mixture of soap and conditioner. Her sister looked halfway normal for a change. Bernie's eyes were averted as she methodically rubbed a piece of her dress between her thumb and pointer finger. Bell couldn't help but wonder when her sister would begin to speak again. Brushing her bangs back, she pretended to bump Bernie's shoulder. She looked up, and Bell smiled at her. The corners of Bernie's mouth twitched briefly in response.

Arriving at their destination, Alex climbed out of the limo and gave each of his sisters a hand as they followed his lead. Bell's long navy dress dragged across the floor of the car when she scooted out the door. She smoothed the dress down and linked arms with Alex. Bernie stood by the door, her arms folded across her chest, staring at the building in front of her, shaking her head.

"Come on, Bern," said Alex. She took his other arm, and they walked through the doors together. They hadn't even made it to the second door when Bernadette fell to her knees and let out a guttural cry. Bell knelt beside her and wrapped her sister in a tight hug. Pulling Bernie up, she led her to a bench to the side of the doors.

"We can sit here as long as you need," she said, holding Bernie's hand. Bernie squeezed her hand so hard Bell had to choke back the pain that radiated through it. "It's okay. You're going to be okay. I know this is hard." Reaching out, she brushed back the stray hairs hanging in her sister's face and wiped away her tears. Bernie leaned forward and buried her head in her sister's shoulder as she continued to wail. All Bell could do was hold her and wait.

Fifteen minutes passed, and Bernadette's cries began to quiet. She wiped her tears away and shook her hands out. Then, turning to Bell, she reached for her hand again and pulled her to her feet, leading the way into the funeral home. No one had arrived yet. The room was quiet. Fresh chocolate chip cookies and coffee masked the smell of old musty furniture. The pastor greeted and escorted them into the church to see that things were in proper order.

At the head of the room stood a table with three urns; each had been carefully handpicked to suit its occupant, and a corresponding framed photograph stood next to each. Off to the side were several bouquets of flowers, and in the background was a video that included three sections of photos of each person's life.

"Is everything as expected?" asked Pastor Roy.

Bell couldn't open her mouth to form words. A tear ran down her cheek. She turned and looked at him. He lightly touched her arm. "If you think of anything you need, don't hesitate to ask. I'll give you three a moment alone."

Once the pastor had left, Alex said, "It looks nice, I guess. I mean, as nice as a funeral can look."

"Yeah," said Bernie.

Alex and Bell turned and stared at her. She stared back for a moment and then stepped off toward the flowers. She ran her fingers over the soft, silky petals of a rose. Leaning forward, she inhaled its sweetness. Alex and Bell followed closely behind in anticipation of her next move. They watched as she read a few of the cards attached to the bouquets, then turned her attention toward the urns.

Bell was curious to hear what her sister thought about the choices she and Alex had made regarding the funeral, but she wasn't going to ask at this time. She was pleased that Bernie had said a single word out loud. She watched as Bernie ran her newly manicured fingers over their father's urn. It was made of dark, rich mahogany wood. She paused momentarily, pulling her hand away.

"Wow, that's smooth. I'm sure he approves."

"Yeah, I hope so," said Alex. "I took forever to make the final decision, but he was so fond of mahogany that I felt it was the only way to go. The real issue turned out to be finding the proper shape. I liked the smooth curves of this one the most. It's simple and majestic looking."

"You did a nice job, Alex," said Bell.

"They're actually quite beautiful," said Bernie. She moved over to their mother's urn. Bell noted that her sister hesitated to touch this one, but after a moment she lovingly placed her hand on it and said something that Bell couldn't make out. Alex was standing closer to Bernie, so Bell nudged him.

"What did she say?" she whispered.

"She said: *Mom, I love you, but you can be a real pain in the hiney. This decision couldn't have been easy for Bell and Alex, but I think they did well. I hope you're pleased.*"

Bell accidentally let out a brief giggle. Alex lightly swatted her arm for it. She walked over and stood next to her sister.

"It's pretty, isn't it?" she asked.

"It is," replied Bernie.

The urn was a dark blue lapis with sterling silver. The silver was in the shape of flowers and vines. It was ornate and breathtakingly beautiful. It fit Mariska's lavish life, and it was her favorite color.

Bernie stepped sideways, so she was in front of Bradley's urn. She picked it up and hugged it to her chest. Tears ran down her face. Bell barely caught the words coming out of her sister's mouth.

"I'm so, so, sorry. This should've never happened. I should've been with you instead of Martin, and I should've told you every day how important you were. I love you, and I'm so sorry I wasted our time." She continued to hold his urn tightly in her arms. She sat down on the floor and cried silently.

Bell sat down next to her and put her hand on her sister's arm. She looked at the urn. It was black, dark purple, and silver. There was a band of silver around the neck, center, and bottom of the urn, while the majority of the body was black metal with what looked like thin purple crystal embellishments. Bradley's favorite color was purple, and he had a strong love of crystals, so this particular choice in urn made sense.

Bell watched Bernie's face contort in pain. "It's okay, Bern. You can say whatever you want to him. He's listening," she said confidently. She firmly believed their loved ones were there with them, even if they couldn't be seen.

Alex looked at his watch. "We have about fifteen minutes before people begin to arrive."

"Let her be," said Bell. "She needs this." She looked at Bernadette, who was staring down at the urn in her arms.

"You picked this out, didn't you?" she asked Bell.

Bell had tried to reach out to Bradley's father to see if he wanted to be a part of the decision-making, but he had responded with a voice message saying she would know better than him about how to honor Bradley's memory. His voice had cracked, and the message had been cut short. Bell felt sorry for him, as she knew they had only just met. "Yes. I figured he would like it and that you'd approve."

"You were right." She hugged the urn one last time, carefully stood, and placed it back on the table. Bending down, she kissed the top. "I'll never forget you, Bradley Cordine, or how well you always treated me. You've stolen a piece of my heart, and nothing will ever fill that hole," she said. Turning away, she looked at her brother and sister for direction.

"Should we go sit down until people arrive?" asked Alex.

"Yeah, let's do that," replied Bell.

The three siblings linked arms and, without a word, walked out the door and into the adjoining sitting room, where they would begin counting down the minutes until they could return to the safety and quiet of Alex's home.

The funeral and visitation lasted three hours. The siblings laughed, cried, conversed with guests, and grew increasingly drained as time went on. Bell felt trapped in one spot the entire time, but luckily, Matthew was standing next to her. At one point, she had to cut off a guest mid-sentence and leave them to talk to Matt just so she could make her way to the restroom, which proved to be a task in and of itself. Over a thousand people had been filtering in and out of the visitation and packing the room from wall to wall, offering condolences to the family and saying their goodbyes. The faint smell of sweat wafted across her nostrils every now and then, involuntarily wrinkling her nose. She'd wanted to check in with Bernie, but that became impossible once people arrived. She could only wish her siblings strength as the night progressed.

The funeral home had finally emptied at nine o'clock, and it was time to go home. Andre, Alex's driver, pulled up to the door, and the siblings trotted toward the car in their heels and leather loafers as thunder crashed and water began to pour from the sky. They dove, one by one, into the limo, collapsing into the leather seats. Bell reached for a water, as her throat was thoroughly parched from speaking to all the guests. She was astounded by the number of people who had ventured out to say their goodbyes. Every single person had wanted to express their feelings to the children of the victims. Never had she felt so overwhelmed by others' sadness.

As the limo navigated the streets toward home, the only sound to be heard was the faint swishing of the wipers as they pushed back the rain. Bernie sat between Alex and Bell. Once situated in the car, she had reached for each of their hands and squeezed them tightly. The tears flowed silently down her face. Bell looked over at Alex and saw that his expression matched Bernie's. The storm may have been outside, but it was raining inside the limo as a waterfall of silent emotion washed away their pain.

The quiet continued as the siblings exited the limo and entered the house. Without so much as a wave, they each took off to their separate rooms. Bell was tired of people and only wanted to be alone to cry a few more tears and fall asleep. They'd finally put their loved ones to rest. The following day, they were to visit their father's cousin, Mitch, the lawyer, to discuss the division of assets. She wasn't the least bit excited about the excursion. It was one more thing to check off a list.

Lying in bed, she thought about all the work it would take to clean out their mother's home. She wasn't looking forward to that either, but someone had to do it. Drifting off to sleep, she heard Liberace playing in the background and could see diamonds floating through the air. She could smell her mother's perfume. Looking around, she saw her mother, Mariska, leaning against Liberace's piano, dressed in a very expensive and very short red cocktail dress.

"You did well, darling," said Mariska. "I couldn't have asked for a nicer send-off." "Thanks," said Bell, "I'm glad you liked it."

"Don't worry, darling. You'll get through this, and you'll help your siblings see the light again."

"How can you be so sure?" asked Bell.

"You're strong, like me. Plus, I know your future," she said, smiling radiantly.

"Thanks, Mom. Will you visit us?"

"I'll try, darling, but Liberace and I are quite busy these days." She watched as Mariska plucked a large diamond from the air.

"Hmm, that's odd. These diamonds appear to be fake," reported her mother. "I would never allow such a thing into my home."

"Maybe Liberace brought them," said Bell.

"Don't be silly, child. Liberace would have brought bigger, brighter, and clearer diamonds. Not fake ones." She laughed.

Bell stood contemplating the diamonds as Bernie walked into the room in a bright blue shimmery evening gown. She pointed her finger at Bell. She was still wearing her wedding ring. Bell watched as Bernie held her other hand in the air, and a large butcher knife appeared, the handle balancing on the tip of her finger. Her sister opened her hand, and the knife slid into it.

"Just remember what I told you. Diamonds can be pawned, but zebra are forever," she said as she threw the knife, and it embedded in one of the floating diamonds directly in front of Bell.

Bell jolted awake. Sweat dripped from her brow, and a chill ran through her. Try as she might, she couldn't recall what had happened. The dream faded as instantaneously as it had begun.

Chapter Three

Bell awoke at seven in the morning feeling refreshed and ready for anything. She had slept fairly well, aside from the weird dream she couldn't recall. She brushed the thought aside and chose to stay positive.

Her sister was most likely still sleeping. The smell of bacon met her nose as she crept over to her sister's door and knocked. Bernie didn't answer. Opening the door, Bell peered inside. She couldn't actually see Bernie under the mound of blankets she had thrown on the bed. Unable to resist, Bell opened the door farther and scooted inside. Reaching out, she poked the mound of blankets.

"What do you want?" asked a muffled voice.

"I want you to join us for breakfast," said Bell.

Bernie pushed back the covers, yawning and stretching her arms above her head.

Groaning, Bernie said, "Is it morning already? I feel like I just went to bed."

Bell's brow furrowed. "Didn't you sleep well?"

"I slept fine. I just can't believe it's already daylight again. I feel like I could sleep for days."

"Unfortunately, you can't. We have to go meet Daddy's cousin, Mitch."

"Booo," she grumbled and propped herself up on one elbow. "Why?"

"He has the wills, and he wants to go over the division of assets. Trust me, I don't want to do this anymore than you do, but it's got to be done. One more step in the process of moving on."

Bernie let out a sigh. "I guess."

"By the way, if you intend to stay here more long-term, we can maybe invest in some different décor for this room. I mean, I know Elvis is cool and all, but the memorabilia and Elvis-inspired bedspread don't seem to fit your personality.

"You've seen the bathroom, right? Elvis is on the rugs. Apparently, someone also made Elvis soap dispensers, a toothbrush holder, hand towels, and a shower curtain. It's definitely much more of the King than I need to see on a daily basis," said Bernie.

Bell nodded. "Yeah, I'll mention that to Alex."

"Maybe I can talk him into Marilyn Monroe or adding in some other celebrities to make it more interesting."

"Now you're thinking," said Bell. "At least get the Marilyn Monroe bedspread. Marilyn and Elvis were both iconic, and you see them in art together all the time. It fits. Anyway, let's go eat breakfast and then head out to meet Mitch."

"I'll be out in a couple of minutes," she said.

Bell headed back to her room. She needed to make herself presentable as well.

She could hear Alex bustling away in the kitchen. The food he was cooking permeated the air and filled her with joy. She knew, without looking, he had opted for his favorite gluten-free pancakes with dark chocolate chips, organic scrambled eggs with natural cheddar cheese, turkey bacon, sliced apples, and organic coffee. This was his go-to meal any time he had to make breakfast.

The Price family had always been big on making healthy food choices, with occasional splurges here and there. Alan didn't want his kids to be deprived of the best food, but he also wanted them to go out and have a pizza with their friends now and again. He was the one who had gotten Alex hooked on this particular menu.

While the siblings were frequently out and about for meals, they still attempted to make healthy choices. Their restaurant, the 365th Street Jazz Club, served the highest quality food. All of their menu options were organic and hormone-free, with a good deal of gluten-free and vegan items as well. The club hadn't always been that way, but with the health crazes hitting the United States, Bernadette and their father had decided it would be a great change for the restaurant. Bradley had done most of the buying of their food supplies. He'd been a huge asset in locating the best organic, vegan, and gluten-free suppliers. Bell had no idea what they would do now that he was gone. He wouldn't be easy to replace on any level.

Alex hummed a tune while he cooked. Bernie walked into the room, followed by Bell.

"Good morning, my little sunshiny people," he said with too much enthusiasm.

"Alex, where does your excitement toward life come from? You're always a ball of fiery energy in the morning. How do you do it? Especially with the current circumstances," asked Bell. She couldn't believe how fired up Alex could be the day after their loved ones' funerals. They ran most mornings together, and he always brought his "A" game unless something distracted him, which rarely happened. She wished she had his view on life. If he was upset, he rapidly got over it. Nothing would bring him down. She could easily surmise what his answer would be. They were close, like twins, even though they didn't share a bloodline.

"Belinda, life is a gift, which we still possess. It would be a horrible waste to ignore it when we're still here and able to make a difference in the world. We still have each other," he rationally replied. She frowned at him for using her full name. She hated being called Belinda, and both of her siblings knew of the aversion full-well. They did it to mess with her.

"Toss me a pancake," said Bernie.

Alex grabbed a plate, and with a flick of his wrist, he tossed the pancake up into the air. It landed with a squish on the plate. Bernie reached out and grabbed the pancake off the plate and proceeded to eat it with her hands.

"No plate or even a fork? I see how it is," said Alex, shaking the spatula at Bernie. "You think loss allows you to eat like an animal, huh?"

"Ha! Alex, she always eats chocolate chip pancakes that way," said Bell.

"Alrighty then," he said, raising an eyebrow.

"Another pancake over here, maestro," said Bell.

"No plate for you either?" he asked.

"Nope, that's one thing we have in common. We both like to eat our chocolate chip pancakes with our hands."

"Well, thank goodness that's the *only* thing you have in common," said Alex, rolling his eyes.

Bell and Bernie looked at each other, trying to keep straight faces. Then Bernie let out a snort and the two fell apart in a fit of laughter.

"I don't know what he's talking about," said Bell.

"Me either," replied Bernie.

"Okay. On a more serious note. Can I interest anyone in a plate with some other food items on it?" asked Alex. "I didn't make all of this food for myself alone."

"Sure, Alex, I'll take the works," said Bell. He promptly handed her a plate of food he'd already put together.

"I would like another pancake and some coffee, please," said Bernie. Reaching out, she helped herself to a mug.

"Eat up, sisters. We have business to which we must attend."

Alex piled food on his own plate and then walked around the breakfast bar to take a seat at his large oak table. The girls joined him. The rest of breakfast was quiet, but they had made progress. They were sharing a meal together, and Bell felt happy about that.

At nine o'clock, the Price family arrived at *The Law Office of Lawrence and Price*. Bell had seen Mitch Price on occasion, but he wasn't a regular part of family gatherings. He was in his early forties and one of the best estate planning lawyers in Tulsa. He wore dark sunglasses most of the time, making him look like he was hiding something, but in reality, he was a good man who worked hard for his clients.

Mitch greeted his family with a sad smile and ushered them into his private office.

"Never in a million years did I think I would handle the affairs of Alan and Mariska so soon. This is a horrible tragedy, and I cannot even comprehend how this feels to the three of you."

"It feels shitty," said Bernie.

"Bernie!" scolded Bell.

"Well, it does," she said.

"I agree with her," replied Mitch. "It's shitty. I honestly didn't think I'd ever have to attend to your father's affairs. I thought for sure he'd outlive me. He's always been the healthiest one in the family."

Alex looked at Mitch and nodded his head. Bell was frowning at Bernie. She didn't approve of swearing. It was a rare occasion when she let such words fly. In the end, she couldn't blame her sister for her outburst.

"Have the police made any discoveries regarding the death of Bradley?"

"They believe it was Martin's partner, but beyond that, there are no real leads," replied Bell.

"Obviously, we want this person in custody, but if we can't catch them, then I hope they've moved on. It's unfortunate that another tragedy took place just after you lost your parents. If you need anything or have any questions regarding laws, please don't hesitate to ask."

"Thanks, Mitch," said Alex. "We appreciate your kindness."

Mitch nodded. "You're welcome. Anyway, let's get this over with, shall we?"

"Yes, that sounds good. This world has become much too heavy as of late," replied Alex. "We need to grieve and move on."

"Understandable. Anyway, this is actually quite simple," stated Mitch. "I'll pay off all bills outstanding at the time of death for both of your parents. Once their debts have been paid, the remaining money will be donated to Habitat for Humanity International. While I know this doesn't sound much like your mother's plan, I assure you she was on board with this decision, and all the proper documents have been signed. She wanted to do something thoughtful with her money."

"Wow, that's impressive," said Bell. "I never thought mom would do something thoughtful for anyone outside of our family. It's nice to know she had it in her." Bell smiled, thinking about her mother and how she seemed to have a small soft spot in her.

"Yes, I agree," said Mitch. "Now, moving on to the houses," he said while removing his dark glasses. "Bell is to receive Mariska's property, and Bernie was to receive Alan's. Alex, they did not include you in this part of the assets because you already have your own home."

"I'm glad they didn't. One house is plenty," he said with a laugh.

"Bernie, since the fire destroyed most of your property, aside from the bungalow, you'll receive money from insurance. You can either sell the property or rebuild, whichever you deem fit. If you need any help or advice, I will further assist you," he said. "Any belongings left in the homes are to be separated equally between the three of you, which includes the claimed items lost in your father's house fire. We've separated the businesses out to each of you as well. Bernie will run the 365ᵗʰ Street Jazz Club, Bell will oversee the Price & Fitz Modeling Agency, and Alex will take control of the Price & Fitz Department Store, though I know both the agency and store work hand in hand. If there are any disagreements, your parents decided they would allot you one hour to decide who is to take charge of which business, and if an hour is not enough time to remedy this situation, it will be determined in a court hearing."

"I think we all agree that we each have been given the business we prefer to run," replied Alex. Bernie and Bell nodded in agreement.

"That's great. It makes life easier when a family is on the same page with these types of things. You would not believe the sibling rivalries that have come to light in this office."

"I'm sure there are tons of people out there who can't stand their family and will fight over a loved one's assets just because they're angry, but we're not at all like that. The three of us are very close, and we generally agree on most things in life," said Bell.

"Since you agree on who's running each business, I'd like to add that the profits are to be split amongst the three of you. If one of you decides to leave the business, you must first offer your business to your siblings to see if they want to run it. If they agree they do not want the business any longer, then the three of you may sell it. The sibling who sells their business still receives profits from the other two companies. The profit sharing ceases only if all three businesses are sold to a buyer outside the family."

"Well, that's an interesting concept," said Bernie.

"Your father wanted the three of you to always be provided for and remain close to one another. I think he's trying to make that happen through the businesses."

"I don't think we need to worry about any of us giving up control of our business any time soon," said Alex. "He recognized which would suit each of us best, and because we each have the business we love most, I'm sure he assumed we'd continue to work and stick together on our decisions."

Bell had dreamt of one day taking over the modeling agency, so she was ecstatic that her parents saw her as the right fit. During the work week, if she wasn't modeling, she helped her father with scouting new models or any other number of tasks. She'd developed a strong infatuation with the business from a young age, which was why she never pursued a college career. Her parents had assured her she would always have a spot at the agency once she gave up modeling. Her future would be secure.

"Next item of discussion is that of your trust funds. The age still stands at thirty-five, and the accounts from overseas will also be allotted to you at that time." Mitch looked up from his papers and at the siblings. "Since your situation has been improved regarding Martin and there's no foreseeable danger, those funds continue to be withheld. If, down the line, any of you run into a sticky situation, my office will reevaluate and, if necessary, the funds will once again come back into play. Now, if everyone is in agreement on everything, we'll sign papers, and then you'll be free to go," said

Mitch. "Oh, I almost forgot." He reached into his desk drawer and pulled something silver out. "This is for you, Bernadette. It's Bradley's sterling silver cross and chain. He had a brief will which stated that everything should be donated, except this keepsake, which he wanted you to have." He reached out toward her, and she apprehensively took the item from his hand.

"I didn't expect him to leave anything to me," she babbled as she ran her fingers over the cool metal of the cross. "Very odd that he put this in his will and that I'm the person he thought of."

"He cared about you," said Mitch. "His will was fairly new. He came to me about a year back, and we created it. His cousin had passed at a young age, which made him think quite a bit about his own mortality. He decided a will wasn't such a bad idea. He told me he didn't have a lot as far as items of value, but the cross had been with him most of his life, and he wanted it to go to someone he loved. That person is you."

"Wow," said Bernie. "He cared that much for me even back then?"

"Even though you were guarded, he understood you cared about him. He should've told you his feelings sooner, but it's no one's fault," said Alex. He squeezed Bernie's shoulder.

"Sometimes we withhold our feelings because we think it's in the other party's best interest, or we have plenty of time. It's a common thought pattern. Anyway, let's move on to the paperwork," said Mitch.

While Mitch rifled through papers, Bell put an arm around Bernie and whispered so only she could hear. "If you ever doubted his true feelings, Bernie, this speaks volumes. He was never without that cross, and now he's giving it to you. He'll always be with you in some way." Bernie bit down on her bottom lip and nodded.

Bell leaned her head against the cool glass of the limo. Her eyes drooped as she thought about how thankful she was for her father's meticulousness when it came to handling legal documents. Not everyone had a will at his age or a nephew who was a lawyer. If it weren't for their father, their mother's estate would have been an even bigger mess.

Bernie was the only one who had to jump through hoops. She was still married to Martin, but the divorce papers had been filed, and a court date was pending. While Oklahoma was a no-fault state, it was unlikely Martin would get anything from Alan or Mariska's estates since he was the reason for their demise. Unfortunately, her assets were tentatively frozen. Mitch immediately opened the emergency fund for Bernie so she could take care of her bills, even though Bell knew she'd be the one paying them, as Bernie was too busy dealing with her OCD and PTSD.

"Anyone hungry?" asked Bell. Alex was snoozing to the right of Bell. She watched as he opened a tentative eye.

"I could definitely eat something," he said.

"Maybe," added Bernie.

"It's already 2:30. Why don't we order a pizza. Then, if we're hungry later, we can eat popcorn or something," suggested Bell.

"Sure, that sounds good. I haven't had popcorn in forever," said Bernie. "I miss the butter."

"You haven't exactly eaten a whole lot in the past three weeks," commented Alex. "You're beginning to look anorexic."

"I guess I have some catching up to do," said Bernie.

"Bern, I don't think it works that way," replied Bell. "You definitely need to put on a little weight. Alex is right. You're looking a little under the weather from an outsider's standpoint."

"Whatever," she said back, "I'm down with pizza and popcorn. Besides, no one in the industry has ever said a model needed to gain weight, right?"

"Girlfriend, you're in denial. There are plenty of underweight models. Take Linz, for example. That girl needs a sammich," said Alex. "Probably a whole pie. Maybe some chocolate cake, too." He laughed. "Now I'm making myself hungrier. Chocolate cake sounds delightful."

"Are you going to make one? I don't think Sammy's Pizza sells chocolate cakes," said Bell. Scrolling through her phone, she looked for the restaurant's number.

"I don't have to." Alex grinned. "I keep a frozen one on hand for situations like this."

Bernie's eyes widened. "Seriously?" she asked. "Where did said cake come from?"

"Girlllll. You know it came from Angela's Bakery. She makes the best chocolate cakes, hands down," said Alex.

"Oh, yeah, I know her chocolate cakes. They're amazing, and amazingly expensive. You're spending over a hundred dollars on an eight-inch cake?" Bell wasn't overly surprised by this. Her brother knew how to spend money when he was in the mood.

"How do you know how much this cake costs?" Bernie eyed her sister.

Bell let out a sigh. "I know the price because I've bought one before."

Bernie pointed her finger at Bell. "So, what you're saying is, you're a hypocrite?"

"In my defense, I had no idea I was buying a cake that expensive. Alex clearly gets his taste for expensive chocolate cakes from Mom. When you were away on one of your swimwear shoots six years ago, we threw Claire, our model agency receptionist, a baby shower, and I was to bring the cake. Mom told me she called it in, and all I had to do was pick it up and pay for it. I was shocked when I found out I was paying one hundred and eighty dollars for the ten-inch cake. I almost refused it, but I didn't have a backup in place, and I didn't want to disappoint Claire. I definitely gave Mom a piece of my mind later. She, of course, thought I 'was being ridiculous,' but you know, Mariska, no regard for other people's financial positions."

Bernie had a disgusted look on her face. "Well, that was a crummy play on her part. We didn't have nearly as much money back then."

"She did reimburse me, but at the time, I thought I was going to be stuck paying for the over-priced cake," said Bell.

"I know they're expensive, but I love them all the same," said Alex with a sigh.

Holding her phone up to her ear, Bell motioned for her siblings to be quiet. "Hi, this is Sammy's Pizza, correct?" The person on the other end had answered so rapidly their words had been inaudible. "I'd like to order a large pepperoni and pineapple pizza. That's for Alex Crimson, on Tanzanite Lane." She paused for a moment and listened. "Yes, that's the correct phone number. Thank you." A moment later she hung up.

"Yum," said Bernie. "Pizza is sounding tastier by the minute."

"That was perfect timing. We've arrived, and our pizza will be here in twenty minutes," said Bell. "We should have just enough time to get changed, remove our makeup, and sit down for dinner." She looked at her sister, whose eyes seemed to hold a spark she hadn't seen in a while. She was happy to hear Bernie express a desire for food. It had been rough getting her to eat.

The siblings exited the limo and headed up the walkway. Approaching the door, Bell noticed something stuck to it. "What is that?" she asked. Alex pushed past her, and she followed him closely. He stopped short of the steps. There, in the center of the door, was a note with a knife sticking out of it. The note looked as if it had been written in blood.

Bell gasped and froze in her tracks. "What is it? Alex, what does it say?"

Bernie stepped up to the door. "I know," she read aloud. Looking at Alex, she asked, "Know what?"

He promptly marched up to the door and, with a firm grip, yanked the knife and the note from it. Turning his back to the house, he held up his hand and waived the knife and note in the air. "You're a funny one, Tyler. I told you I didn't eat the last cookie! I don't know why you keep demanding that I did! If you're going to worry about how many cookies are available and who ate the last one, then I suggest you ask Gerald to make extra next time! Don't think for one moment that I won't be coming back at you! You too, Kirk! I never thought you'd take Tyler's side! You better watch your backs!" Tyler was standing across the street with their mailman, Kirk. Both of the men were laughing uncontrollably and waving back at him.

"What's going on?" demanded Bell. "This is a prank? I nearly peed myself I was so freakin' scared!"

"I'm sorry, girls. Look," he said as he held out the knife and paper. "It's not real. See? It's just the handle of a knife. It wasn't really sticking out of the wood on the door." Crinkling his brow, he frowned and shook his head. "You know how I play poker with the guys a couple of times each month? Tyler and I have been razzing and pranking each other on and off for weeks. It started one night when we were at his place. It's nothing but a game between us. Although he was seriously miffed about those cookies." Alex laughed. "His husband makes the best chocolate, chocolate chip cookies I've ever tasted. I didn't eat the last one, but I definitely took it with me and threw it in the freezer." He grinned mischievously. "Kirk is also a member of the group, and until now, I thought he was an ally because he's helped me carry out a few of my own pranks. Tyler must have had him stick it to the door when he delivered the mail."

"After all we've been through, I didn't need a scare like that, and neither did Bernie," said Bell. Her eyes were dark as she stared back at her brother. "Now, let's go inside." She opened the door to the house, and they proceeded inward. Reaching around the corner, she flipped on the lights to the expansive entryway. The smell of lavender and vanilla relaxed her as she crossed over to the mudroom. Leaning over, she opened the lid to Alex's freezer and peered inside.

"Yep," she called out. "There's a chocolate, chocolate chip cookie in here." She laughed. "Or, at least, there was." She broke off a chunk of frozen cookie and popped it into her mouth. The cold, sweet treat made her mouth water in delight. "Oh, this is delicious."

Bernie walked in behind Bell and snatched the cookie from her hand. "I so need this," she said," and popped a large piece into her mouth. "Mmm," she moaned. "I see why he took it." She pressed the cookie back into Bell's hand and lightly nudged her to move over. "Now, where's that cake?" she said as she began shoving frozen foods aside. "Oh, here it is." She pulled the cake out, and Bell closed the lid. "Is it wrong to emotionally eat? I feel it may be warranted after all we've been through."

"I'm with you, sister," said Bell. They proceeded to the kitchen.

Alex walked into the room, now sporting black sweatpants and a red t-shirt. Bell looked at him with amusement. Even when he dressed down, her brother still looked fashionable. He could have gone out for a night on the town in that ensemble, and it would have been okay because he was rocking the Prada loungewear. Soft, luxurious, and cozy, but stylish as heck.

Walking up to Bell, he pointed at the cookie. "I believe that's mine."

"Finders keepers," said Bernie, waving the frozen chocolate cake over her head.

"Now wait just one minute," said Alex, "I believe everything in this house was once found and stowed here by me. This is still my house. Therefore, these items have already been found and most definitely claimed. I don't believe 'finders keepers' works when it's in another man's home." He frowned at them as he went for the cake.

Bernie put the cake box under her arm and went into a defensive football stance. "Whatcha gonna do about it, big brother?" She laughed. Bell jaunted around the breakfast bar to stand in defense of her sister and the frozen cake. The doorbell rang before Alex had a chance to react.

"I'll grab it," said Alex, ignoring his sisters and turning toward the door.

"That's right, you run away!" called Bell as Bernie tossed the cake onto the breakfast bar. It slid halfway across the counter and stopped short of the edge. The girls gave one another a wide-eyed look. "That was close," said Bell. Bernie stifled a laugh. "We should get changed. The pizza's going to get cold." Both girls ran off in the direction of their rooms as the smell of gooey, cheesy, fresh pizza filled their nostrils.

When Bell returned, she had on her father's old oversized black t-shirt and her grey ripped-up baggy sweatpants. She understood that her sister didn't approve of this ensemble, but it was comfortable and comforting. She couldn't part with the ratty old clothes, especially now that their father was gone. She knew Bernie would no longer object to keeping the old rags.

Bernie walked into the room. She had on a pair of Alex's Armani sweatpants, which were cinched tightly at the waist due to the weight her sister had lost, and a red 365th Street Jazz Club tank top. She hadn't taken the time to buy any new clothing since she'd fled from Martin. It was the last thing on her mind.

When Evie Wellington, the lingerie designer, heard what had happened to Bernadette, she sent over some bras and panties as a gift. Bell and Alex stopped at the club and picked up shirts from their marketing stock just so Bernie would have something to wear. They could never have expected that their sister wouldn't have replaced her clothing after three weeks. Bell had to give Bernie a dress to wear to the funeral, which wasn't a problem, but she couldn't stop herself from worrying about the lack of functionality coming from her sister. She was thankful that Bernadette was finally getting words out and showing her sense of humor once again, though she was sure that it was thanks to the drugs Andra had given her. Heck, she was pleased with the idea of her sister wanting to eat. If the drugs made it happen, they were a Godsend in Bell's eyes.

Alex set three plates and three beers on the breakfast bar and opened the pizza box. "Yummy," he said. "This truly hits the spot."

Bernie reached into the box and grabbed the first slice. Turning away, she swiped a beer bottle with her left hand and walked out of the kitchen and into the living room.

"You think she's okay?" whispered Alex.

"Yeah, I think it'll take a little more time, but I believe this is a start," Bell replied with sincerity. "We need to provide her with a sense of normalcy and comfort. I fully intend to press her to go back to counseling. I think it's important."

"I agree with you. She has to get her feelings out. The last thing I want is to see her have a nervous breakdown," said Alex.

"Come on, she's going to wonder what's taking us so long." Bell picked up her plate of pizza and her beer and walked away.

After dinner and cake, Bell could no longer sit still. She walked over to the fireplace and flipped the switch to turn it on. Reaching overhead, she hit the power for the stereo and cranked up her favorite radio station. The DJ announced that there would be a dance party going on all night. She was stoked. Dance party night was her favorite. "Who wants to have a dance party with me?" she asked excitedly.

The music brought back a memory of their mother. Years ago, when they were growing up, they'd had a family cat. Her mother delighted in dancing with the cat. Bell wasn't sure the cat loved it, but for some reason, Sammy the cat put up with it. Probably because Sammy loved their mother. Bell smiled. Sammy had been an exceptional animal.

Alex reached out and lightly shook Bell's shoulder. "Heck yeah!" he said. "I could use some exercise, and dancing is the best form. It'll help relieve some stress, which is something we all need!"

"Come on, Bernie, you know you want to!" The song *Turn Down for What* began to play, and Alex and Bell started dancing around the living room. Bell was smooth when she danced, and Alex was capable of fluid dance moves, as well as robotic. He had taken dance classes six years earlier. According to his teacher, he could have been a professional dancer, but Alex liked modeling and chose to stick to that.

Watching Bernie out of the corner of her eye, she noticed a smile erupt. It wouldn't be long, she thought to herself. As if she had read Bell's mind, Bernie gave her a look, jumped up from the couch, and began dancing around the room. She knew how to move her hips and always looked beautiful when she danced. It was no wonder she attracted so many people to the dance floor when she was out at the clubs. Her rhythm was contagious, and she had been compared to *Shakira* on more than one occasion.

The three continued to dance and jump around to several more songs. Bell thought it was nice to let loose. It had been a long time since she was able to enjoy a moment with both Bernie and Alex. She needed more stress-free moments, such as the present. She was tired of the pain and drama and of being sad and mopey.

After the eighth song, all three collapsed onto the couch.

"Man, that felt great," said Alex. "I'll consider that a replacement for the run I missed this morning."

"Yeah, I haven't danced in months," commented Bernie with a tired smile.

"Let's agree to dance and let loose more often," said Bell. "I know we need to mourn our losses, but we also need to find the happy things in our lives. We need to laugh, dance, and be silly because our loved ones want us to. Life is much too short. Let's not waste it."

"Yeah—" Alex was cut off by a loud crash. He flung himself over his sisters to make sure they were protected. "Don't move," he whispered urgently. Bell surmised that he was listening to see if anything else was going to happen. When nothing else came through the window, he slowly pulled himself away and crawled toward it, getting down on his hands and knees. From the side, he peered out into the yard. Darkness had crept in.

"What do you see?" asked Bernie. "Is anyone out there?"

"No, I don't see anyone," he replied, "though it's tough to tell in this light. Bell, call the police." He walked over to the wall across from the window and bent down. Reaching out, he plucked an object from the floor. It was a baseball with a note attached to it. He pulled the note away from the ball and unfolded it. Reading out loud, he said, "*Peacetime is over.*"

"Oh, my, God," gasped Bernie. "Did they sign it?" her voice shook, and her face paled as she backed further away from the window.

"No. It isn't signed. I'm not sure what it would say if it was." Alex's demeanor was all business.

"Who's it from?" shrieked Bernie. "Who? Is it Martin's partner? Or is it your neighbor again?" Bernie backed herself up against the wall and dropped to the floor, hugging her knees.

Bell dialed 9-1-1 into her phone and waited as it rang. She watched Alex walk over to their hysterical sister. Trying to calm her, he wrapped her tightly in his arms.

"Are we in danger?" she squeaked.

"I don't know, Bernie," said Alex, his tone was tired. "I need you to pull it together for us. We have no idea what we're looking at here."

Bell was still waiting for someone to pick up. "The ball was catapulted through that window. It's lucky it didn't hit any of us," she said in awe. Finally, someone picked up on the other end. "Hi, this is Bell Price. I'm calling from my brother Alex's house. Someone threw a baseball through the front window. There was a threatening note attached to it." She paused to listen to the operator. "Okay, thank you." She hung up the phone. "There should be an officer on the scene within ten minutes. In the meantime, they said to stay inside the house."

Alex and Bernie were now seated silently on the couch. Alex was still hugging her. Bell walked over to her sister and sat down on her opposite side. Turning, she placed her hands on her shoulders. "Listen, we're not going to let anyone hurt you. You need to be strong. I know this is scary, but we need to try to remain calm. Until the police arrive, I think it's best we go into a different room where we cannot be seen. Perhaps the kitchen would be better?" she asked Alex.

"Yeah, I think you're right," he said. "The kitchen keeps us near the exits but away from the windows. We'll know the second the police arrive. Bell, why don't you call Matt? See if he'll come over.

I'd feel better if we were to look at this situation from all angles and not just sheer paranoia and fear."

Nodding her head, she said, "I already texted him. He'll be here in fifteen minutes."

The trio headed for the kitchen. Alex walked over to the sink and started loading dishes into the dishwasher while Bernie and Bell took seats at the breakfast bar. Bell didn't know what to think about the situation. Who could be out there watching? Was all of this linked to Martin? An uncomfortable chill ran through her body as the paranoia grew. Without realizing it, she began chewing on the nail of her left pointer finger.

After the incident with Bradley, the Price family worried that Martin's accomplice was still coming for them, but after a week of investigative work, Detective Wells decided that Bradley had been the only target. The department believed the shooting was a way of silencing and stopping Bradley from remembering who had kidnapped him. Since no one else could identify the shooter, Wells thought the Price family to be safe. Bell had been leery about putting her paranoia to rest. What if he was wrong? She couldn't afford to lose any more family members. The pain was unbearable as it was. If Bradley was the only target, why didn't the shooter leave after Bradley was down? There would be no need to fire other shots. Wells said the shooter was probably caught up in the moment and trying to create a further distraction for their getaway.

Looking over at her sister, Bell could tell Bernie was letting her fears dance around inside her head. The look on her face was panicked. She feared her sister would retreat back into her reclusive state.

"Hey, Bern, why don't you take your Xanax? It'll help you relax. It's about time to take it, anyway. Also, Alex, don't give her any more beer. She probably shouldn't be drinking."

"I feel fine. The light buzz I had is gone," said Bernie. "Toss that bottle here, please," she motioned to Alex, and he threw her the bottle of pills. She popped one into her mouth and washed it down with a bottle of water, which Alex also handed her. Averting her eyes, she shook her head. "I can't do this anymore."

"I know, we can't either," stated her brother. "I don't know what's going on, but we'll figure this out. I promise. No one else is going to die," he said with confidence.

The next several minutes were quiet as they waited for the police to arrive. Finally, after what felt like an hour, the doorbell rang. Bell hopped up from her stool and proceeded toward the entry. Opening it, she found a handsome grey-haired older officer and the middle-aged Detective Wells standing on the other side. Looking at the grey-haired officer, Bell noticed a distinct resemblance to Bradley. She hadn't met him in person, but from the look on his face, it had to be him.

"Officer," she nodded, "Detective. Come on in." Her brother and sister stood behind her, watching as the gentlemen entered the house.

"This is Officer Thompson," said Wells. He's Bradley's father. Alex gasped and then reached out and shook Thompson's hand. Bell noticed Thompson's pained look had instantly turned to that of concern, which reminded her of the expression their father would get when he was worried about his children's safety.

"You're Bradley's father?" asked Bell.

"Yeah," replied Thompson. Bell could hear the sadness in his voice, but the look of concern stayed present.

"How come we've never met you?" demanded Bernie. She looked like an angry cat ready to attack. Bell reached out and gently squeezed her arm, raising an eyebrow as she looked at her. Bernie sighed, and the pained expression returned to her face.

"I transferred back to town a few weeks before Bradley's death. If he never brought me up, it was because he didn't know I existed. His mother never told either of us about the other until she was on her deathbed."

"Wow, that's sad," said Alex.

"Yeah," replied Thompson. "Bernie, he did tell me about you. He took my cruiser while I was in the bathroom and messaged me, saying it was an emergency. He had to save the woman he loved."

Bernie stared back at him, and a tear ran down her face. "I'm glad he got to meet you. He mentioned you when I asked about the police cruiser. I never got a chance to ask any further questions. I should have made a point to ask."

"That's okay, dear. I'm sure he understands. Anyway, let's focus on the current situation. Why don't you and I talk more about this later?" Wells had given him a look to indicate that he should wrap up the current conversation.

"That sounds good. I definitely have some questions," she said. Thompson squeezed her hand.

Leading the way, Bell said, "The living room is over here."

The entire entourage followed her into the next room. Alex and Bernie took their places around the perimeter, still taking care to avoid the windows as much as possible. Detective Wells walked over and took a look at the window. Bell handed Thompson the baseball and note. He looked at it tentatively, then walked it over to the detective. Bell noticed both men were wearing gloves, something she hadn't thought about.

Wells reached out and grabbed the articles from the officer and stared at them for a moment. A frown crossed his lips. "I assume you've all put your fingerprints on these?" asked Wells. His tone held a note of irritation.

"Not all of us," said Bell. "Bernie didn't touch them."

"Oh goodie," he replied. "Next time, be more careful when inspecting the evidence. It makes it hard to get prints off an item if everyone and their neighbor has held it."

Bell couldn't help but notice that the detective seemed more owly than usual. She didn't appreciate being treated like an imbecile. She watched him examine the room, the window, and the objects again. Walking over to the sofa, she dropped down onto it with a squish. She may as well be comfortable while they waited.

Five minutes passed, and Wells returned his attention to the trio. "Now, tell me what happened from your viewpoint," he requested.

Bell pushed herself back up. "We'd been listening to music and dancing to let off some steam. After eight or nine songs, all three of us were drained, so we sat down on the sofa. We had no more than sat down when the baseball came flying through the window. Alex got down on his hands and knees and crawled to the window to see if anyone was out there, but due to the darkness, he couldn't see anyone."

"Alex, is that correct?" asked Officer Thompson.

"Yes sir, mostly. When the ball came through the window, I threw myself over the girls to keep them protected, then after a minute, I crawled to the window to see if anyone was out there," he replied.

"What happened next?" asked Wells.

"I crept over to the object to see what it was. Picking it up, I noticed the note, which I unwrapped and read aloud to my sisters. Then I asked Bell to call the police, and we retired to the kitchen to stay clear of the windows until your arrival."

"Smart thinking, son," said Thompson.

Wells puffed out his cheeks and squinted as he nodded in agreement. "Officer Thompson and I are going to go outside and look around to see if there's anything we've missed. We'll speak to you shortly," said Wells. He turned and left the room with Thompson trailing closely behind.

"Wow, is it just me, or is Wells in an exceptionally crummy mood?" asked Alex.

"It's not just you," said Bernie quietly. "He was so much nicer the last time we saw him."

As they sat in wait for Thompson and Wells to return, Matthew walked in. He wore a gray polo shirt with a black leather jacket, black Dockers, and black Doc Martens. No matter what he wore, his clothes always looked good. What didn't look good, was the expression of concern on his face. He hurried over to Bell.

"Oh, thank goodness you're here, Matt," said Bell, standing up to greet him. "We don't know what's going on, and we're all a little freaked out."

"I'm here now," he consoled, wrapping her in a warm embrace. "We'll figure this out. I'm going outside to talk to Wells and Thompson. I also want to see if I notice anything they might have missed, but first, let me take a look at those." He pulled a pair of leather gloves from his back pocket and put them on. Reaching out, he picked up the baseball and note Detective Wells had left on a nearby coffee table. "Not a lot of information to go on," he said.

"*Peacetime is over.*" His reaction was similar to that of Detective Wells.

"What do you think about this whole incident?" asked Bell.

"Well, let me take a look outside, and then we can talk more. I can't give you much if I haven't checked things out from every angle." He kissed her on the cheek and headed outdoors.

"I simply cannot stand waiting," said Alex. He was now pacing back and forth in front of the broken window. "It feels like we do a lot of waiting these days. Why can't they just tell us what happened? Shouldn't they know? The show *CSI* makes it seem so easy."

Bell rolled her eyes at him. "Alex, I don't think that's quite how it works. We have to be patient, just a little longer. I'm sure they'll come back inside shortly and tell us what they believe is going on."

"What if they can't give us anything? What if they don't know?" asked Bernie.

"Well, hopefully, they'll keep looking until they find something solid," she replied to her sister. "Alex, please stop." She took a seat on the couch next to Bernie. "Your obsessive pacing isn't helping. It's making me more anxious."

He stopped and looked at her for a moment and then let himself sink into the nearest chair.

"Maybe we should go back to dancing?" he stood up and walked back to the stereo and turned the music on. "That'll teach whoever to screw with us." He laughed. "I mean seriously, maybe if we act like we don't care, they'll leave us alone."

"Maybe you have a point," said Bell. "Or maybe that'll make them more angry and provoke a stronger response."

"Which will make you happier," asked Alex, "music and dancing, or cowering in fear?"

"Well, obviously the music and dancing," said Bernie. "But that doesn't mean we'll be any safer. It may mean that we make ourselves even bigger targets, and I, for one, am not keen on that idea."

"We don't even know who's doing this or why," stated Bell. "Seriously, whatever is going on, or whoever this person is, we need to make an agreement here and now. We'll stick together and make decisions as a family. The situation we just went through with Martin nearly got us all killed due to our inability to work together or involve the proper authorities from the start."

"Why'd you have to say that?" asked Bernie. "I feel crummy as it is."

"Bern," said Alex, "we aren't blaming you. We all dealt poorly with the Martin situation. We've learned many valuable lessons, and while we lost loved ones, we'll never blame you. That man made it his life's work to prey on women and rich families. This could have happened to anyone. Please get this in your head. It's not your fault."

A tear ran down Bernie's face.

"I agree with Alex," noted Bell. "You're our sister, and we love you. If anything, we're sorry we didn't find a way to stop the madness sooner. We never wanted you to go through such a horrible ordeal. We feel guilty as well."

"Okay," said Bernie as she got to her feet. "Who wants to dance?"

Alex and Bell stood up and walked toward their sister.

"Put your hands in," said Alex as he reached his hand out. Bell and Bernie placed their hands on top of his. "Repeat after me: *We're family, we're strong, and we will remain united and work together no matter what.*"

The three siblings repeated the words together, and then, at the end, Alex yelled, "Go team!" in a high-pitched voice.

Forty minutes had passed before Matthew, Detective Wells, and Officer Thompson returned inside.

"Well kids, we scoured the property and found nothing," said Wells. "I don't know what this incident was, but my best guess is that someone is messing with you. Did you anger one of your neighbors?" he asked Alex.

"Look at me," he replied. "I'm an attractive gay model with a chauffeur and a high-end fashion designer boyfriend. My neighbors, along with many other people, have any number of reasons to love or hate me. Take your pick. Earlier tonight, the neighbor across the street did pull a prank on us, but that was all in good fun; this is not. There's a distinct difference."

"Yeah, I suppose you've got a point there. It could be a hate crime. I'll be talking to your neighbors to find out if they saw anything suspicious."

"A hate crime," stated Bell. "That's honestly what you think this is? What about the shooting at the station? Don't you think it's possible they're connected, and just maybe Martin's partner is still out there and coming after us?"

"I think it is highly unlikely that these situations are intertwined," said Wells. "Thompson has a vested interest in this case, too. He's been on me to check out every single detail and possibility. The evidence to state otherwise is just not present." Thompson nodded in agreement.

Bell frowned at him. "I'm still not sure I agree with you on that. Martin is a sneaky and persuasive person. People believe what he wants them to believe."

"Either way," replied Wells, "Officer Thompson will be staying outside the house for the entirety of the evening to make sure nothing else happens. If you see or hear anything suspicious, please make sure you report it immediately." He turned his attention to Matthew. "Are you staying here tonight?" he asked.

"Yeah, I think that would be best," said Matthew, placing his hand lightly on Bell's shoulder. "I want to make sure everyone feels safe."

"Okay, but first thing tomorrow morning, I'd like it if you'd stop by the station for further discussion. The chief would like to meet you."

"Oh, interesting," said Matthew.

"Don't worry," said Wells, "you aren't in any trouble." He laughed.

"Humph, well, that's good. I guess I'll see you in the morning," said Matthew.

"Great, I look forward to it. Anyway, the rest of you lot stay out of trouble, okay? Remember to notify Thompson immediately if anything else happens. And, Bernie, don't talk Thompson's ear off all night. He has a job to do."

"Don't worry," said Bell, "We'll definitely let him know if anything happens, and I'll make sure Bernie lets him do his job."

"Good deal, kids, I'm heading out," he said, turning for the door. Thompson nodded toward the siblings and followed Wells.

"Dang," said Bernie. "We have a bodyguard sitting at the end of our driveway now."

"I wouldn't call him a bodyguard. He's more like a deterrent," said Matthew.

"He's Bradley's father; did you know that, Matthew?" asked Bernie.

"What? He's Bradley's father? Nope. Didn't know that. Why didn't I know that?" he asked.

"Because they had just met two weeks prior to the shooting," chimed Alex.

"Wow, that is unfortunate timing," replied Matt.

"Well, whatever he is, I feel safer for the moment, but what happens tomorrow when he leaves?" asked Bell.

"We'll deal with that situation when we get there," stated Alex. "I say we turn on a funny movie and wind down. We don't need any more negative excitement today. Who's up for *Airplane*? Leslie Nielsen makes everyone laugh," he said with a chuckle.

Chapter Four

Bell couldn't stop thinking about the note. What did it mean? She stared up at the ceiling, counting the glowing stars she had placed there. She'd barely slept. Each time she fell asleep, she was jolted awake by the creaking of the house or one of her siblings getting up to use the bathroom.

The group had stayed up late watching movies. None of them wanted to close their eyes any sooner than needed. Bell didn't know if she believed the incident was a hate crime or that it wasn't related to Bradley's death. Why wasn't Thompson pushing it more? Was there truly no evidence of who had been outside their house the night before?

Rolling over, she found herself face to face with Matthew, who was sound asleep. She stared lovingly at his handsome face. She was so lucky to have him. She felt sad about Bernie's loss and was curious to know more about Thompson. They would have to find some time to corner him later and find out more about his and Bradley's relationship.

Reaching out, she brushed her fingers lightly over Matt's short black hair, and leaning in, she kissed his lips softly. His eyes fluttered open when he felt her touch.

"Good morning," he said with a sleepy smile. Reaching out, he slid his arms around her waist and pulled her closer. "How are you feeling?"

"A little anxious." She couldn't seem to stop chewing her bottom lip. It was beginning to taste slightly metallic. "I didn't sleep well."

"Anything I can do to help you relax?" he asked. "Maybe I can massage some of that tension out of you?" He pressed his fingers into her shoulders.

"Do you have a meat tenderizer under the covers somewhere?"

"Not exactly," he grinned, "but I'm sure I have other tools that could maybe do the trick."

"Like some form of full-body massage cushion, maybe?" she asked playfully.

"Hmm, not quite what I was thinking," he replied, reaching down and squeezing her bottom. Moving his hands upward, he massaged her lower back gently while pressing his body tightly against hers.

Bell could feel the electricity pulsing through her as Matthew's fingers worked their way into her lower back. Pushing him away, she sat up and swung her legs over his body, positioning herself just above his waist. "You have some kind of jackhammer to bang the knots out of my body for me?" She grinned menacingly and stared into his eyes. "Or maybe you have the key to my relaxation," she said while rocking from side to side.

Matthew threw his hand over his mouth to cover a deep, throaty laugh.

"You know it, baby," he replied with pseudo confidence, as things had already begun to deflate from Bell's lack of seriousness.

She jumped off the bed. "I'm going to make coffee," she declared and bounced out of the room.

"Troublemaker!" Matthew called after her.

She smiled to herself as she walked into the kitchen. She understood he meant well, and honestly, under normal circumstances, she might have been down for what he prescribed, but today, she couldn't seem to get past the anxiousness that was buzzing within her. They still hadn't taken things all the way, and she didn't want their first time to be amidst a crisis. He was patient with her, and she could tell he was truly invested, which was why her heart fluttered any time he touched her.

She filled the coffee maker's basket with grounds and hit the brew button just as her phone rang. She trotted over to the island where she'd left it sitting the night before. "This is Bell," she said.

"Bell, it's Hector. I'm checking in to make sure you remembered the show tonight. I know things have been crazy, and Alex has been a bit elusive lately, but please tell me you're still coming? Also, I'm short a model. Is your sister available?" he exhaled loudly into the phone, then said, "I'm so stressed out. This is my biggest show of the year, and I need it to be perfect. What will I do if I'm short a model?" his voice raised two octaves. "This is terrible! I cannot believe this is happening."

"Hector! Breathe, okay? Things will be fine." She couldn't promise the same for Alex since he'd failed to inform her of the show, but she would be there and help Hector in any way possible. "What time and where is the event being held?" she asked.

"What? Alex didn't give you the details?" Bell could feel his horror seeping through the phone.

"I'm sure it slipped his mind. There's been a lot going on with the funerals and our sister. Last night, someone chucked a rock through Alex's front window, so we had to deal with that."

"A rock? Who would do such a thing?" he asked. "Is everyone okay?"

"Yeah. We're okay, but there's concern as to whether we are being targeted by Martin's partner or if it was a hate crime."

"That's awful. Keep me posted," he said, and then, "The show is at the Zarrington Theatre at 8 o'clock this evening, but I need you, and hopefully your sister, there at 6 o'clock to get ready. Is that doable?"

"Yes. I think so. I can't promise you Bernie will be up for it, but I'll try to work it out. I'll text you when I have further information."

"Good. I look forward to seeing you," he said and hung up the phone.

Matthew walked into the room and grabbed the freshly brewed pot of coffee. Pulling two cups from the hooks beneath the cupboard, he poured Bell a mug and then himself.

"Thanks," she said, carefully grabbing the steaming mug from him.

"So, what was that all about," he asked. "An event?"

"Oh, Hector, of course. Did you know I'm supposed to be in a runway show tonight?"

"Nope."

"Me either," she replied and shook her head in wonderment. "Alex needs to start making notes on what he schedules. This is the second time he's forgotten to inform me of a show in recent weeks."

"Yeah, that sounds about right. Things have been pretty crazy. It's easy to forget when you're under extreme stress."

"Is it, though? We're models, after all. This is our livelihood."

"Yes, but in extreme circumstances, you could forget your name," said Matt.

Shaking her head, she said, "Those would have to be pretty extreme circumstances."

"All I'm saying is go easy on him. He's under a lot of stress, too. I'll be amazed if he even remembers he's in the show."

"Humph." He was right, but she hated it when Alex acted like an airhead and forgot to tell her things.

"Speak of the Devil," said Matthew as Alex walked in.

"Your ears must have been burning," said Bell. "I just got off the phone with Hector. Did you know we're in a runway show tonight?"

"Get out! What? I had no idea," replied Alex.

"Don't play with me, boy," said Bell with a stern look. "How could you forget to tell me something like that?" After the words had left her mouth, she realized she'd totally disregarded Matthew's advice.

Alex wrinkled his face into a frown. "I'm sorry, Bell, it slipped my mind. It's undeniably my fault. I'll let Hector know that I forgot to tell you."

Bell pointed her finger at him. "Yes, and you'll talk Bernie into doing the show as well."

"Whoa," said Alex. "Why does Bernie need to do the show? Are you not going to attend?"

Rolling her eyes, she said, "I'm going, of course, but Hector is still short a model."

Alex raised his eyebrow as he glared back at Bell. "Don't you think you're asking for a miracle?"

"What miracle?" asked Bernie as she made her way into the room.

Bell grabbed a mug and nudged Alex. "Ask her," she prodded while pouring coffee into the mug.

"There's a runway show tonight at the Zarrington Theatre. It's one of Hector's shows. I completely forgot about it, but Bell and I are both modeling. Hector needs one more person, and we think it should be you."

Bell handed the cup of coffee to Bernie, who walked over to the kitchen table to take a seat next to Matthew.

"No," said Bernie. "I don't want to. I'm not ready," she squeaked.

"Listen, I know you're feeling uneasy, but we'll both be there with you. I think you need to get out of the house and do something normal again," said Bell. She'd put on her best concerned face, but she didn't believe it would be easy to convince her sister.

"Why? Why do you want me to go? Can't someone else do it? Ask Audra."

Alex shook his head. "Audra's already in the show, so she's out of the question.

"Geez, Alex, you're using the models from Price & Fitz, and you didn't tell me?" barked Bell.

"The schedule was clear, and you were busy dealing with other things," replied her brother.

"Seriously, I need you to run things like this past me before making a decision."

Alex ignored Bell's comment. "Bernie," he said, "you love modeling. Don't give up your passion because of fear."

"Do you think I want to feel this way?" she asked, the coffee cup shaking in her hands. Bell realized her sister was one step away from screaming and hyperventilating.

"Calm down and breathe. I know you don't want to feel this way, but getting out is part of healing. You'll take a Xanax, the last one, and you'll do this show because you're strong and brave."

"I don't feel strong or brave," she said quietly.

"Listen," chimed in Matthew, "we'll all be there. Your sister's right; you can't let this break you. I know that strong, confident woman is still in there somewhere." He grinned.

"Bernie, I think right now the best things for you are to go back to counseling and to try to start working again. You just need a little confidence building and to be surrounded by people who care about you. We have been through a lot of traumas, too. We will help you in any way we can," said Bell. "Whether you do the show tonight or not, I want you to promise that you'll go back to therapy."

"Yes, Bell. I'll go back to therapy, and yes, fine, I'll do the show. Anything is better than being alone in the house after what happened last night."

"Good thinking," said Alex. "I don't want you here alone either."

"It's settled then. We'll head out at five-thirty. We have to be there by six, but the show isn't until eight o'clock. Matthew, will you be joining us?" asked Bell. In all the discussion, she'd nearly forgotten he was there. He had been so quiet. Taking things in as always. It was one of the things that made him a great investigator.

"I wouldn't miss it," he declared as he got to his feet. Leaning over, he kissed her on the forehead. "I've got to go. They want me at the station this morning. I should probably make myself presentable."

"Okay, I'll see you later." Bell blew him a kiss, and with a smile, she breathed out a sigh as she watched him leave. He wore a ripped pair of blue jeans, red high-top Converse All Stars, and a red cotton muscle shirt that advertised Captain Morgan. The man was hot, no doubt about it. It didn't matter what he wore.

After Matthew left, the day seemed to race by. Bell and Alex had immediately left for their morning run. After breakfast, they spent the remainder of the morning filling out paperwork with Bernie for entry back into therapy. The afternoon was spent cleaning Alex's house, at which point Alex had conveniently disappeared. He'd agreed to meet Hector early in preparation for the show. Bell understood it was important for him to be there for his man since Hector had been so good to their family over the past months.

Before long, the cleaning was complete and it was time to head to the Zarrington. Bell chewed her nails as she thought about the show. She knew her arch nemesis, Emmy Lou Baker, from their local newspaper, would be there waiting for the chance to drag her name through the mud. Emmy loved any dirt she could dig up on Bell. It started when Bell broke a heel and fell off the catwalk the prior year and continued when she caught wind of the horror story regarding Martin. Add Bradley's untimely tragic death, and it was the sweet, creamy icing atop the mass media cake.

The article Emmy wrote pulled in press from all over the US. They followed the Price family around and camped outside their homes. Emmy Lou Baker was thriving, and Bell's stomach soured any time she heard the insidious woman's name. Pausing for a moment before walking toward the door, Bell crossed herself and prayed Bernie would make it through the night without giving Emmy any further highlights to gloat about.

"Bernie! We've got to go!" Bernie was in her room with the door closed. Bell could hear her pacing and shuffling things about. If it had been Bell in her situation, there would have been loud thuds as she threw things around, trying to find the right outfit. She wasn't nearly as graceful as her younger sister. Bell didn't know what to expect when her sister emerged from the room.

Bernie looked pale and thin as of late. She wanted things to return to how they once had been, even though she understood nothing would ever be the same. Time was the solitary thing that could heal, but getting Bernie out of the house and back into a routine was the first step to recovery.

Bell held her breath as Bernie's door began to open. Unbelievably, her sister was dressed to kill. She had on a flowing purple dress made up of satin and tulle. The straps were thin, and the neckline cut down to two inches above her belly button and covered just the right amount of cleavage. The back of the dress scooped down just above her butt and flowed outward when she walked. She had on dangling diamond earrings and a y-necklace with several diamonds resting directly between her breasts. On her feet, she wore black strappy stilettos; each had a diamond on the band, which sparkled when the light caught them.

"Dang girl, I guess this is some serious business tonight," said Bell. "I feel like I need to change clothing now."

"You should change," replied Bernie while spritzing herself with what appeared to be Bell's perfume. "Here, I borrowed this," she explained, handing the bottle to her. "I guess I'm back on the market again, and I should look and smell good if I ever want to find another man. Once the new man finds out about Martin and my past, he'll most definitely run screaming for the hills, and the cycle will repeat itself, but at least I'll look and smell good in the process," she said. Her mouth curved into a frown, and for a moment, Bell could see tears glistening at the corners of her sister's eyes. Bernie blinked them away and stared back at her sister.

Reaching out, Bell put a hand on her sister's shoulder. "Don't say that. Things can only improve, right? Anyway, what *exactly* are you wearing?"

"It's a Hector piece. It was sent over this morning. Didn't you get a package?" Bernie pointed toward the kitchen. "Alex set them on the buffet. I thought you knew."

"No, I definitely missed that conversation. Okay, well, I guess you'd better heat up the steam iron for me. This dress is bound to be wrinkled if he sent them over in boxes."

"It's in my bathroom. I bet it's still hot. I'll turn it back on." She walked back into the bedroom as Bell set off toward the kitchen.

Sure enough, there sat the box on the buffet. Her name was scrolled in large, beautiful letters across the top. She tore into it like a child at Christmas. The dress was silver and very sparkly. She pulled it out of the box. Upon further inspection, she realized it wasn't actually a dress but a romper of sorts. It had the same plunging neckline and back as Bernie's dress, but with long loose sleeves and flowing shorts. The whole torso of the romper was adorned with tiny white crystals that shimmered in the light.

Bell proceeded back to Bernie's bathroom.

"Here's a hanger," stated her sister.

"Thanks."

"That is an interesting piece," said Bernie. "I like it," she smiled genuinely and held out the steam iron. "It shouldn't take much to remove the wrinkles. This fabric is fairly easy to work with."

"It's nice to see you smile," said Bell. She grabbed the iron and set to work, steaming the garment.

Ten minutes later, she was dressed in her sexy new Perrago couture and ready to go. She'd chosen diamond studs and nothing more. Her outfit was so sparkly she didn't feel it needed a long, dangling necklace. She'd slipped on the matching pair of silver stilettos, and then she and Bernie were on their way out the door.

Even though Alex was not riding along, he had sent Andre to pick them up.

"Good evening," said Andre as he opened the door to the limo. "You ladies both look ravishing." He smiled with adoration. He'd known the Price family for five years and was more than just a limo driver. He had become a friend and confidante, too.

"Thank you, Andre," said Bernie.

"So, are you ready for this?" he asked. He held Bernie's hand firmly and helped her into the car.

"No, but at what point will it become any easier?" she asked.

"She just needs to rip the bandage off and do it," said Bell.

"I guess that's one way of dealing with it. Well, young lady, I'll be parked outside if you need to go anywhere." He winked at Bernie.

Bell climbed into the limo, and Andre shut the door behind her. They pulled out of the driveway and were on their way to the show. *Nothing is going to stop this freight train*, thought Bell. She knew she had to keep pushing Bernie, or she'd go right back to her hermit-like state.

Andre eased the limo up to the curb outside the Zarrington. Several other cars were dropping off models for the show. Looking out the window, Bell saw Linz and Audra walking with three more models. She'd seen them more frequently as of late. They were the newbies in her agency, and despite Alex's blatant lack of regard for her end of the business, she was thrilled Hector was borrowing them for the evening. She noted that Linz looked even thinner than the last time she saw her. Alex was right. That girl needed to eat something.

"Come on, lady, let's get in there and rip the bandage off!" She could tell Bernie wasn't feeling the vibe, but she hoped the excitement would catch on as they entered the building.

"Lead the way. I'm right behind you," said her sister. "Bye, Andre. Thank you for the ride." Andre closed the door as the girls walked away.

"Break a leg," he called after them.

"He knows we aren't actors, right?" laughed Bernie.

"Who knows," said Bell. "Sometimes I'm not sure he even knows what city we live in. He's a little scatterbrained at times."

"Yeah, you can say that again, but seriously, why would you tell a model to break a leg?"

"I'm with ya. If we break a leg, we can no longer work. Can you maybe say, *unbreak a leg*, so I feel better, and I'm no longer jinxed?" asked Bell. "Last thing I want is to break a leg. It was bad enough when I fell off the stage last year."

"Um, okay. Drama much?" asked Bernie, shaking her head. "You need to get over that. It was an accident. Anyway, unbreak a leg, and good luck out there. Does that work for ya?"

Bell scowled back at her. "Thanks, that makes me feel a whole lot better."

"Whatever," said Bernie, motioning her hands in the air. "So, where do you suppose Alex is?"

"I'm texting right now." Bell had her phone in hand as it began to ring. "Hello?"

"It's me," said Alex from the other end. "Oh." He laughed. "I see you!"

Bell looked up as Bernie grabbed her arm and pointed at Alex, who had glided through the doorway to the atrium. She hung up the phone and stowed it back inside her shimmery black Coach clutch.

"It's about time you two arrived," said Alex. He held his hands up in the air and motioned to the space surrounding him. "Isn't this great? Hector fully outdid himself this year. The theme is Enchanted Garden. Aren't the flowers extravagant?" he asked. Pausing, he took in a deep breath and sighed it out.

Bell looked around and let the sweet smell of the flowers infiltrate her senses. Roses, Jasmine, Gardenia, and Rosemary?

Bernie had wandered over to a nearby flower bed with a water fountain in the middle. "This is almost as impressive as the garden at the Bellagio in Las Vegas. This had to take days to build."

"It took four days, which is less than the Bellagio, but this isn't as large of a production. The garden in the Bellagio is definitely one of my favorite places to visit. The flowers are divine, and they smell heavenly. I just can't get enough of it," said Alex.

Bernie flicked some water out of the fountain toward her brother.

"Hey, watch it, or you'll be going for a swim. Hector isn't going to be pleased if this tux gets wet. Speaking of, we should get moving. You both need to get to makeup and hair. You won't be wearing those dresses for the show, but he does want you to wear them out after. He likes having his clothes displayed during the hours surrounding an event."

"He's kind of a freak like you," laughed Bell.

"Don't you know it," said Alex. With lightning-quick reflexes, he snatched Bernie's hand out of the water.

"Hey!" she shouted in protest.

"No time to play. We have to go." He stepped off toward the hallway, and the girls followed closely behind.

Bell looked around the hall as they walked. For whatever reason, it was lit exclusively by twinkling purple fairy lights. She liked the look, but it was unnecessary, considering they were walking through the back hallway solely designated for the staff and models to get around.

Alex looked back at Bell. "Do you like the lights?"

"They're fun, but isn't all of this a little over the top? I mean, members of the staff and show are the only people allowed back here, right?" She thought back to the earlier conversation she'd had with Bernie. *What if someone breaks a leg?* she wondered.

"This adds to the transformation. He wants his models to feel the spirit of the event and get into character. He feels it will make for more confident models and a more believable show."

"All I believe is that Hector's a little nutty," said Bernie. Bell nodded in agreement and gave her sister a high-five.

"Don't pick on my man. I know he's different, but he's an artist and a hard worker."

"Did I hear the word artist?" asked a soft male voice. Hector had appeared, as if on cue, through one of the side doors and was now walking beside them.

"Yes, sir. We all think you're an amazing artist," replied Alex with admiration. He held his hand out for Hector, who grabbed it and squeezed.

"Isn't this great? I'm so excited. The space has truly taken on a magical feel. Melanie did a great job on the garden, right?"

"It's stunning," remarked Bell.

"We were musing over how wonderful your mood lighting is." Bernie laughed.

"What's so funny?" asked Hector. "You don't like the fairy lights? I thought they were an excellent addition." He pouted.

"Ignore them. You know you've been accepted into the family when my sisters decide to pick on you."

"On the contrary, we are quite impressed with how you surround everyone in the show with the same feeling you present to the audience. It isn't very often you meet a designer with that sort of ambition and desire to create a specific mood. Bernie and I both love it, and we're excited to be here wearing your beautiful clothing. Thank you, Hector." Bell reached over and squeezed Hector's shoulder, and he smiled back at her.

"You're welcome. By the way, you get to keep everything from tonight's show, so yay!" he squealed.

"Wow, you're so sweet," said Bernie. "I hope you don't figure out what a dork Alex is and leave him." She laughed.

"Hush you!" snapped Alex.

"Bernie," said Bell, lightly hitting her sister with her purse. "All joking aside, we are happy you two found one another."

"Yes," said Bernie in agreement. "You have been there for us in so many ways over the past month, and we appreciate it."

Bell's heart warmed at the thought of Hector and Alex, and she recognized that Bernie, despite locking herself inside her room for the majority of the time, was right. Hector had been there for them. He'd brought food and taken care of everything with the businesses with a little help from his friends so the family could do what they needed to do to grieve and move on. Though eccentric, Hector was a great man capable of running a business and creating beautiful things at the same time. Alex was lucky to have such a well-rounded guy in his life.

Arriving at the hair and makeup stations, Bell noticed that Audra and Linz were about to sit down. There were three other models there as well. Each was a regular freelance whom Price & Fitz would hire on occasion, but as of late, three regular spots had opened inside the agency, and they needed replacing. Hector was trying to get her to hire them, but Bell preferred to meet each possible hire in person so she could evaluate how serious they were about their futures. After seeing the list of models for the evening, she decided it would be a perfect time to evaluate them in their natural element and then speak to each after the show.

"Hey, Bell," called out Linz. "Nice that we get to be involved in Hector's show, isn't it?"

"Yeah, I agree," said Audra. "I love the photo shoots your company sends us on, but it's always nice to be a part of the runway shows."

"I'll admit it was nice of Hector to include Price & Fitz," replied Bell.

"Hey, Bell, did I hear you are headhunting?" asked Linz. "You know Jordan, Torrence, and Lee," she noted while pointing to each model in turn. "All three would give their left pinky to join Price & Fitz."

Bell noticed that Torrence scowled at Linz. She apparently didn't feel the same about giving her left pinky.

"Nice to see you all again," replied Bell. She shook each of their hands. "I am indeed looking for some new models, and I will be watching each of you closely to see how you present yourselves before, during, and after tonight's show. We will discuss expectations and my thoughts after the show, and then I'll let you know Monday at the latest if we would like to work with you on a regular basis."

"Sounds fair enough," said the willowy model. Bell recalled her name was Lee Cartier, like the diamonds. Her dark eyes drank Bell in. She had beautiful caramel skin and long, wavy raven hair with red highlights. Her legs went on for what seemed like miles. She wasn't into women, but if she was, Lee had an exotic and intoxicating beauty about her.

Next to Lee sat Torrence Keats. She had chin-length bleach-blonde hair, dark brown eyes, and perfect pouty lips. Her alabaster skin was flawless, as were her well-manicured nails. She had a tight body, but she was a little on the short side for a model. Bell wouldn't be able to send her to certain photo shoots, but she could definitely put her in runway shows. At five feet and five inches, she wore some giant heels to make up for her shortcoming. It didn't matter that Torrence was short; if she could play nice, look good, and do as expected, Bell would let it slide. Looking at her one last time, she noticed a silver ankle bracelet that appeared to have some sort of cat charm on it. *That will have to go before the show,* thought Bell. It definitely wasn't up to Hector's code.

The third person was a pain in the butt. Jordan Blake. He was known for his poor attitude and flirtatious behavior. Jordan was a tall, sexy Viking of a man, but when it came to behaving himself, he simply didn't know how. Jordan had befriended Alex a few months earlier and was consistently trying to break into a regular modeling gig. The problem was that he couldn't keep it in his pants. He'd sleep with anyone. It didn't matter as long as they made him the center of attention. Alex had asked a favor of Bell. He wanted Jordan to be a regular model for Price & Fitz. Bell had straight out said no. Alex threw a fit, and then Hector got involved. Hector cut a deal with Bell. Jordan was a shoo-in, and Bell couldn't believe she'd stooped to such a level.

The agreement had been that Hector would promote and use the Price Fitz Modeling Agency and their agency alone, starting with January of the upcoming year. Tonight's show would tell her a lot about what she could expect from working with Hector in the coming year, but either way, the deal was already done. Bell prayed Alex and Hector would stay on good terms. If things went south, she had no idea what would happen. She knew Alex wasn't one to stay in relationships very long, but he had already been seeing Hector for nearly five months, which was record-breaking. His longest relationships prior had lasted three months at most.

"Why don't you three sit down for make-up?" said Hector. "I have a few things to which I need to attend. I must check in and make sure the dark forest is running properly." He winked at Alex, turned away, and sauntered back toward the hall.

"For having so much to do, he sure has a poised walk," commented Bell. She'd taken the middle seat out of the three empty chairs, and a short, round, middle-aged woman had set to work painting her face.

"Yeah, he never runs unless there's an emergency." Alex frowned and patted his heart. "I'd love to see him run. It's a shame."

"Nice," said Bernie. "I'm shocked you're dating someone who doesn't share your love of running." She raised an eyebrow at her brother.

He looked at her and shook his head. "We have plenty of other things in common," he said curtly.

Bell peered back at him. "Like what?"

"Yeah," said Bernie, "Like what?"

"Are you for real right now? Haven't we gone through enough lately? Now you're going to drill me on what I have in common with the man I love? Dang, I thought we'd had enough sadness and drama for a while."

Bell stared at him. He looked hurt. She didn't mean to upset him. He was right, after all. There had been way too much sadness and drama. Hector being in Alex's life was a positive thing.

"Alex, please don't be mad. After what I went through with Martin, we just want to make sure you're in a good place," said Bernie.

"Oh, I'm sorry, honey," he replied sincerely. "I'm sure of all people, you know how rough it's been. I get why you'd want to check in." He drew an invisible heart in the air and pretended to throw it to her. She reached up and caught it.

"I love you too," she said with a smile.

"To answer your question, we both love fashion, modeling, old black-and-white movies, traveling, and who knows what else. We're still learning about each other. I know it seems like this relationship has been longer than others, but we have been taking everything slow. Time is hard to come by lately."

"You said you loved him. Is that true?" asked Bell.

"Oh, I don't know." Alex blushed. "I mean, I might. I don't want to say too much, though. I don't want to scare him away."

Bernie grinned at Alex. "You really think you could scare him away by saying you love him?"

"No, but I'm afraid to chance it. He's such a stunning, successful, and well-mannered man. His charm lights up the room when he walks in. I feel like I'm the lucky one in this relationship."

"Alex," scolded Bell, "he's the lucky one. Any man would be lucky to have you. You're very charismatic, and everyone at the club, as well as Price & Fitz, loves you. I've never known you to say such things. Must be love if you're feeling that humbled."

"Well, perhaps you're right." He smiled sheepishly. "Anyway, I guess it's time for me to head over to wardrobe since you ladies obviously have much more going on with your hair than I do." He chuckled.

"Okay, see you later," said Bernie. She drew him an invisible heart and threw it back at him.

"Thanks, kid."

After Alex was out of sight, Bernie looked to Bell, narrowing her eyes. "Do you think Hector is really the one?" she asked.

"Only time will tell, but I have to be honest, I think our big brother is going to be bitten by the commitment bug pretty soon."

"You think so?"

Bell shrugged. "Yeah, didn't you see the look on his face? He's totally smitten with Hector. I'll be shocked if some sort of engagement doesn't take place."

Bernie raised one corner of her mouth. "How does that make you feel? I mean, things will change, won't they?"

"I guess, but as you well know, that's what happens as we become mature adults."

"Are we just now hitting that point?" asked Bernie.

"In some ways," said Bell. Her tone was regretful. "But you chose to speed things up when you went into a relationship with Martin. I believe he forced you to grow up much quicker due to what he put you through. Because of Mom and Dad's deaths, Alex and I needed to grow up in terms of responsibility toward running the businesses, but relationship-wise, we're both only just catching up. I get the feeling we've been much too oblivious to the world outside of the businesses and modeling. We've gone through life feeling secure and not questioning anything. Look where that's gotten us," she said pointedly. "We hadn't dealt with death or manipulation, aside from our mother. You thought the biggest problem in the world was your lack of a good man. Now how do you feel?"

Bernie shook her head as she stared at her feet, and then she said in a quiet voice, "I feel like I've lived an entire lifetime in less than a year. I didn't know people like Martin existed. Why would I? We don't pay close attention to the news or spend much time watching television or browsing the internet. Most of my online ventures involve ordering something or checking my email."

"Exactly. We have been a bit sheltered. I'm done with that. I want to know what's going on around me, and I want to help people if possible." She reached over and lightly touched Bernie's arm. "I want us to enjoy life but be aware of it and cherish what we have."

"I agree. Before Martin, I had no idea how much freedom I actually had. I didn't realize what a blessing it was to be able to wear what you want or do whatever you feel like whenever the mood strikes. I didn't know what it meant to feel pain or to lose someone I loved."

"Well, now you do, and now that we're aware, I need you to go back to counseling. I'm worried you won't be able to achieve a sense of normalcy if you forgo therapy." Bell smiled encouragingly at her sister.

"I'm planning on it," said Bernie. "You helped me fill out all the paperwork this morning, and I didn't even complain. Please give me the benefit of the doubt. I know you're right. I'm moving forward with it," she said sharply.

Despite the paperwork, Bell thought convincing her to comply would be a fight. "I'm glad to hear it."

"Tell Alex he can stop worrying as well. I don't need you both tiptoeing around me. Andra made it clear that this is an important step. I gave her my word, and now you have it as well, so please, stop pushing."

It took an hour and a half to get make-up, hair, and clothing taken care of, but the siblings were finally standing backstage, and Hector was giving them the lowdown on how the night would proceed. There were twenty-five models and thirty-four outfits, which meant nine models needed to change rapidly into a second outfit backstage. The process was always maddening when a clothing change was involved. To help minimize the chaos, the nine models were each given two assistants who would strip them of their first look and slide, slip, shellac, button, snap, or tie them into their second. They would then be sent back onto the catwalk in perfect timing to strut their second ensemble. Each of the siblings would take two turns on the runway.

Bell could hardly contain her excitement. Hector's new line of clothing did not disappoint. She stared at herself in the mirror, taking in the gorgeous detailing. She wore a black oversized cowl neck dress that barely covered her lady parts in front and flared out like a cape in the back. The underside of the dress was purple. Her shoes were lace-up stiletto boots, and she wore a black birdcage with purple flowers on her head, which covered part of her face. She did a twirl and a grin spread across her face. When she saw the second outfit she would show, her eyes went wide, and she began clapping and jumping up and down.

Somehow, the second ensemble was more exhilarating than the first. She'd wear pinstriped pants adorned with decorative zippers and black suspenders. Her top, a silk purple blouse. And on her feet, black strappy stilettos. The pieces that got her going were the gorgeous black fedora with purple and teal feathers she would wear on her head, and the purple umbrella she would carry in her hand as she marched like a mafia queen down the runway.

Turning from the mirror, she took in her siblings' outfits. "Oh, my goodness! You all look amazing!" she squealed. Their clothes were equally impressive. Alex wore a sparkly dark grey suit with a black dress shirt and a long coat that billowed out from his body when he walked. Hector accessorized him with a purple tie, and a dark grey fedora containing teal and purple feathers. His shoes were black leather. She could see his second outfit hanging next to him. It was a pair of skin-tight black leather pants with multiple zippers that ran parallel to the ground. His shoes were black leather combat boots, and his shirt was a half-unbuttoned teal silk shirt with zippers that matched the pants. His accessories were a black leather tie and a matching black leather briefcase.

Bernadette's first outfit was a frilly halter dress made of black lace with hundreds of teal feathers around the halter and flowing down the lacy skirt, which stopped at her calves. She wore gothic combat boots on her feet. On her head, she wore a hat that perfectly matched her dress. Her second outfit, hanging next to Alex's, was a black dress that matched Alex's leather pants, along with a teal vest and teal strappy stilettos, and a purple and black cocktail purse.

"This has got to be one of the best shows I've ever been a part of," gushed Bernie. Her siblings nodded their agreement.

"Hector has outdone himself, once again," said Alex.

The siblings were all smiles as they stood backstage and waited for the music to signal the start of the show. Alex grabbed his phone to do a shout-out on social media. He was so excited about the line that he wanted to document it and tell everyone to check it out. He grabbed Hector as he sashayed by so they could take a photo of the four of them. Bell watched as Alex beamed at Hector. It was a warm moment that she was proud to be a part of.

Once the music began, the crew snapped into action. Each model strutted professionally down the runway and did a brief pause and turn at the end. Clothing changes were fast and efficient, and each model found themselves back out on the catwalk in but a moment's time. Bell couldn't help but feel a little sad walking down the runway. She knew some of her biggest fans would never be in the audience again. She missed her crazy mom and adoring father, but she kept looking ahead, even as a couple of tears fell from the corners of her eyes.

At the end of the show, each model followed Hector back on stage and took a bow. The show was twenty minutes long, and from the roar of applause, it appeared to be a success. Bell smiled while taking her bow between Hector and Bernie. She squeezed both of their hands to show she was proud of them. Hector gave her a nod.

As Bell exited to the back of the stage, she heard Audra's voice calling after her.

"Bell, you all should come out with us tonight. We're going dancing at this new club called the Buccaneer Ballroom. It's pirate-themed! There's even a ship," she gushed. "They play a huge variety of dance music, and they serve some awesome fruity drinks. It should be a blast."

"Sounds fun." She smiled. "Let me talk to the crew and see what they want to do."

"See, there you go. You're already speaking like a pirate." She laughed. Bell stared blankly at her. "Crew, Bell. Crew."

"Oh!" Bell laughed at herself. "Argh, I get ye." Audra's nose wrinkled as she shook her head. Then, waving Bell away, she and Linz headed off toward the hall.

Looking over at her sister, Bell noticed she seemed a bit flustered. "Are you okay?" she asked.

Bernie turned toward her, and tears were running down her face. "I miss Dad!" she wailed.

"I know, honey. I feel the same way," said Bell. "Trust me, he's here with us." *If this is the only sad moment tonight,* thought Bell, *we'll be in pretty good shape.* She'd held concern that Bernie might have a breakdown in the middle of everything, but her sister had held it together quite well.

"Ladies!" yelled Alex as he walked in. "How was that for exhilarating?" he asked, but then abruptly stopped as he noticed the look on his younger sister's face. "Are you okay?" He wrapped her in a hug. "I know. It's okay. You can let it out."

She cried softly into his silk shirt for a moment and then pulled away and wiped her eyes clear of tears. "I'll be okay, I promise. We should get out of here."

"What's the plan?" asked Alex.

"Audra invited us to go out with them. I do need to talk to the newbies at some point. Perhaps we should go, and I can kill two birds with one stone," replied Bell.

Alex looked at her with intrigue. "Where are they going?"

"The Buccaneer Ballroom. Ever been?"

"Yes, I've been there. It's a blast," swooned Alex. "I would love to go back. Bernie, I think you'll really like the place."

"What's so special about it?" she asked.

"Well, as I've been told, it's like a pirate ship," said Bell.

"Oh, sweet. Count me in. Can we wear pirate apparel?" asked Bernie.

"You can, but I wouldn't advise it tonight. We should definitely be wearing our Hector Couture out," replied Alex.

"Bummer," said Bell. "Dressing up would have been fun."

"You are dressed up, just in a different way," replied Alex. He gave Bell an exaggerated grin.

"There's always next time." Bernie looked at both of her siblings. "Let's get crackin'!"

Returning to the dressing rooms, they hurried to change clothes. A short while later, they were joined by Matthew and Hector, who was all aglow after a successful show. Matthew was interested in the club but had to decline the after-party because he needed to finalize some paperwork for a case he was wrapping up. Hector couldn't wait to go to the club and informed the group that he already had a limo pulled up to the doors and waiting.

Stepping out of the theatre, Matthew turned to Bell. "You were absolutely stunning on the catwalk tonight, though honestly, you're always stunning." He beamed at her. "I'm sorry I can't join you. I'll be at your place when you get home later."

"It's okay, I understand. Duty calls." Bell kissed Matthew goodbye and then piled into the limo with her siblings and Hector. Popping open a bottle of bubbly, Hector made a toast to success.

Everyone was laughing and having a wonderful time as they pulled up to the club. The other models had arrived just before them and were waiting in the VIP section that had been put aside after a quick call made by Hector. They had bottle service and their own cozy couches inside an area made to look like the captain's quarters on a ship. The smell of desserts and fruit and cheese plates filled the air as they were laid out across a long table. Everything looked great, though Bell was simply happy to be away from the house and with both of her siblings for a change.

"Isn't this great?" asked Linz.

"Totally," replied Alex. He looked like he couldn't wait to get out on the dance floor. He was already rocking back and forth to the beat.

"I should take care of business before I get too crazy," said Bell. "Lee, why don't you and I speak first?"

Bell took a seat, and Lee walked over and sat down in the plush chair next to her. The young woman exuded confidence, which was one of the things Bell loved about her.

"I think you were amazing out on the catwalk tonight. You seem to be naturally poised. The crowd loved you. I want to offer you a regular position with Price & Fitz. What do you think?"

A smile radiated across Lee's face as she sat forward in her seat. "Wow, Bell, that's wonderful news. I've always respected your company and your father's hard work. He was a great man. It would be an honor to be a part of Price & Fitz."

"Fantastic!" replied Bell. "I'm excited to have you join our team. We can sign the contracts on Monday, if that works for you."

"That sounds perfect. You won't regret this, Bell. I can't wait to sign!"

"We'll chat more in a bit. In the meantime, will you please send Torrence over here?"

"Sure, no problem," replied Lee. She was still beaming as she walked away.

Bell looked at the rest of the group lounging on the couches and noted how much she wished Matthew was present. Ever since the shooting, she felt a little unsafe out in public. She considered herself lucky to have him in her life.

Torrence wasted no time in bounding across the small area toward Bell. She was clearly excited to find out what her future would hold.

"Hi, Bell. You wanted to see me?" she asked as if she didn't know what was going on.

"Yeah, I would like to offer you a contract as a regular model for Price & Fitz. I need you to understand that you will primarily be a runway model, though I will also do my best to find you other gigs. Your height, as you know, can sometimes be an issue, but I'm going to offer you whatever work I can. I also expect you to follow the rules for each show, which means you don't add unapproved adornments to your outfits. Jewelry should be approved prior to a show. This will be stated in your contract. Do you understand?"

"I understand," she answered while anxiously chewing her lip. "I will take whatever I can get at this point."

"I know you've struggled with finding regular work. My hope is that with Price & Fitz, you'll feel like family, and you'll be treated as a key player," said Bell. "Now, go have some fun." She smiled warmly. "Welcome to Price & Fitz."

After Torrence was out of sight, Bell decided to approach Jordan herself. Reaching out, she tapped him on the shoulder. He was talking to Hector. Hector looked at Bell and grinned.

"You'd better go with her," he said to Jordan. "From what I hear, your fate's in her hands."

A concerned look passed over his eyes when he turned to face Bell.

Sitting down, she looked up at him with a stern expression. "You did a halfway decent job out there tonight. You handled yourself professionally, but listen, Jordan, I don't have time for games or troublemakers. This is a serious agency that creates serious models.

You may think you're a model now, but Price & Fitz will take you to the next level. Don't think for one second that I don't know your history or the rumors that follow you. If you can behave yourself, then I may have a job for you. If you can't follow the rules, though, I may as well not even waste my time. You have an okay walk, but it could use some work. This will require discipline. What do you have to say for yourself?"

"I say whatever milady wants; milady gets." He smiled and flashed his teeth, bowing in her direction.

"Knock off the theatrics. I'm looking for a serious answer." Bell scowled at him. "Can you do this or not? Because if you can't, I don't care how many Hectors back you, I'm not going to accept you into my agency."

"Yes, Bell, I swear I'll behave myself," he replied.

Pausing, she contemplated his response for a moment and then, forcing a smile, said, "Welcome aboard. Please don't make me regret this." Jordan grinned and happily shook her hand. "Now get out of my sight before I change my mind." He immediately sauntered back to Hector. Bell knew he was trouble, but she had promised to give him a shot.

Looking out over the room, she saw Lee walking her way. She again took the seat next to Bell.

"So, how'd that go?" asked Lee.

"I've added three new models to the agency, so that's exciting. I have low expectations for Jordan and his capability to follow orders, but we'll see where things go. I hope he proves me wrong."

"Yeah, Jordan's a knucklehead," said Lee with a laugh. "Want one?" she was holding two glasses and held one out to Bell.

"What is it?" she asked.

"It's Rum Punch, girlfriend. It goes down smooth." Lee swirled the liquid in front of her.

Bell plucked the cup from her hand and took a big gulp. "Mmm, that is tasty and refreshing."

Lee reached out and grabbed her free hand. "Come on, let's go dance!" she shouted, pulling her toward the jam-packed dance floor. "I have a reason to celebrate!" Bell smiled at her enthusiasm. Why couldn't every model react like that?

"Bernie!" yelled Bell, "I'm gonna go dance! Come join us!" Bernie and Alex both looked at Bell being escorted toward the floor. They smiled in her direction, and Bernie motioned that she would be there in a minute.

The bass was pounding out a sensual rhythm that made her movement feel effortless. Lee still held her hand and danced closely with her. She was beginning to wonder if something more than she had anticipated was going on, but she was in too great of a mood to let it bother her. Bernadette suddenly appeared, grabbing her by the elbow and twirling her out of Lee's grasp. Bell somehow managed to not spill her drink in the transition. Lee raised a contemplative eyebrow in Bernie's direction but went on dancing.

The night continued, and Bell and Lee danced and spoke about many topics. She felt a strong bond was growing. The whole group told stories, laughed, and drank rum punch. One crazy night out was just what she'd needed, and as a bonus, it looked like it was just what Bernie and Alex had needed as well. Her siblings seemed to enjoy the music and camaraderie as much as she did.

During a much-needed break from dancing, the group piled back into the VIP area to rest in luxury on the cushy chairs. Bell took a seat on one of the sofas. Lee squeezed in on one side and Alex and Bernie on the other. It was a cozy fit. Hector sat in the chair next to Alex, running his finger back and forth across Alex's forearm. The other models had filled the remaining empty chairs and were chattering away.

Lee turned toward Bell and reached up and brushed some stray hair away from Bell's eyes.

"Listen, several of us are planning a trip to the Dominican in a few weeks, and I think it would be fantastic if you and your family joined us," she said. "It's been nice hanging out with you tonight, and I know you all have been through some serious trauma over the past several months, so maybe a getaway would be good for you all." Looking into her eyes, she smiled warmly at Bell.

"Who's going on the trip?"

"Audra, Linz, Jordan, Torrence, and Hector have all joined the list. It will be a lot of fun and give us more time away from work to get to know each other and build closer relationships." She continued to gaze adoringly into Bell's eyes. Without the alcohol, the situation would have felt awkward, but Bell was feeling overly relaxed and didn't put much thought into it.

"I don't know." She turned her face away from Lee and looked over at her siblings. They weren't paying any attention to the conversation. Looking back at her new friend, she nodded her head in contemplation. "Yeah, it does sound fun, but I'll have to talk to Bernie and Alex about it later. I don't think any of us are in a position to make any major commitments tonight." She laughed.

"Of course not," said Lee. "You think about it over the next couple of days and get back to me." She cupped Bell's chin with her perfectly manicured fingers. "It would mean a lot to me if you joined us."

The contact forced Bell's attention over to her. Bell didn't know what to think about Lee or how to respond to how she was acting. She adored Matthew and had never experienced any form of desire toward another woman in the past, yet something about Lee was exciting to her. She didn't know where this was coming from. She grabbed Lee's hand away from her face and, squeezing it lightly, said, "I'll definitely let you know within a day."

"Sounds good. Shall we get back to the dance floor?" asked Lee.

"Ya know, I think I'm gonna call it a night."

"Oh, no, it's not even midnight yet," she protested.

"It's been a long day. I kind of want to crash." Getting up, Bell smiled back at her. She also wanted to run from the slightly awkward feeling she was having. "I'll get back to you regarding the trip," she assured.

Lee stood up and gave her a hug. "Okay. Have a nice night."

"You too," replied Bell as she watched Lee head back to the dance floor.

Bell turned to her brother and sister, who were laughing uncontrollably at something Hector had said. Hector looked up at her and grinned.

"Ahh, bonita, how is your night going?" he asked in his usual suave and sultry way. It didn't matter who Hector spoke to. He always sounded as if the subject of his attention were the most important person in the world at that moment.

"I'm a little tired, but you might be able to coax me into staying up longer if we either go to the club or back to our house and chill." Her voice was cool and rational. She didn't want anyone to know that she was feeling a bit flustered.

"I'm a little tired myself," said Bernie. "Why don't we go back, throw on our pajamas, and chill with some wine on the patio? Maybe we can have a fire?"

"I could go for that," chimed Alex. He had already jumped up and, grabbing Hector's hand, spun him in a circle. Looking into his eyes, he said, "Are you down with that, mi amor?"

"Oh my," said Hector. "Well girls, I think he just said he loves me." Hector looked elated.

"Now wait a minute," retorted Alex, "I said my love, not I love you, and there is a difference." Hector's smile faded as he gazed back in disbelief. He looked like he had been slapped.

"Now," said Alex, "I'm saying 'I love you.' Do you hear me, Hector Perrago? I love you! I will tell the whole world!" he howled.

"Alex, how much have you drank tonight?" Bell wasn't sure if she should be concerned or not.

"He's had two drinks, that's it," sang Hector. "He loves me." With that, he spun away and began prancing toward the exit with Alex in tow, telling everyone he passed that Alex was in love with him.

"That didn't take long," said Bernie.

"Nope." Bell playfully punched her sister in the shoulder. "I love you, Bern." And then, grabbing her hand, she pulled her off the couch to follow Alex and Hector to the limo.

Back at the house, Alex had hurried to set up for the fire. He had both a propane fire ring and a regular fire pit. Bernie hated using *fake* fires, so he moved all the chairs to the wood fire pit and was now organizing tables for beverages between them.

Hector was in the house grabbing glasses, and Bernie was already opening up two different bottles. One was the champagne they had been drinking in Hector's limo, and the other a bottle of Rex Goliath pinot noir. She had to hand it to her sister; she was gifted in knowing what her guests preferred to drink, at all times. Alex and Hector would drink the champagne, and she and Bernie would drink the Rex.

Bell thought about the red wine and remembered learning early in life that a cheap bottle of wine doesn't always mean an inferior wine. Her father, while he could afford any bottle of wine he wanted, still loved Rex Goliath and bought it time and time again because while it was inexpensive, it tasted like so much more. The wine grew on her and held a special place in her heart.

"Bell." Her sister nudged her shoulder. "Hello?" She was holding a glass of wine out, and Bell was failing to grab it.

"Oh, sorry." She took the glass from Bernie. "I guess I was dazing out thinking about Dad and the wine he drank."

"That happens. Earlier this evening, I saw a man that reminded me of him, and it took me back to my wedding and how we all were dancing and being silly together. It's still so fresh." She took a seat in the chair next to Bell. "I've been so wrapped up in myself that I haven't even asked you how you're doing with all the loss. I'm a horrible sister, and you've been so patient with me. How are you doing?" She stared intently at Bell.

"Well, someone has to keep this family going, so I've made it my own personal job. I know this whole thing was much more traumatizing for you than for Alex and me. We all went through hell, but we weren't locked away in a room for days on end and beaten, and we didn't lose our significant others. You lost not one but two relationships, as well as Mom and Dad. So, in answer to your question, I'm doing as well as can be expected, and I'm thankful that you are functioning as well as you are." She reached out and lovingly squeezed Bernie's wrist. "I thought we had lost you on more than one occasion, so I'm beyond elated that you're still with us. Whatever happens, we can get through this together," she smiled.

"I really am quite lucky to have such a strong sister to pull me back to reality. I'm not feeling okay. I know it will take time. Hopefully, therapy will help me find some peace. Thank you for not giving up on me, Bell, before and after all the craziness that happened over the past year." She was chewing on her nails again. Bernie reached up and swatted her hand away from her face. "Stop that. Dad would not approve." She let out a small laugh.

"You're right about that." Bell's look turned sour. "He'd be giving me one of his lectures about having to replace yet another set of nails, and if it happened one more time, he would take my trust fund away to pay for all the damage."

"Yes, indeed. And I'd get the other end of the lecture," said Alex. "He'd look at me and say, 'Alex, can't you get her to stop chewing like that? It's not very ladylike. You talk to her; she listens to you.' And then he'd laugh and tell you to put it on his card, but it was the last time he was going to do so." Chuckling at the memory, he took a seat in the chair to Bernie's right.

"I don't know why he thought you'd be able to fix things. Most of the time I don't even realize I'm doing it until the damage is already done. It's a nervous habit that comes out when I'm stressed."

"Which is apparently all the time," said Bernie.

"Lately, it does seem that way," she replied. Just then, Matthew walked out onto the patio. He was carrying a bouquet of wildflowers.

Leaning forward, Matthew said, "These are for you because I was unable to come out and celebrate after the show." He carefully handed her the bouquet. "I wish I could've done a little dancing with you tonight." He pressed his lips to her forehead and then sat down beside her on the loveseat.

"That's just one more reason for us to plan a date night in the near future." She felt a rush of warmth through her body as she gazed lovingly at him. "You realize we haven't been on an official date yet?"

Wrinkling his face, Matthew said, "No, I suppose we haven't. I promise we'll rectify that soon."

"Wow, I hadn't even thought about it," said Alex. "You two haven't had much chance to just be a couple, have you?"

"No, it's been too crazy. I guess you could say we've been taking it slow due to the circumstances of the past few months," replied Bell.

"Well, if you don't already know, you have my blessing," said Bernie. "Not that you need it at this point. Matthew, I'm sorry for how I treated you when you came to Martin's home. I wish I could take it back."

"Bernadette, you were in love. No one expects to go through the situation you found yourself in. It's natural to question strangers. I'm just thankful you're still with us," he said with a nod.

Alex handed a glass of wine to Matthew, then, looking at Bell, he grinned mischievously. Raising his glass, he gushed, "Here's to the future. The past is gone, and may nothing hold us back from love, adventure, and happiness." The group all raised their glasses in response to his toast.

"Speaking of adventures," said Bell, directing her attention toward Hector who was standing behind Alex, "Lee told me you're planning a trip. She asked if we'd like to join."

"Indeed. We're leaving in three weeks for Punta Cana. Have you ever been?" asked Hector.

"No, we've visited Puerto Plata previously, but not Punta Cana. How many nights is the trip?" asked Bernie.

"Seven," replied Hector. "Decent length stay. I'm just happy I can afford the time off right now," he said, widening his eyes. "My staff is worried I'm going mad! Thus, I'm due for a break. If Alex comes with, that would be a huge plus." He placed his hands on Alex's shoulders and squeezed them for emphasis.

Alex looked up at him. "Oh, I'm there, baby. No one needs a break more than this family, am I right?" He turned toward Bell, waiting for her to jump at the opportunity and agree with him, but Bell wasn't sure it was a good idea. They hadn't traveled for leisure in quite some time. Despite her outer composure, she was paranoid and waiting for the next awful thing to happen. She couldn't let her siblings know about the fearful thoughts. She was the rock in the family, and she needed to keep them afloat with positivity and structure, or at least that's what she had been telling herself.

"Yes, let's do it!" blurted Bernie.

Bell turned toward her sister in shock. She realized if Bernie was on board, she couldn't very well say no and ruin the excitement. After all, her sister hadn't shown this much interest in anything in months. "Okay, that's settled then. Punta Cana, here we come!" she yelled. Alex raised an eyebrow at her. If anyone could call her on a bluff, it was him.

Bell and Alex had formed a strong bond from the moment Alex had first joined the family. They were silly and crazy and could finish one another's sentences. They loved to run together, and it was rare that they were seen in public without each other. Bernie did her own thing and was less likely to be seen in all the same places. She had spent time away at college and also traveled more because of her swimsuit modeling gigs. The two scenarios combined had forced her to become more independent.

"Bell," Alex cut in. He was now behind her, whispering in her ear. "Are you okay? Do you want to go chat inside?" Bell noted that the others were all focused on Hector who was describing the accommodations that awaited them on their trip.

"No, Alex, I'm okay. I'm just a little nervous because they haven't caught Bradley's killer, and the whole rock-through-the-window incident brought that reality to the surface. Maybe that's all the more reason to get out of town for a while?"

"I think it's as good a reason as any. One of us is due for a stroke or heart attack if we don't find a way to decompress. Besides, like the toast I made, life has to go on. I know you know that." He wrapped his arms around her and squeezed. "You won't be alone. You've been so strong through all of this, but it's time for a break, and I believe we could all use some sunshine."

"I said we're going, so we're going," replied Bell.

"It'll be fun. You'll see." He patted her on the shoulder and walked back to his seat.

The remainder of the evening was a relaxing blur of wine, stories, and discussion on the excursions and activities they would plan during their trip. Everyone was excited; even Bell was getting there. She knew it would take time to heal, but perhaps this would be the start for her. She realized it could be one of the best things for them, and who was she to hold them back from an adventure away with friends. What could possibly go wrong?

Chapter Five

The day of the trip arrived, and the siblings ran around Alex's house like they were on fire. The limo would pull into the drive at any moment, and everyone felt as if they'd forgotten something, or at least it appeared that way since they all seemed to exhibit the same frantic behavior.

"Stop! Everyone stop what you're doing!" yelled Alex. He watched his younger sister briefly, tapping his foot as he waited. "Seriously, stop, Bernadette." Hearing her name, she turned and stared at him with a crazy glint in her eye.

"I just need—"

"No! You don't just need nothing!" he yelled. "We're going to a warm climate for sun and relaxation. If you have your swimwear, flippy floppies, sunscreen, sundresses, a hat, and sunglasses, you're packed. This is ridiculous. How much stuff do we need for a week on the beach? Come on, let's go," he said, motioning toward the door. Then he paused. "Holy cow, I forgot dress pants!" he yelped and ran for his bedroom.

"He's right, except for the dress pants comment. What could we possibly need that we haven't already packed?" asked Bernie. "I mean, who's going to come looking for us down there, anyway?"

"Oh, don't even," protested Bell. "You know that a group of models on vacation will attract the paparazzi. We have to look good all the time, so make sure you have what's suitable for any event because I can guarantee someone's going to be watching. I wouldn't be surprised if that snake, Emmy Lou Baker, were to show up."

"Oh, come on, you think Emmy is going to get on a plane just to harass us for a week on the beach?"

"Heck yes! I'm quite positive her life's goal is to ruin my career. It's a load of bull hooey!"

"Okay then. I think I'm ready to go, so I'm heading out the door now and climbing into that limo. I suggest you rein in that boy because, believe it or not, he's the one that has the most issues with forgetting to pack something."

"I'm going," replied Bell through gritted teeth. She loved her brother, but no matter how much he made it sound like they were the ones with the problem dropping things and going, it was always him. He was a queen through and through. Hector was the more masculine one in the relationship, but she loved that about Alex. Many girls would give anything to have a bestie like him, but

Bell actually had him, and she loved that they could do all the fun girlie stuff together.

"Hey, Alex, wrap it up." He was digging through his closet like a madman. "You're done. I mean it. If you don't cease and desist and move your tush to the car, I'll pick you up and carry you out of here."

"You wouldn't!" he shouted back. "You couldn't! I'd like to see you try!"

"Alright, you asked for it." Bell charged at him like a wild animal and, wrapping her arms around his legs, took out his center of gravity, forcing him to fold over her shoulder. Flailing and laughing, the two toppled to the ground in a pile of silly squeals.

"I guess I haven't done that in a while." She laughed.

"Ya think?" he replied through laughter. "Are you okay? You didn't hurt yourself, did you?"

"I think I'm okay," she said as she looked herself over.

Adjusting his shirt, he got to his feet and pulled her up. "Okay, that was fun and all, but you're right, we should go." He turned and grabbed his bag, and they headed for the door.

Climbing into the limo, Bernie raised an eyebrow at them. "What happened? I thought you were right behind me."

"I had to carry him out here," said Bell.

"No way, you didn't!" screeched their younger sister.

"She tried." Alex laughed. "But she didn't get far," he said while playfully swatting Bell's shoulder.

"Yeah, I went down like a wheelbarrow full of bricks. You putting on weight, donut boy?" asked Bell with a wink.

"Whoa girl, you better watch yourself," he replied. "I haven't been to the donut shop in months."

"Oh, I suppose not," replied Bernie. "You got yourself one handsome designer instead." Bell nodded in agreement. Hector and Alex made quite the power couple. Hector was well-loved and sought after, by many admirers, too.

Alex nodded in appreciation of Bernie's response. "Can't dispute that one," he said. I'm a very lucky man." Looking at his phone, he noted the time. "I hope Matthew is ready to go because we're definitely running behind this morning."

"I wouldn't worry about Matt," said Bell. "He's always punctual. He's probably wondering where we're at. Luckily, his place is close to the airport."

"How long is the flight, Bell?" asked Bernie.

"Looks to be six hours and twenty-two minutes with one stop in Atlanta. Maybe we should've driven to Atlanta and gotten on there?"

"Nah, this is fine. Drinks on the plane," said Bernie with a high-five to Alex.

The siblings were in a rare mood. Everyone had finally relaxed, and they couldn't wait to get to their destination. Bell decided Alex was right; the trip was much needed.

Six hours and twenty-two minutes later, the entire entourage arrived in Punta Cana. The sun was shining, and the beach was buzzing. Alex had already changed into his swim trunks at the airport. Bernie, against Bell's wishes, had changed into her swimsuit in the van that was transporting them to their all-inclusive. Bell wasn't into changing in public and had opted to wait until after check-in. It was one thing to change backstage during a show, but a totally different thing to bare all in public. Her sister held no qualms about nudity ever since fleeing from her ex-husband. Bell found this mildly disturbing.

Unlike the siblings, Matthew had worn his suit onto the plane, so he was also ready to go.

"What shall we do first?" asked Matt.

"I think it's about time to check in, so I say we do that so those who haven't changed can go to our rooms and do so. After, we can meet at the swim-up bar," replied Lee, sporting a bright red sundress and a large floppy hat. Bell again noted how the girl had legs for miles. Dang, she was a beautiful woman. Musicians created songs about legs that long.

Matthew turned toward Bell and, wrapping his arms around her, pulled her in close. "What would you like to do, Princess?" he asked. "I want this week to be all about you relaxing and letting loose."

"I agree with Lee. Let's check out our rooms and change. Maybe see how comfy the bed is." She winked.

"Hmm," said Matthew, "I like where your mind's at. He swatted her playfully on the behind as their group entered the hotel they'd be calling home for the next seven days.

Bernie sashayed up to the desk, followed by Lee, and proactively requested their accommodations as the rest of their entourage stood gawking at their surroundings. The two women took all the key cards and handed them out one by one to each of their friends.

"Thanks for making the reservations, Lee," said Linz. "That was nice of you."

"Hey, no problem, I'm just excited everyone was able to come along," she replied.

"Let's get a move on," said Bell. "I want to see the room and get back outside to enjoy this beautiful sunshine." She grinned.

"Okay people. You heard her. Everyone skedaddle," said Alex as the group made for the elevators.

Matthew, Bell, Alex, Hector, and Bernie were all on the twelfth floor together. Alex and Hector had a suite on the south end of the building, and Bell, Bernie, and Matthew had a two-bedroom suite on the North end. The other half of the group had been placed on the ninth floor since they'd booked their trip earlier. Bell was happy her family was on the same floor and easy to find.

Arriving at their room, Bernie shoved open the door and charged inside to investigate. Bell knew her little sister would be the biggest critic of the space. Therefore, she always let her make the call as to whether accommodations were up to standard. She watched as Bernadette swooped from room to room, inspecting everything. She and Matthew stood and waited. There was no point getting cozy or exploring until Bernie gave the okay.

Popping her head out of one of the bedrooms, Bernie cheerily stated, "All clear! I'm taking this room. You may commence with the unpacking and changing."

"Not so fast, young lady," said Bell. "Is that the room with the whirlpool in it?"

"Of course, it is." She said matter-of-factly. "Don't worry, your room has a whirlpool as well. Speaking of which, I'm going to go enjoy mine right now." She disappeared into the room, closing the door behind her.

"Phew, that was close," said Matthew. "I thought for sure we were going to lose that amenity."

"No, I knew there were two, but I wanted to see if she was paying attention or if she just took the room she wanted without regard. She has a tendency to always take the whirlpool, which honestly, I can't say I mind because she uses it every day, whereas I may use it once or twice during a trip."

"Well, I'm definitely interested in a little whirlpool time with you, my dear." He reached out and grabbed Bell's hand. "Will ya just look at this place," he mused. "The tropical atmosphere is heavenly. The plants and the breeze from the balcony bring in all the wonderful scents of flowers and the ocean. How could you not feel great here?" He took a deep breath, held it for a moment, and slowly let it out. "It purifies the soul."

"Come on," said Bell, "let's check out the bedroom. Maybe I can help you further purify your soul." She winked. "Bernie will be more than twenty minutes in that tub, so I think that means we can do a little unwinding ourselves," she grinned mischievously.

Matthew led her into the bedroom decorated in shades of purple, green, and blue. The room was vastly covered in a floral motif with bamboo furnishings. Walking to the balcony, Bell pulled back the sheers and opened the door. The view was beautiful, and Matthew was right; the breeze smelled intoxicating, which helped put her in a more relaxed mood.

"I'll be right back," she said. "I want to go freshen up a bit." Carrying her purse into the bathroom, she closed the door behind her. Opening it, she pulled out a piece of lacy lingerie. She cleaned herself up and began putting on her new outfit. The top was a black see-through shelf bra that barely covered her nipples and had crisscrossing bands connected to a pair of lacy see-through panties. She put on a banded garter belt and neatly connected it to a pair of sexy lace stockings. Her feet were adorned with black stilettos. For an added touch, she put on a dangling diamond necklace hanging between her breasts.

Gazing into the mirror, she applied some bright red lipstick. Blotting her mouth with a tissue, she looked at herself approvingly.

Making herself feel sexy was the first step in achieving intimacy with another person. Turning away from the mirror, she smiled and reached for the bathroom door.

When she appeared in the entry to the bedroom, Matthew's jaw dropped. She could tell he hadn't expected her to come out like that. He didn't even know she owned lingerie. Placing one hand on the back of her neck with her elbow in the air and the other on her hip, she struck a pose. "What do you think, sailor?"

He flashed a smoldering smile. "I think it must be my birthday because you're all wrapped up like a gift meant for me."

"Oh, no, you're mistaken. This is my swimsuit," she said.

From the look on his face, he was absolutely caught off guard by her comment. "Wha— oh, I guess I shouldn't have assumed."

"Oh, my goodness, you should see the look on your face, darlin'. I'm joking. There's no way I'm headed to the pool looking like this." She realized the error she'd made. He probably didn't know any better regarding what a model would or wouldn't wear to the pool, and she was sure her comment wasn't helping the moment any.

"You better scoot your sexy little butt back into that bathroom, give me a minute to recompose myself, then try that entrance again," he said with a sheepish laugh.

"Ay Ay, captain." She turned and walked back into the bathroom. She shouldn't have joked. Man, did she feel awkward when it came to sex and relationships.

"Okay, Bell, get it together, girl," she said sternly to the mirror. "I'm going to do this right." She turned away and marched back into the room and was surprised when she nearly ran into Matthew, who was standing waiting for her in a neon yellow G-string. Her jaw dropped open as she took him in.

Wrapping his arms around her, he pulled her close, and she could feel the ripples of his six-pack against her flat tummy as well as his strong arms holding her safely. He ran his fingers down her back and cupped her bottom, squeezing lightly. She grabbed his head and crushed her lips to his. A spark of excitement ignited and ran through her body, stopping in her nether region. She felt so alive. All her receptors were on fire and screaming to feel every inch of him.

Firmly grabbing hold of her, he scooped her up, and she wrapped her legs around his waist. Carrying her over to the bed, he gently set her down. Straightening up, he put his thumb and forefinger on his chin, assessing the situation. "Damn, girl, you are hot!" Leaning in, he whispered, "I want to make you feel things you've never felt before."

"I think I'm already there," she replied breathily.

Gently pushing her back on the bed, he ran his hands tenderly down her face and then proceeded to softly kiss a trail from her neck, down her stomach, to her right thigh. Her head was light and she felt as though she could pass out from the exhilaration of his lips. She wanted him inside her, and she wanted him now.

Reaching upward, he began to peel her out of the sexy lingerie. Tossing the garment aside, he took a moment to look her over. She was now wearing nothing but stockings, a necklace, and stilettos.

"I approve of this apparel," he said with a wink. Bell couldn't help but let out a laugh.

Leaning forward, he grabbed her hips and gently turned her over onto her stomach. Reaching underneath her, he placed his hands on her breasts and gently massaged while kissing her neck. She could feel his erection pressing against her bottom. Licking her lips, she let out a light moan. She didn't know how much more she could take. "I need you now," she said breathlessly.

"Are you sure?" he asked.

"I am. I'm so ready!" she said with eagerness. She felt his fingers gently slide between her legs, the sensation making her body shudder. She wanted more. Nothing else in the world mattered at that moment but the need to make a carnal connection with him.

"Yes, I think you're ready," he replied. She could tell by his voice that he wanted her, too. Grabbing her by the hips again, he flipped her back over and leaned in, kissing her passionately. "I want to be able to see you," he said as he slowly pressed himself into her.

"Oh, you're definitely seeing me," she whispered as he thrust in rhythm. "I don't think anyone has ever seen me the way you're seeing me right now," she assured, her arousal beginning to build with sensation. It had been a long time since she'd shared such an intimate moment with anyone. She didn't want it to end, but she was uncertain whether she could control herself for much longer, as her body was already beginning to arch and tremble with ecstasy.

At six o'clock, Bell finally emerged from her and Matthew's room into the common area of their suite. Bernie's door was open, and she came bustling out in a tropical cotton sundress and red sandals. Her fiery red hair was piled atop her head in a messy bun. She looked pretty as usual, but her posture had a calmness that Bell hadn't seen in over a year.

"You two take a nap or something?" she asked with a wink.

"Or something," replied Bell. She couldn't stop herself from smiling. Her body felt like it had released ten years of pent-up anxiety and stress.

"Oh, that's great," said Bernie. "Good for you!" Bell could tell she meant it. Her sister was always on her about jumping back in the saddle regarding relationships. Being abused previously and then seeing Bernie's situation hadn't helped, but Matthew seemed genuinely respectful, and he had made her feel safe from the moment she first met him.

Walking into the room as he buttoned his shirt, Matthew said, "If it's okay with you, Bernie, I'd like to steal your sister away for the remainder of the evening to have a nice quiet dinner and discuss a few things."

"No worries," said Bernie. "I'll check in on everyone and make sure they're staying out of trouble, and I'll let them know you wanted some alone time before joining up with the lot of us."

"Thanks, Bern," said Bell. "I appreciate it." She smiled at her little sister, and then she and Matthew walked hand in hand out the door. She was famished and glad they weren't waiting for the rest of the group to go to dinner. She was sure the others would wonder why they never showed up at the pool, but then again, they were on vacation and entitled to do whatever they wanted with their time. She and Matthew had needed some quality alone time.

"I called down to the seafood restaurant, and they had room for us, so I had them put us on the list. I hope that's okay," said Matthew.

"Yeah, seafood sounds great. I could go for some surf and turf," Bell said enthusiastically. She was still on cloud nine from their bedroom escapades and couldn't wait to finish dinner and return to them.

Matthew didn't speak the entire elevator ride down to the first floor. He just grinned adoringly at her the whole time. Grabbing her hand again, they exited into the main corridor leading to the little outdoor restaurant where they would be dining. Bell could smell freshly baked rolls with butter. Her mouth began to water as she took in the beauty of the restaurant and the ocean it overlooked. Turning back to Matthew, she stifled a laugh.

"If you don't stop grinning like that, people are going to start wondering what your secret is," said Bell.

"I can't help it," he replied. Brushing a stray hair away from her face, he looked her in the eyes. "I love you, and I can't believe how lucky I am to be the man you've chosen to be with. I mean that. I was genuinely scared I might lose you in the car accident when you were fleeing from Martin. I'm so thankful you came out of it okay. I'm not asking you to marry me right now because I know you like to take your time, but I want you to know that one day I will, and if you're interested right now, I'd like for us to move in together."

"Yes!" she blurted. "Let's move in together. I'm not just saying that because you make me feel safe. I love you too!" she squealed. "This is just as good as a proposal," she said, grinning wildly. Their vacation was off to a perfect start. First, they made love, and now they were planning to move in together. Bell could picture life with Matthew, and it made her heart swell.

The hostess led them to a table and handed them each a menu. "Your waiter this evening will be Spike, and he'll be with you momentarily. In the meantime, may I get you something to drink?"

"I believe some Champagne is in order," said Matthew. "We have a lot of celebrating to do." He smiled at Bell and her face flushed.

"Wonderful! I shall return shortly with that bubbly," she said with a smile.

"Thank you," said Bell as the hostess turned to leave.

Reaching out, Matthew grabbed Bell's hands in his. "I have something else to discuss with you. I'm going to be traveling much less," he said. "I've decided to quit working as a private investigator. I'm going back to being a police officer. Detective Wells recommended me, and Chief Jacobs approved. I start as soon as we return home, and eventually, I will become a detective."

"Wow, Matt, that's great news. I'm so happy for you, and for us. This is the best day ever," she gushed.

"It kind of is, isn't it? What could possibly make it any better?"

"Dessert and more love-making," she said as their waiter, Spike, arrived carrying their Champagne.

Grabbing the glasses from Spike, Matthew handed one to Bell and said, "Here's to dessert and more love-making at the request of the young lady." Spike chuckled as he walked away.

They clanked their glasses together and laughed. The night was young and full of endless possibilities. The only certainty was that they would be taking their dessert to go.

The next morning, Bell felt rested and very satisfied with her first night in Punta Cana. The group had decided for their second day to embark on a catamaran party boat adventure. Jordan and Lee had never been, so Bell offered to treat them to the excursion. She figured it would be a small enough venue for everyone to get to know each other a little better. The drinks would also help with relaxing the situation. Nothing was better than being on a boat on the water with good friends, food, and drinks.

"I'm so excited about this," said Torrence. She wore an orange, red, and white animal print monokini; a swimsuit that Bell would have also picked out for herself. Bell was dressed in a purple fringe bikini, and Bernie was wearing its twin in black. "I love boats. It has been forever since I've been on one, and this will be a lot of fun because we get to relax at Saona Island, snorkel at the reef, and then come back at sunset and party it up with some icy drinks. It's the perfect combo."

"Yes, it is," said Bell. Looking over, she was delighted to see that Matthew, Hector, Jordan, and Alex were taking all sorts of silly muscle photos and posing with a giant Marlin that one of the fishermen had landed. He even took a picture with them and their silly muscle pose. Bell noted that he was grinning from ear to ear, and she wondered if the photo was more a highlight for him than catching the fish.

"Where are Linz and Audra?" asked Bernie.

"Oh, they're coming. We cannot let the boat leave without them. Linz was having some lady issue, so Audra stayed to wait for her," said Lee. "Hey, why are we letting the boys have all the fun. We should get some of our own photos."

"I agree. Do you want the fish, or..." Bernie was cut off by Torrence.

"Oh, yes! Look, that dude has iguanas!" She took off at a trot toward him. Positioning her back to the guy, she took a selfie. She had no more than snapped the photo when she was suddenly smacked hard on the butt. Jumping and screeching, she turned around to see that the man had hit her with the iguana's tail.

Scowling at her, he said, "No money, no photo," and held out his hand.

"Oh, shoot," said Torrence, "I'm so sorry. I don't have any money on me." Scowling at her, he took the iguana's tail and made like he was going to hit her with it again.

"Alto!" said Lee. "Aqui," she said, thrusting a couple of pesos into his hand and pulling Torrence away.

Torrence rubbed the back of her suit where the iguana's tail had hit her. "I did not expect that. Those tails hurt."

Bernie and Bell stood off to the side, trying to contain their laughter. Lee rolled her eyes at Torrence, and the sisters lost control of their laughter.

"Knock it off, you two," insisted Lee, who was attempting to stifle her own laughter.

Torrence shook her head in embarrassment. "It's fine. Thanks for paying him. I owe you."

"Man, did you jump." Bernie laughed.

"Well shoot, that thing hurt. I didn't even think about him doing that for money."

"You have to realize, even though things may be cheaper down here, they make money off tourists any way they can," said Bernie.

"I've never been south of the United States," admitted Torrence.

Bell reached out and hooked an arm around Torrence's neck. "Well, girlfriend, now you know." Turning toward Lee, she said, "You speak Spanish?"

Lee nodded. "Yeah. I had to learn in school."

Bell nodded and then turned back to Torrence. "So, you want to go back for round two? Perhaps we can nicely ask and pay him to let us hold his iguanas. He has three, but you don't have to touch them if you don't want to, Tor."

"Awe heck, why not," she replied. "I'm a glutton for punishment."

Walking back over, Lee asked the man if they could pay him to have a picture. He was all smiles and very willing now that he could see the money. Instead of Bernie, Bell, and Lee each taking an iguana, the man placed one on Torrence's shoulders, one on her lap, and one at her feet, and the other three ladies crouched around her, giving the thumbs up. The man snapped their picture and, grinning, gave them the thumbs up to let them know the photo was a keeper.

"Gracias," said Lee and Bell at the same time. The girls pulled Torrence up and headed back toward the boat as Linz and Audra had finally arrived.

"Is it time to go yet?" asked Hector.

Alex walked up beside him. "The captain says we can board the catamaran now."

"Sweet," said Torrence as she ran off toward the boat.

"Follow that blonde," said Alex.

"And follow that blonde," said Hector with amusement.

"And follow that snarky clothing designer who has stolen our brother away from us," said Bernie. Hector turned around and playfully whacked her with his towel.

"Ouch, it was a fly-by-towel whacking," commentated Bell. "How will she respond?"

"Like this," said Bernie. She grabbed the towel from Hector and whacked Bell with it.

"Ow," said Bell. "Retaliation!" She grabbed her own towel and hit Bernie back.

"Okay, crazies," said Lee, "get on the boat. We don't need anyone falling into the drink before we even have a drink or leave the dock, for that matter." She linked her arms around both girls' necks and towed them onto the catamaran. Audra and Linz giggled from behind as they followed.

"Never a dull moment with you lot," said Audra. "You're a bunch of big kids."

Hector looked at her and nodded in agreement. "That is very true."

"Hello, party people! I'm your captain, Mac. We will be disembarking shortly. Once we have left the dock, you are free to order a drink from Wendy at the bar. Bathrooms are down the stairs, but watch your step because rough waters are always a possibility. If you have any questions, please don't hesitate to ask. We are here to serve you and make this adventure memorable."

After the boat pulled away from the dock, the group wandered out to the front of the catamaran and put their beach bags down.

Linz sprawled out lazily on the ground. "What wonderfully sunny weather this is. I'm definitely a sun baby," she said. She looked deathly thin, her swimsuit hanging loosely against her body.

"Me too," replied Bell. She sat down next to her on the boat's netted white polyester floor. "Comfy, isn't it?"

"Yeah, it is. I could fall asleep out here it's so comfy," said Linz.

"Linz," said Bell. "Are you feeling okay?"

"Yeah, why do you ask?" she replied.

"Well, some of us are concerned that you aren't eating properly. You've become awfully thin."

"I'm fine. I've been battling a thyroid problem," she said. "It's a constant struggle."

Bell wasn't sure she believed her, but she didn't want to press the conversation when they were supposed to be enjoying themselves. Bell looked at Bernie, who had been listening to the discussion. Bernie shrugged and shook her head in uncertainty. Linz had gone back to her sunbathing and was no longer paying attention to the sisters or their friends.

"I'm concerned," whispered Bell. "She's part of our agency now. We have to look out for our own."

"Yeah, she's definitely lost weight since last year when I saw her in Ixtapa. Let's look into it further when we get home. Don't ruin the trip over it," requested Bernie.

Alex walked up to the girls, took one look at their somber expressions, and exclaimed, "Let's go to the bar!" just as the boat hit a wave and pitched forward, sending him toppling down onto the netted flooring next to Bell.

"Nope, you've clearly had too many already." Bell laughed.

"Funny," he rebuked as he popped back up and reached both hands out to pull Bernie and Bell to their feet.

The group happily trotted over to the bar.

"A round of Dirty Monkeys, please," said Bell.

"Oh, that does sound good. Nice call," remarked Lee.

The bartender, Wendy, set to work making the frozen beverages, and the group filtered back to the front of the catamaran except for Lee, Jordan, and Torrence, who decided to wait for the drinks. Jordan was saying something that made Torrence laugh like a schoolgirl. Bell had no doubt he was trying to work his charms on her so he wouldn't have to go to bed alone later that night.

"Does Jordan ever give it a rest, or is he always hitting on someone?" Bell asked no one in particular.

Linz shook her head. "He never stops. He started modeling last year at the same time as we did, and he's always chasing tail, whether it's a man or a woman. He doesn't care. I honestly think he might be terrified to be alone or something."

"Maybe he's afraid of the dark," said Audra.

"That's no joke," replied Bernie. "I'm terrified of the dark. I hate it because my imagination always runs rampant, especially if I'm alone."

"I can't imagine what that must feel like to you after this past year," said Bell. She hadn't thought about how horrible it would have been to be locked away in the dark, not knowing what might happen next. The thought sent a shudder through her body. She had noticed the light on in her sister's room most nights. "It's so much easier when you have someone around to sleep with and make you feel safe, but that doesn't excuse Jordan's behavior."

"Nope, he's definitely a *use 'em and lose 'em* type of person, which makes me a little angry," said Audra. "I fell for it when we first met. I thought he actually liked me. I made the mistake of dating him, which was just a game on his end. Once I slept with him, it was over. He never called me again, but he acts like we're still friends, and since he's in our modeling agency, I put up with his stupid antics. That isn't to say I don't warn other people about him if I get the chance."

"Good for you," said Bernie. "I think if someone is going to act that way, they should be prepared to face the consequences, and they should expect that eventually, their poor behavior will earn them a reputation which precedes them."

Bell nodded in agreement. "Amen to that."

Jordan, Lee, and Torrence returned with the drink order. Jordan was carrying a tray, and Torrence had her arm linked through his. Bell rolled her eyes in Bernie's direction, and Bernie gave her an agreeable look in return. Lee began handing out drinks. Once everyone had a beverage, Torrence raised her glass.

"A toast to fun, sun, and being alive!" she yelled.

"Here, here," said the group in agreement as they clunked their plastic cups together.

Bell stopped mid-motion and sniffed the air. She looked to her sister, who had begun to bring the cup toward her face. Bell immediately clamped her hand over the top of it. "Do not move," she said sternly. "Give me your cup." Bernie handed her the beverage, and Bell tasted it. "This has coconut in it. Why is there coconut in this drink?" Bell addressed the group. Everyone shook their heads in confusion.

"What's wrong?" asked Lee. "I mean, there shouldn't be coconut in these."

"Well, there is, and she's deathly allergic to it," replied Bell.

"Did someone request coconut? Do your drinks have coconut in them?" She began grabbing drinks and sniffing them. "This isn't right. They all have it, but coconut is not an ingredient in a Dirty Monkey. It should smell more like a mudslide."

"Relax, Bell. It was an accident, I'm sure," said Bernie.

"You could die. You do realize that, right? I can't lose you too." Her voice cracked.

"Yes, Bell, I do realize that, but I'm not dead, so I think we're okay. Let's just go talk to the bartender. I thought we had informed them to keep the coconut off the boat, but we obviously need to double-check."

"I'll go with you," said Matthew. He helped Bernie to her feet. "Bell, why don't you stay here? You are clearly upset. We can handle this." Alex sat down next to her and patted her on the back.

Bell let out a loud and exasperated sigh, "Fine, just let me know what you find out."

"You know I will, sweetie," replied Matt.

The two walked back toward the bar, leaving Bell behind to calm down. She was upset. Bernie could have been in serious trouble if she hadn't caught the smell in the wind.

"So, you sniff drinks on a regular basis?" asked Alex.

"No, but I do know that a dirty monkey doesn't have a coconut smell to it. It should smell like chocolate and banana."

A few minutes passed, and her sister and boyfriend returned.

"The bartender says there wasn't supposed to be any coconut on the boat. She doesn't know how it happened, but what should have been the crème de banana was actually a pina colada mix. She removed it from the bar and put it aside so this mistake won't happen again. Bernie has decided she will stick to beer for the remainder of the trip."

"Good idea," said Bell.

Bernie put a hand on Bell's shoulder. "Thanks for having my back. Now that I've had a moment to process, I agree with you. That was a little scary. Thank goodness I keep an EpiPen with me now."

"You know I'll always have your back, and I'm thankful for that EpiPen," said Bell.

The remainder of the boat ride went smoothly, with tons of laughs and photos. Linz told some funny model jokes that cracked everyone up. Alex, unfortunately, got stung by a jellyfish while climbing out of the water after snorkeling. Jordan instantly came to his rescue, wanting to pee on him, but Alex protested strongly. Hector, Bell, and Bernie sat back and laughed at the spectacle as Alex tried to get away from Jordan.

The captain tweezed, scraped, and poured vinegar on the wound to make sure no more stingers were attached. Alex took a few shots of tequila to numb the pain. He was as happy as a clam for the rest of the excursion, though Bell contemplated how wonderful he'd be feeling later in the evening if he continued slogging tequila.

The day's adventure was coming to a close. Everyone appeared to be tired out from the sun and fresh air. Barely anyone spoke as they sat on the front of the catamaran, watching the last rays of sunlight disappear below the horizon. The siblings got together and had Hector take a photo of them. Alex intended to put the picture on his mantle once they got home. He always replaced his mantle photo after each trip.

After the photo, Bell cuddled up in Matthew's arms to relax and enjoy the view. "I could get used to this."

"Me too," he replied. "Perhaps when we retire one day, we can get a boat."

"Oh, I like that idea," said Bell. "We can be one of those couples who live on the water."

"Eating fresh fish every day and singing songs about the sea," added Matthew.

"Okay, now you lost me. I can barely carry a tune. After a couple of days of my singing, you might abandon ship." She laughed.

Cupping her chin, he turned her head so he could see her eyes. "On a more serious note, what's our housing plan going to be?"

"Yeah, that's been on my mind too. I think we should move into my mom's house while cleaning it out. We can always decide to get a different place later, but right now, it's mine, and no one is living in it."

Matthew nodded. "That's not a bad place to start since work needs to be done."

"Honestly though, her house is a little excessive. She chose some odd and crazy expensive art. But it's gorgeous nonetheless. You may want to stay once you see it."

"Okay, let's try it out." He leaned forward and kissed the top of her head. "I love you, Bell."

"I love you back," she replied. "Best trip ever."

"Best trip ever," he agreed.

It was the second to last day of the trip, and the group had just retired to the poolside bar after a long day of playing beach volleyball when it happened.

Bell was telling Bernie about her and Matthew's plans to move into Mariska's home together when suddenly Bernie dropped the cup she was drinking from and turned white as a ghost.

"Bernie! Bernie, what's wrong?" prodded Bell. Bernie was choking on the water she'd been drinking. Raising her hand, she pointed.

Bell turned and saw Linz lying on the ground. Hector had rushed to her side and was feeling for a pulse. Shaking his head, he began screaming orders to find a doctor. Torrence started compressions while Alex administered mouth-to-mouth. No one knew what had happened. Jordan was trying to console Audra, who was babbling hysterically. Lee was nowhere to be seen. Bernie and Bell sat gaping helplessly as the situation unfolded.

A medical team arrived and loaded Linz into an emergency vehicle. Jordan and Audra followed along with Hector, who spoke fluent Spanish. The rest of the group went back to Bernie and Bell's suite to wait.

An hour later, they received a deflated phone call from Hector. "Linz didn't make it. We're on our way back. An officer will notify her family in person, and her body will be flown back to the US. I wish I had better news."

"What happened to her? What caused her to arrest to begin with?" asked Alex.

"Without an autopsy, we don't know. Most likely, her family will opt for one. We'll have to wait for the results to come back." His voice quivering, he said, "I'm sorry, Alex. I wish I could have done more, and that I could give you a better answer. I'm so sorry." Pausing, he said, "I'll see you soon."

"Hector, we did the best we could. It's not your fault" said Alex.

"I'll see you soon," he repeated and hung up the phone.

The room felt as if a flood had dragged it under. Bell couldn't breathe, and she began to panic. Matthew immediately rushed to her side. Leaning his forehead against hers, he spoke softly and soothingly. He had her take in breaths to the count of three and let them out slowly to the count of six until she finally was able to calm herself. Lee had joined them shortly after Linz was taken away. She now sat on the couch looking like stone, aside from the trail of silent tears rolling down her cheeks. No one wanted to move.

"Worst trip ever," said Bell through hot tears.

Leaning in, Matthew pulled her close. "Worst trip ever," he agreed.

Chapter Six

Two weeks had slipped by since the untimely passing of Linz. The entire modeling agency had shut down on the day of the funeral to pay their respects. Everyone was still in shock. Audra had taken it the hardest. She disappeared into her home and wasn't seen again until the funeral. She came out to say goodbye to her best friend one last time and then vanished from the public eye once again.

Bell noted that Audra wore a gold 'best friends' charm around her neck and placed Linz's matching necklace inside the coffin with her friend when she paid her last respects. The two girls had been like sisters and were inseparable for most of their careers. She could understand why this was so painful for Audra. She had joined her at Linz's side and held her hand in support as the tears flowed freely from their eyes. Bernie stayed at the back of the church. She couldn't bring herself to come any closer. Alex ventured to the front briefly but then rejoined Bernie. Bell couldn't blame her siblings for how they were acting. The pain of losing Linz had reopened the wounds of all the other losses the family had suffered over the past year.

Linz's family had been informed that she had suffered a heart attack due to the eating disorder she had battled for many years. From Bell's perspective, none of them seemed surprised at the outcome, though they were all clearly mourning. This wasn't the first time a fellow model had died from an eating disorder, and it made Bell rethink how she wanted to run the agency. She was kicking herself for not taking action with Linz sooner. If agencies didn't invest in their model's well-being, this would continue to be a regular theme. She vowed to pay closer attention to her models and ensure they maintained healthy habits. If they didn't sustain a healthy lifestyle, they wouldn't model for Price & Fitz.

Matthew and Bell started moving into their new home the day after the funeral. Matthew was amazed by the house as Bell thought he would be. He couldn't believe the extravagant taste Mariska had. Liberace, indeed, would have thought some of her belongings were a bit much. Matthew wandered from room to room with his mouth agape, absorbing the vastness of Mariska's art collection, which could only rival her clothing and jewelry collection.

"I think selling off these alone could make us quite wealthy," said Matthew. He was holding a pair of genuine sapphire-laden stilettos. "Who wears shoes like these?"

"My mother, that's who," said Bell. "Both she and my father came from old money. I always wondered how far would be too far when it came to her crazy spending habits. Apparently, they never reached the point of no return. The businesses definitely helped keep them well above water."

"I still say it's lucky that Dad took the time to teach us about money," said Bernie. She had her arms full with a box of clothing from Bell's car. "Not that we are ever going to want for anything, but it was still a good idea on his part. Every kid should be taught about money." Bernie set the box down and looked at Bell. "You all have some serious work cut out for you." She waved her hands around to encompass the entirety of the room. "This is not going to be easy to sort through or get rid of, and you obviously have nowhere to put your belongings until you deal with mom's extravagant menagerie of collectibles, so you better get to it."

"You're not going to help us?" asked Bell with wide eyes and raised brows.

"Ha, you funny sista," replied Bernie. "You know I'm not going to be involved in this. It's a good thing she didn't leave the house to me because I'd have been like, 'No, thank you very much,' and walked away with a smile, or I would've opened the doors and said take what you want, it's free, and she would have been rolling in her grave. She'd probably find a way to come back from the dead just so she could show how much she disapproved."

"Yeah, she'd become undead just to get the point across," said Bell as she rolled her eyes at Bernie.

"And then someone would have to stake her, and the party would be over once again," replied Alex from the edge of the room.

"Dang," said Matthew. "Y'all have some kind of morbid animosity toward your mother."

"Oh, trust us when we say we loved our mom, and we miss her dearly, but she was her own piece of craziness, and there is no denying that," said Alex. "Besides, she knew exactly what she was, and she never denied it, so she'd probably laugh at this conversation."

"Isn't that something?" mused Matthew.

"Believe me, he's telling the truth," said Bell. "We all love her because she was our mom, but she was a unique person. Where did we put that bottle of Merlot?"

Alex picked up the bottle and walked into the kitchen to grab glasses and a corkscrew. Setting the glasses out in a line, he poured each of them some wine. "Come grab a glass," he called out. His sisters and Matthew each grabbed a glass and raised it up. "Here's to Mom, may she rest in peace. And here's to Bell and Matthew, who will be taking over this palace and making it their own. You have your work cut out for you, but we wish you a happy future here."

"Aw, thanks, Alex," said Bell. "That means a lot."

"No need to thank me. I'm outta here," he said with a laugh. "No one wants to be a part of this mess," he called over his shoulder as he headed out the door.

"Yep, I'm leaving too. Good luck!" Bernie followed him down the walk and left the couple to debate the disarray they were left to deal with.

Wrinkling his face, Matthew frowned as he looked things over once more. "Where precisely do we begin?"

"In the bedroom." Bell winked. Grabbing him by the hand, she led him down the hall.

"Perhaps I've misconstrued our situation. I think everything will be okay," he said enthusiastically.

Bernie leaned her head against the cool glass window of the limo and exhaled deeply. "Who are we meeting at the club?"

Squeezing Bernie's hand, Alex said, "You haven't been up to the task of running the club, which meant Bell and I had to keep on top of things to stay afloat. We're trying to find someone to take on the position of the new bar manager. Believe me when I say I know Bradley is not an easy person to replace within the business. He did a lot more than I ever realized, so I think we may need two people. A manager and a bartender, unless we're lucky enough to find someone as talented as Bradley."

"Yeah, I knew he wouldn't be easy to replace, considering his vast array of talents," she said, tears forming in the corners of her eyes.

Alex nodded, a somber expression on his face. "Don't cry. We'll figure something out. It'll take time for you to get back into the swing of things at the club. Anyway, we're meeting a guy named Aiden McDermott. I already had a phone interview with him. He passed that test, as far as I'm concerned. He's from Ireland and has dual citizenship because his dad was American and his mom was Irish. He sounds pretty amazing, but I'll let you be the judge of that since you're the one who has to work with him the most. You do understand that my time helping out here is on a temporary basis, right? I expect you to fully take over within the next month."

"Yeah, I know. I'm trying. It's difficult walking in there knowing both Bradley and Dad are gone. Hopefully, the counseling will help me pull myself back together."

"That's all we can hope for at this time. Anyway, are you ready to meet this guy? He's waiting in the VIP room."

"Yeah, let's get to it," said Bernie as she headed for the door. Alex picked up the pace and skipped ahead of her to be the first to enter the VIP room. Bernie followed him in and abruptly stopped. "Excuse us for a moment," she said to the dark-haired, not-so-cleanly-shaven stranger waiting patiently on the sofa. She pulled Alex back outside the room. Though she hadn't gotten a real close look at Aiden, she easily recognized that he had a scar below his right eye and above the right side of his upper lip.

"What's up?" he asked. Concern filled his eyes.

"He's wearing a purple tie," said Bernie. She instantly reached for the cross hanging from her neck. Gripping it hard, she could feel the outline pressing painfully into her hand. "He also has some very noticeable scars."

"The tie," contemplated Alex, "is that a problem? It's a color, Bern. Many attractive people wear the color purple, and as for the scars, I don't know what your point is. Pull yourself together and let's get this over with," he urged while grabbing her in a tight hug. "It's going to be okay, just don't overthink it. We have to hire someone, and this is the first person I've screened who seems to match what the business needs."

"Okay," she mumbled, swallowing back the urge to cry. "I just need to stand here for a second and wrap my head around things. I'm scared, Alex. Things have not felt right, and I'm becoming increasingly worried about who we can and can't trust these days. Lots of strange things have been happening, and I'm not certain they're all random coincidences. How did he get those scars?"

Alex ignored the scar question. "If I'm being honest, I'm on the same page as you. I don't think they're all random, but at the same time, maybe we're being overly paranoid due to what we've gone through over the past year. That's not to say we shouldn't be cautious either way. People are capable of some strange and extraordinary measures when they're driven by lust or revenge."

"Just promise me that if this guy seems off, we won't hire him."

Alex reached out and put his hand on his youngest sister's shoulder. "Oh, honey, you have my word." He turned away and opened the door. Bernie reluctantly followed him in.

"Hello, Aiden, I'm Alex. We spoke on the phone. Sorry about that. We forgot to deal with something that needed immediate attention, but everything is good now." Aiden stood and shook Alex's hand and then turned toward Bernie.

"I'm Bernadette," she said as Aiden reached for her hand. Accepting her hand, he held it gingerly and bowed formally in her direction.

"Wonderful to meet you both," he replied in a heavy Irish accent.

Bernie and Alex took seats opposite Aiden, who had taken a seat back on the sofa.

"So, Aiden, tell us a little about yourself," said Bernie with forced enthusiasm.

"Let's see. I grew up in Ireland. I attended college in the United States and received a degree in Hotel and Tourism. After school, I took time out to travel to other countries I hadn't previously been. During my travels, I did volunteer work and took on temporary paid positions with different hotels that were just starting out. I then spent a couple of years managing a small bar back home called O'Hare's Pub & Grub, and now I'm looking for a new place to call home and become a regular part of for a while.

"I see," said Alex, "Why here?"

"I love the US and have several buddies who live here. My aunt and uncle are in Kansas, and my brother lives in Tulsa because he married a young woman from there. Our parents are both deceased, but my father was from Kansas, which Alex may have told you, is why I have dual citizenship."

"When you say for a while, what does that mean?" asked Bernie.

"Generally, it means two or more years. I hope to stay much longer, but we'll see how it goes. I don't have a whole lot left in Ireland to make me want to go back."

"Well, we're definitely looking for a long-term commitment with this club. We need someone who is going to step up and manage as well as do a little bartending and catering to our VIPs. Do you feel you can meet the demands of this position?" asked Alex. "Have you tended bar before?"

"Yes, I do, and I have. I'm more than ready to step up and help you out with whatever you need. I'm honestly looking for a more permanent place. Plus," he smiled at Bernie, "I find nothing more exciting than bartending and listening to some good old jazz."

"Perfect." She smiled back at him. "We may need you to do the hiring for our musicians as well."

"I'm all over that," replied Aiden.

"How do you handle stressful situations?" asked Bernie.

"I do quite well. I've been in my fair share of stressful situations. In the middle of a wedding banquet back in Ireland, I had a cook pass out and stop breathing. I had to make some very quick decisions and delegate tasks to get a proper medical team on site. We kept the kitchen in production, and we were able to revive her and get her help, all while stopping the wedding party from finding out the extreme nature of the situation that had taken place."

"Geez, that's not an easy task," said Alex.

Bernie and Alex fired off several more questions, which Aiden answered calmly and to completion. The interview moved along rapidly as Aiden described how capable he was of running the club.

"Bernie, do you have other questions for Aiden?"

"No more questions at this time. Do you have any questions?" she asked Aiden.

"No, but I'll definitely let you know if any others come up for me. Alex went over most of the information on the phone, so I feel fairly well informed about expectations."

"Great," she replied. "Thank you for coming in. We'll reach out to you shortly to let you know if we would like to move ahead with the hiring process." She reached out to shake his hand. He again grabbed it and bowed toward her. She had calmed by several degrees as the interview was in progress. Aiden had a way of making her feel relaxed and safe.

"Thank you for taking the time to interview me," he said sincerely.

Alex shook his hand, and then they escorted him from the building.

After Aiden was outside, Bernie turned toward her brother. "Do you feel good about him?"

"Yes, I do. He's polite. He has the right mannerisms. He looks great, so the ladies will no doubt like him. He has a Bradley-like finesse as well. I feel Dad would have approved. I think you should offer him the job tomorrow."

"Yes, he does have a Bradley-like finesse. You said yourself that he's the best fit we've found."

"Girl, I saw how you looked at him."

"You saw nothing," she snapped, reaching for the cross hanging from her neck. She didn't want to feel anything toward another man, but Alex was right; something about Aiden was magnetic.

"Fine, I'll pretend it was nothing, but sometimes you can't stop the chemist's train from reaching the station."

Bernie wrinkled her face at Alex. "What's that supposed to mean? I'm pretty sure you have that saying wrong."

"It means that sometimes chemical attraction cannot be stopped; on a different note, you always deny your feelings."

"No, I don't."

"Yes, you do." He smirked. "Just relax, be cautious, but allow yourself to feel. Feelings can be good, after all. Feelings help a person heal."

"Easy for you to say. You've never been kidnapped and beaten, and as far as I know, you never caused the death of people you loved." The look on her face turned cold, and the pain again crept in.

"Come here," he insisted, wrapping her in another big brother hug. "You're fine. We're fine. Everything is going to turn out fine. We'll be vigilant, but that doesn't mean we can just stop living our lives. You deserve to be loved, and you're making progress in every way. It takes time. You've got this."

"I hear you. I really do. This is why I'm in therapy," she said, reminding herself and swallowing back the pain. "Anyway, moving on, we need to discuss Dad's house and how we'll deal with all of that. Let's go sit down and have a glass of wine while we hash out some details," she said with determination. Alex followed her toward the bar even though she could tell he wasn't happy about the topic of discussion. He had put it off several times already, but Bernie recognized that now was the time, and if she had to move on with hiring someone to run the bar, then he had to deal with their father's house.

After retrieving two glasses of the house Pinot Grigio, she and Alex took seats at one of the small booths across from the bar. The club hadn't yet begun its business day, so it was ghostly quiet. Bernie looked around. The main colors were deep shades of purple and blue with silver mixed in. Her parents had done well with the décor. Framed photographs of music legends adorned the walls of the bar. There were several large round blue and silver booths along with bar top tables.

The place was sectioned off into five different areas: VIP, restaurant, showroom, bar, and game room. The VIP room was furnished with plush blue and purple oversized furniture, pillows, and metallic tables to set drinks on.

The game room held three pool tables, three dartboards, and a shuffleboard table, as well as an old-fashioned bar and pinup girl signs, most of them funny. Despite being funny, they were surrounded by upscale silver and black frames that gave them a classy look. The walls were painted gray, and purple lights were strung across the vaulted ceiling. It felt expensive yet light and whimsical feel.

The showroom held several high-top tables with plush blue chairs. There was a stage with a purple curtain, and the walls held silver antique lights with crystals, which gave off a slight shimmer. There were also several booths around the perimeter of the room and a small bar in the back left corner. The entire room accommodated one hundred people. It was meant for intimate performances.

The restaurant was the most stunning part of the club. The center of attraction was the large mosaic blue and turquoise water fountain, which shot water ten feet in the air. The tables throughout the room were black with turquoise linens. Several crystal chandeliers hung throughout, and all were connected by strings of crystals to one larger chandelier which hung directly above the water fountain. The room shimmered and sparkled from the crystals and candles that were lit on each table and in sconces on the walls. People came to the restaurant for dates and special events and they trusted that their guests would feel important and well taken care of.

Bernie took a sip of her wine and looked at Alex. "I've been thinking. I feel like the three of us should go through Dad's house together and pick out anything salvageable that we want to keep. After we take what we want, providing there is anything left that's in decent shape, our best option is to hire an auctioneer to get rid of the remaining items and donate the money to a charity. I know Mom and Dad would appreciate that."

"Have you mentioned any of this to Bell?"

"Not yet. I wanted to see what your thoughts were first. You know how she struggles with getting rid of anything that isn't clothing. Too much sentimental value for her to deal with. I mean, let's face it, I've tried to throw that old ratty shirt of Dad's away many times, and she always finds it. On top of that, we should help since the money is to be split amongst us."

Alex leaned forward, resting his chin on his hands while contemplating the situation. Watching him, Bernie could see the pain in his expression. She wasn't the only one suffering, though she knew Alex worked hard to keep it together for his sisters. He picked up his glass and sipped some wine. Placing the glass on the table, he raised his eyebrows slightly at her, and she could see he was coming around to her suggestion.

"We need to arrange a time to meet Bell at the house and go through things together."

Alex nodded his head. "Yeah, I agree with that. If we let her go by herself, she'll likely pick up some old heirloom, cry for an hour, and get nothing done."

"I bet it'll be one of Dad's old tobacco pipes, even though she was always getting on him about smoking."

"Yup, I can see that happening." He laughed.

"All I care about is that we are in agreement on how to handle this." Bernie furrowed her brow.

"What is it?" he asked.

"I think we better get back over to Mom's and put this plan into action before she goes around hoarding everything over there as well."

"Good idea!" said Alex a little too enthusiastically. "The last thing I want is for Bell to start turning into Mom. It's best if we coax her to get rid of some stuff before she gets too attached. I'm sure Matthew will be in agreement. We can enlist his help in controlling this situation, so she doesn't go overboard. After all, they're going to be living together from now on. He should have a say in what his own home will look like."

"I think you'd better knock before going in," said Alex. "You never know what those two are up to." He grinned.

They were back at Mariska's house, and the place looked dark. Bernie rang the doorbell and waited. No one answered, so she proceeded to thump her fist loudly on the door. Still receiving no answer, she tried the handle, which was not locked. Gently pushing the door open, she peered through the crack like a spy. "Hello? Is anyone in there?" she called out.

"Hey, put your clothes on!" yelled Alex.

Bernie gave him a dirty look. He grinned in return. "Are they not here?" she asked.

"I don't know. It's awfully quiet. At the same time, though, this house is huge. Maybe we should just go in and make a bunch of noise to state our presence."

"Okay, proceed," she said.

"No, you proceed. I don't want to go first. That's my sister in there doing whatever it is they're doing."

"We don't know that they're doing anything or if they're even here," replied Bernie. The words had no more than left her mouth, and she heard a high-pitched laugh coming from across the house.

"Oh, they're in here," said Alex as he prowled about.

Bernie rolled her eyes. "That has been brought to my attention."

"Bell!" yelled Alex. "Matt!"

"Hey, guys, we just want you to know we're inside the house. Please use discretion!" shouted Bernie. "Come on, this way," she said, grabbing Alex's elbow and leading him toward the other side of the living room. "I think they're in the den."

"Oh man, I hope they aren't doing freaky things in there. That's my favorite room in the house."

Bernie approached the door, which was closed. Reaching up, she knocked firmly. "Hello?"

"Hello?" called Bell from the other side. "Who's out there?"

"It's your meddling sister," said Alex in a high-pitched voice. "I've come to have you committed," he stated in a creepy low voice.

Bell threw open the door. "What are you two doing? You scared us half to death!"

Alex took a step back. "What are youuu two doing?" he asked suspiciously.

"We're looking at Mom's old movie collection."

"Oh, is that so?" he replied. "Okay, carry on."

"What did you think we were doing?" asked Bell.

"Oh, you know, bow chicka wow wow," he teased as he did a little dance. Bell reached out and whacked him in the shoulder with a movie case. "Ouch."

"Well then, knock it off," she scolded as she shot him a dirty look.

"What are you drinking?" asked Bernie. Bell was holding a crystal flute.

"Oh, it's an Asti. Would you like some? We were continuing our celebration of moving in together, although Matthew hasn't actually brought any of his stuff over yet."

"Yeah, I'll start tomorrow," he noted.

"Sure," said Bernie, "we'd love some Asti."

"Okay then, go grab some glasses," she replied.

"On it," said Alex, bounding off toward the kitchen.

"What brings you back over so soon?" asked Bell.

"We wanted to discuss something with you."

"Oh, what's that?" she asked.

"Well, Alex and I—"

"Oh geez, here we go," said Bell.

"Bernie and I," added Alex as he walked back into the room, "feel that the three of us should sort out what we want from each house, together, and then auction off the remainder of the items to raise money for charity. We don't need the money, and we also know you have a problem with hoarding—"

"Wait just a moment," said Bell, "I have a problem with hoarding?"

"Well, yeah," said Alex. "You don't appear to know how to let anything go unless it's last year's wardrobe. You get too emotionally attached to things."

"Hmm, this is interesting," said Matthew. "So, my little lady is a hoarder?" He grinned.

"Oh my goodness," she said. "I kept one shirt of Dad's. One shirt!"

"No, Bell, not just one shirt. You kept matchbooks from clubs where you went on dates, the first glass you toasted with in college, the napkins from the first phone number you were given at a club, and the list goes on to much larger items."

"That was years ago," she protested.

"Oh no, it was not years ago. You also kept the coasters from the concert we recently went to, an ashtray from a runway show we were in last year, and a giant balloon from Evie Wellington's lingerie show. You have a problem."

"Oh, snap," said Matthew. "I guess I should've known about this sooner." He laughed.

"Anyway, Matthew, we want you to know about this little issue so that you can help our sister decipher what is a keepsake and what is not. Also, we don't want you turning into Mariska and trying to keep all of the crazy expensive, ridiculous things she has in this house. No one needs half of this stuff," said Alex.

"Okay, fine, you win," said Bell. "We can sort through it all together and then auction off what's left."

"Good deal, girlfriend," said Matthew. He beamed at Bell.

"What are you smiling at?" she asked. "You get to sift through it all with me."

"Yup, but at least I'll be with you." He winked.

Chapter Seven

It took thirty days to sort through the two estates and auction everything off, but the siblings survived. Bell tried, as usual, to hoard things, but Matthew kindly helped her see what was worthwhile and what was junk or just ridiculously over the top. He was patient with her, and they learned a lot about one another's taste in living. No matter how silly the item was, he didn't bash it. He kindly reminded her of what their goal was, and she was able to move on. He did agree to let her keep the sapphire stilettos as a memento. After all, they were highly impressive, and Mariska had worn them in her prime for a modeling gig at a casino opening in Las Vegas, where Liberace was indeed present.

Bell found Matthew to be minimalistic but with expensive taste, which he directed quite deliberately. He didn't just buy whatever he saw first, but was meticulous and planned things out. He made sure he saw the whole picture in his mind before moving ahead, which was something Bell hadn't been accustomed to. For example, the house had to have a theme, and if the items within the house didn't match the theme, they were auctioned off.

Matthew was into rustic and Bell was eclectic. They decided, in the end, to go with an upscale rustic style. They mixed together wood with metal and crystal to give their home a luxurious farmhouse look. The color palette was grey, brown, black, and white. Overall, the entire place felt clean and comfortable.

Matthew's favorite space was the dining room with its large, shiny wooden tabletop and cushy gray chairs because he loved cooking and sharing meals with his family and friends. Bell's favorite was the living room with its oversized gray suede sectional, dark brown wooden coffee table, and matching entertainment center. In the end, the couple was ecstatic about the result of transforming Mariska's place into their own.

Matthew hadn't lived in such a permanent setting in a very long time. His job had forced him to frequently live out of hotels or short-term apartment rentals. He was happy to be settling down in one location and even more pleased that it was because he had a new job and a wonderful woman with whom he could share his life.

Bell, little by little, had learned that Matthew's entire family was back in California and that he seldom visited. His twin brothers were ten years older than he and both big wig lawyers in their own firm. They loved to pick at him and call his life 'unconventional.'

His parents were retired doctors and spent most of their time bouncing from one yacht to another. They didn't approve of his lifestyle and frequently asked him why he couldn't go to law school and join the firm. They wanted him to be more like his older brothers.

He had told Bell that he was always the black sheep of the family. He worked because he enjoyed helping others, whereas his family sounded more like Bell's mother, who worked simply for the money and the partying that followed. Having Mariska as a mom gave Bell a strong understanding of what life may have been like for Matthew, which in turn made her happy to be the solid part of his world.

"Hey," called Matthew from their walk-in closet, "when are we supposed to be heading out?"

Bell looked up from the mirror where she'd been applying one final layer of mascara. "We should have left five minutes ago."

"I'm ready if you are," he said, emerging from the closet. He was wearing a light grey pinstripe suit with a pale pink tie. Bell wore a matching light pink cocktail dress.

"I don't know why we're trying to match," she stated with frustration. "This is a date auction, so that means someone's bidding on me to go out with them this evening."

"Moral support, baby," he replied coolly. Nothing could get him down. Matt remained positive through thick and thin, and he was the water that floated her boat.

"Yeah, I thank you for that, but this totally bites. I tried to get out of it."

"Hey, this is for a good cause. Remember that. Besides, everyone knows you're spoken for, so they should mind their *Ps and Qs*."

"Yeah, they should, but will they? I feel like I'm falsely advertising myself right now. Morally, this feels wrong."

"Sweetheart, just relax. It's for charity. Perhaps you'll get someone who wants to pick your brain about business. Besides, we aren't married or engaged, so I give you the freedom to go out and have fun tonight. I know you're coming home to me and that you'll be on your best behavior." He patted her on the butt like he was sending her up to bat.

"I guess, as long as we're on the same page."

"No guesswork involved, my lovely. Now," he wrapped his arms around her waist, "give me a kiss."

Standing on her tiptoes, she pressed her lips tightly to his. She knew this wasn't their last kiss, but she couldn't help herself.

"Come on," she insisted, "we best get this train rollin', or Bernie's going to have a conniption."

On the other side of town, Bernie was indeed having a conniption. She and Alex had spent the early hours of the morning decorating the club for the date auction. They'd arrived before sun up and hastily set to work readying the stage and making it look like a runway for the auction. The flowers scheduled to arrive at nine that morning had not arrived yet, and it was nearly ten. She nervously waited as the florist checked the delivery schedule and route of the delivery van.

"Hmm. I see he left here on time but ran into a traffic jam in Tulsa. He appears to be moving now. I'm so sorry for the inconvenience, but these things sometimes happen. I promise the flowers will be there shortly," she assured Bernie.

"Well, it shouldn't happen," said Bernie. "I don't have time for any delays," she added with frustration.

"Listen, tell you what, since you're one of our larger clients, I'll knock twenty percent off your next order. Again, I do apologize for the inconvenience. These situations are unforeseeable."

"Thanks," said Bernie. Alex motioned toward the door. "Oh, looks like the flowers are arriving now. We'll talk soon."

"Good deal. You have a great day," she replied with too much enthusiasm.

Alex met the florist halfway across the room and directed him where the flowers needed to go. Bernie took a deep breath. Everything was going to be fine, she mentally reminded herself. As she breathed in, the floral scent helped to calm her nerves.

"Hey, where's Bell?" asked Alex.

"I'm sure she's on her way, though running late as usual. The *only* time that girl is on schedule is when someone else picks her up. By the way, thanks for coming in early and helping me decorate and get things in order. Aiden had an appointment this morning, so I couldn't rely on him to be here to direct the setup."

"Speak of the devil," said Alex. "How's it going, Aiden?"

"Hey, I can't complain," he looked at Bernie and gave her a smile. "Sorry I'm arriving so late. What would you like me to do first?"

"Go whip the kitchen staff into shape and make sure everything's on track, and then I want you to set up the hors d'oeuvres and Champagne fountain in the VIP room. We're so behind. I need all hands on deck with this. Once Matthew and Bell arrive, we need to put them to work, too. The doors open at noon, and I am starting to worry we might not be ready."

"Stop for a second," said Aiden, closing the distance between himself and Bernie. "Look at me. Just breathe for a minute," he requested. "Now, repeat after me." She couldn't help but gaze into his soft blue eyes. He had only been with them a month, but he had a smooth way of handling Bernadette and her nerves. "I'm a tough and driven woman who can accomplish anything I put my mind to."

"I'm a tough and driven woman who can accomplish anything I put my mind to," she said with conviction.

"Now, remember that," he said with a nod. Without realizing it, she had reached out and placed her hand on his chest. He looked down at it and raised an eyebrow. Giving her a wink, he turned and headed for the kitchen. She stared after him, mesmerized by his tight butt.

Completely zoned out, it took her a moment before she noticed the hand waving in front of her face. Alex was gawking at her. His brow was wrinkled in disapproval, and he shook his head from side to side. "Honey, this is neither the time nor the place for that, and I'm pretty sure it's considered harassment."

"What? Oh, um, yeah, I probably shouldn't have done that," she said uncomfortably. Her face had turned a bright shade of red. "We're just friends, and of course, I'm his boss, so it's totally inappropriate. He's just trying to be helpful."

"That be pure blarney," scoffed Alex. A menacing grin crossed his lips, "It's not like you two don't have a relationship outside of here. Don't think I haven't noticed how you've been meeting for lunch dates the past three Fridays in a row. *Something's going on*," sang Alex.

"Oh, God, who am I kidding? I need help," she said. "I clearly have a problem."

"Well, let's contemplate that one later, shall we? We have a lot to do, and we need to focus."

"Can I add something?" asked Bernie.

"Fine, go for it, but it's your dime," said Alex.

"I know this might be paranoia, but I feel like someone might be following me. I'm afraid to be alone, so if I go anywhere, I make sure to invite someone along. Aiden makes me feel safe."

"Have you told anyone else?" asked Alex, his eyes narrowing with concern.

"No. I'm not sure Detective Wells would believe me. I get the impression that the station thinks we're being paranoid. They don't seem to believe there's a real threat since Martin's behind bars and Bradley's no longer around to point a finger at Martin's accomplice. You were there; he brushed off the window incident as if it were a random hate crime."

"I'd tell him, Bernie, you never know. If you're really being followed, you could be in danger. Wells should be looking into it. Besides, now that Matthew has joined the force, I'm sure he can help us out. If nothing else, you should tell him."

Alex had barely finished his sentence when Bell's voice broke through their conversation "Hey guys!" She sauntered into the room with Matthew in tow. "What can we do to help?"

"Well, next time, you can show up early instead of late," said Alex, pointing a finger at her.

"Well, next time, why don't you pick us up, and we'll arrive on time," she interjected.

"This conversation is going nowhere," said Bernie. "Start putting flower arrangements and candles on the tables while Alex and I put covers and sashes on the chairs, please."

The group speedily set to work, and though it took some effort, they managed to complete everything fifteen minutes before the doors were to open. All of the models had shown up on time and were ready to be auctioned. With a few minutes to spare, the group could relax.

"Let's have a toast to kick the event off," said Bernie as they gathered by the bar. "Aiden, please pour us each a glass of the Pinot Grigio." Turning back to the group, she looked at Matthew. "Matt, I want to say thank you for everything you've done for our family. You've been a huge support, and I'm so happy you and my sister found one another. Before we kick off this event, I need to tell you something."

"Oh boy, am I in trouble?" he asked.

"No, but I might be," she said with hesitance. "I think someone's following me. I haven't told anyone else because I'm worried they'll think I'm being paranoid, but the other night, coming out of the club, a car was waiting at the far end of the parking lot. I swear that same car was there two nights earlier, and this time, when I stopped to look at it, the driver sped away."

"They haven't approached you or followed you out of the parking lot?" asked Matthew.

"No. Not that I know of."

"Okay, that's good. Maybe it's just some kids parking at the back of the lot and fooling around. You know how teenagers are," he said, "but I'll look into it. Tonight, before we leave, I can do a perimeter check to make sure nothing is out of sorts. If you want, I'll do so for the next week and see if I notice anything suspicious."

"We," said Alex, motioning to himself and Bell, "would greatly appreciate you doing that."

"Bernie, if you're scared, you need to tell us," said Bell. "We aren't going to fault you for paranoia with all we've been through."

"I don't think I'm paranoid. I've had this gut feeling that it's real, and even before I saw the car, it felt like someone has been watching me over the past few weeks."

"Well, don't you fret, little sister. Matthew will take care of us," said Alex. He patted Matt on the back for good measure.

Aiden poured the wine out and handed a glass to each of them. Taking one in his own hand, he raised it and said, "Here's to Bernadette and this beautiful club. May you raise tons of money today and have a blast doing so."

"Cheers!" said the group in unison.

It was nearly two o'clock and guests were seated and waiting in anticipation for the auction to begin. Bell and Matthew sat comfortably in a booth with Alex, Lee, Torrence, and Jordan. They were chattering away about upcoming modeling events and enjoying a glass of wine. Bernie was off giving commands for who would be auctioned when. She had given the job of emcee to Aiden, who was still behind the bar pouring some final drinks. Bernie would soon head toward the bar, prompting him to take the stage, and that would be their table's cue to pay attention because the auction was about to begin.

"How's Audra doing since the funeral?" asked Bell.

"Not well," replied Lee. "I keep trying to get her back in the game, but she can't seem to get past this loss. She's talking about giving up modeling. Last I saw her, she was muttering something about modeling destroying more good women."

"She wouldn't be wrong," said Torrence, "modeling, as we all know, is a very demanding vocation. Many women end up with health issues from starving themselves. I've heard that in some countries, agencies will go as far as to scout women who are leaving eating disorder clinics. Talk about sick."

"Well, as you may know, we've developed a policy that goes into effect next month," said Bell. "Quarterly health checks are now required to continue modeling for our agency. I don't want any more models killing themselves to look good. If you do appear to have a problem, there will be a length of time allotted for you to get it under control with professional help, and then resume your job. I'm not going to be an enabler of poor health. Too many agencies care too little about their models, and Price & Fitz will not be one of them."

Jordan gave Bell the thumbs up. "Girl, I agree with you. If we want change, it has to start somewhere, and losing one of our own is a pretty low blow."

"Yeah, Emmy Baker had a blast with that article," said Bell.

"Oh, please, don't start in on that again," said Alex. "Emmy will always be there to call you out, so you may as well get used to it."

"I don't know if anyone ever gets used to their name being bashed," replied Matthew. "Anyway, sweetheart, you're doing a great job, and Emmy is simply doing her job as well. Maybe you should contact her and make nice. Get her to do an article on the changes you're implementing at the agency."

"I think that's a great idea," said Lee, smiling warmly. "Bell, you should keep your enemies closer."

"Oh, there he goes," said Bell. She watched as Aiden made his way across the room and onto the stage. "It's time to work, guys and gals. We can table this discussion until later."

"Ladies and gentlemen, it is my honor to welcome you to the fifth annual Price & Fitz Model Auction for Charity. Tonight's proceeds will go to St. Jude Children's Research Hospital. The lucky bid winners will be given the evening to spend with their prospective date, and all food and drinks will be on the house. We have picked out some extra special dishes for you to choose from this evening as well as a couple of signature libations. If you'd like to bid in the auction, just hold up your red flag, and I'll put you in the running. Without further ado, let's get this auction started!"

Bell sat back and watched Aiden work. He was a smooth operator indeed. He auctioned off each model while providing comedic commentary that had the audience laughing all afternoon. The first two models went for far less than she had hoped, but the third far exceeded her expectations, which helped even things out. Lee appeared to be the most sought-after model. Who could blame any one of her bidders? She had confidently stolen the microphone from Aidan and taken over her own bidding war. She was smart, beautiful, funny, and nearly as smooth as Aidan. She smiled at Bell from on stage and waved her hands in the air to promote higher bidding. She strutted around the stage, egging the buyers on. The crowd loved it. The girl knew how to get them going.

"Man," said Alex, "I wish we could auction her off to more than one person. These guys are bending over backwards to bid on her."

"Yeah, she's a catch," said Torrence, who looked slightly annoyed. She hadn't brought in nearly as much money as she'd hoped and was letting everyone know just how disappointed she was. "I don't think she's even into men," she commented. "How did she go for so much more than me?"

"Cheer up, girl. It happens to the best of us," said Alex. "Who knows, I'm up next. Maybe I'll go for less."

Bell sat back and watched as Alex marched up to the stage. She was certain he wouldn't go for less. Hector joined the table midway through the auction, and she could tell he was prepared to outbid anyone who attempted to win a date with his man. He was known for his possessive side and appeared incapable of sharing anything.

"Next up, we have Alex Crimson of Price & Fitz. Who would like to start the bidding?" asked Aidan. "Can I get one hundred dollars?" Hector's flag shot into the air. "Very nice. Can I get one hundred and fifty?" called Aidan. Another red flag went up.

"Five hundred dollars!" yelled Hector, waving his red flag in the air.

"Oh, high bidder over there! Can I get six hundred?" replied Aidan, and the other bidder's red flag once again flew into the air.

Bernie had joined the table. "Looks like this could get ugly," she whispered to Bell. Hector was visibly gnashing his teeth and frowning.

The sisters watched as the bidding bounced back and forth between Hector and the other bidder, who decided to stand up so everyone could see her.

"Oh boy," said Bell. "It's Eloise. She has no idea what she's in for, and she's definitely not going to let Hector win."

"She's one of the most clueless women I've ever met," commented Bernie, and then turning to Hector, she said, "Hector, honey, this might be a hard win for you. That's Artemis Jasper's niece, and she's like a pitbull. She's gonna lock her teeth in, and you'll have to get a crowbar to get her off your man." She laughed.

"She knows Alex plays for the other team, doesn't she?" asked Bell.

"I doubt it. She isn't one to waste her time. She's gonna have a heck of a long night trying to win him over." Bernie was smirking with satisfaction. Bell understood her sister's excitement about the situation because Eloise had expensive taste and acted much like their mother. Eloise had also tried to win Bradley over once, but Bradley preferred a spicier woman than her.

The bid had reached fifteen thousand dollars, and neither bidder appeared close to their threshold. Aiden queued up LMFAO's song. *I'm Sexy, and I Know It*, and Alex was going to town dancing around the stage. Other bidders joined in, and Hector's face was beginning to turn a shade of red Bell had never seen on another person before.

"Hector, man, this is for charity. We should be happy he's getting such high bids. This event is going to be a total success because of him alone at this rate," said Matthew. "Don't let it get to you. Let someone else win."

Hector let out a throaty growl from between his clenched teeth. "The problem is he's just too damned desirable. Everyone wants to get their hands on him. It doesn't matter if he's gay, straight, or whatever. They all want a piece of him."

Bell listened as Matthew spoke to Hector. "Yeah, he is desirable, Hector, but he's with you, and he knows it. What are you worried about? Alex seems like a pretty faithful guy."

"That maybe some other rich so-and-so will come in and sweep him away from me."

"Oh, Lordy, that's never gonna happen," said Bell. "He's unconditionally yours. I've never seen him so into another person, besides me," she laughed, "in his entire life."

Bernie put on her business face. "Seriously, you need to relax a little and realize that this is for charity, and no matter who wins, it's an innocent date auction. Everyone has been warned ahead of time that he's in a relationship and that his date is more about a friendly get-together. It's not about intimate relations."

"Fine," said Hector. His bid had reached forty-five thousand, and he decided to pull out as the next bidder called fifty-thousand.

"Let someone else pay the price for Alex. You get him for free all of the time," said Matthew.

"That is true," commented Hector. "I guess there's no harm in letting him go to someone else for an evening."

"Why don't you bid on someone else if you want to give money to the event? Let this bidder spend money on him. That way, we know there'll be another decent contribution toward whomever you choose to bid on." said Bernie with a grin.

Alex finally went to Eloise for seventy-three thousand dollars, and Bell and Bernie looked at one another with wide eyes, then broke into laughter at the same time. "Holy heck! That's a lot of money for a dinner with our brother," said Bell. "I'm gonna auction him off every year from now on. He'll be ninety, and we'll make him shake his booty for charity on stage." She laughed.

"Wish me luck," said Bell. Standing up she made her way to the stage. Matthew blew her a kiss. She had no idea what to expect.

Aiden grabbed her hand and helped her up the stairs and onto the stage. "Here we have the ever-lovely Bell Price. Bell is the person you need to talk to if you desire to break into modeling or simply do business with Price & Fitz, so let's see those bids, ladies and gentlemen. Can I get one hundred dollars?"

Bell watched as several people began bidding the price up. She was shocked to see who some of those bidders were. Jordan Blake was one of them. She couldn't stand him, but Hector and Alex thought he was worthwhile, so she allowed him to stay on at the agency. Scanning the audience, she saw Artemis Jasper. He had just upped the bid to eight thousand dollars. Looking around to see who else was present, she noticed Alex's red flag waving to the beat of ten thousand dollars. She glared back at him. He wasn't supposed to be bidding since he was already someone else's date.

The bid volleyed back and forth and shot up to forty-eight thousand. Artemis Jasper bowed out, but Jordan was still in the running. He won it at fifty thousand. Bell was both appalled and astonished. She was happy she'd reached fifty grand, but not happy that the winner was Jordan, who clearly had no idea how she felt about him. He was nothing but a trust-fund brat who flaunted his looks and money. She realized how hypocritical the dialogue in her head sounded. Others could say she was also a trust-fund brat, even though she tried to act classy and be nice to everyone she met. She didn't use people, though she supposed at times she might come off as slightly vain, however unintentional. Jordan Blake made her skin crawl. Now, she would have to put on a fake smile and pretend to enjoy her evening with him.

Bell exited the stage, and Bernie entered. "Nice work," she whispered to her sister.

"Good luck," replied Bell. She was going to be the last auction of the afternoon, and she hoped the bid would go high because that girl needed a boost.

"All right, ladies and gentlemen, this is the last auction of the evening. If you haven't spent enough money yet, we have an area to make donations at the back of the room. The staff will be glad to help you put your money toward a great cause. Now, let's start the bidding for the lovely Bernadette Price at five hundred dollars!" A chill ran through Bell as she watched several men meet the five-hundred-dollar call. If that didn't make Bernie feel good, she didn't know what would.

Bell watched red flags fly up all over the room. Aiden queued up the song, *Work B**ch*, by Britney Spears, and Bell watched as Bernie began strutting her stuff and dancing on stage. Her jaw dropped. The song was perfect, but she couldn't believe *her* sister was actually getting into it. The crowd was screaming and hollering, and the bid steadily climbed.

"Well dang," said Hector. "It looks like our girl is a hot commodity. From the people I recognize, they look like they're all eligible bachelors bidding."

"This should make her feel good," said Alex. He held his red flag up to make the twenty-five-thousand-dollar bid. Bell jerked his arm back down.

"Stop that!" she said. "You know you aren't supposed to be bidding."

"I know that. It's not like I'm winning this bid. I just want to show my love." He smiled.

"We know you love us," she replied.

"Aw, what the heck," said Hector. "Fifty thousand!" he roared, throwing his red flag into the air.

"Oh, sweet!" yelled Alex. "Bid her up!"

The bidding proceeded on and flew past Alex's final bid

until it reached eighty thousand. Hector put in a final bid of one hundred thousand and won an evening with Bernadette Price.

"Dang Hector, I didn't know you were so into our sister. Are you sure you're dating the right person?" joked Bell.

"I figure she'll feel safer if it's someone she trusts, and who better than her gay brother's handsome and charming lover? I saw how she opted away from paddles and went for flags instead, so that tells me she could use a little extra understanding. I planned to make a sizeable donation anyway."

"You could have bid that on Alex," said Matthew.

"Yes, but as you so kindly reminded me, I get to spend time with him for free." He shot a smile in Alex's direction. "Now I can sit and pick Bernie's brain on other events we might be able to host together at the club." He laughed. "It's a double win in my book."

Breaking into the conversation, Bernie's voice could be heard loudly over the keyed-up crowd. "Thank you, everyone, for participating in the auction this afternoon. Watch your email for an update in the following week as to how much we raised for St. Jude's. Please proceed to the back of the room to pay for your dates and collect your tickets for this evening's dinner and festivities. The restaurant and showroom will be closed between three and five to prepare for tonight, but you may adjourn to the game room, the main bar, or relax in the VIP suites if you're a bid winner. Thank you again for coming and for your generosity. I wish you all a wonderful evening!"

Bell watched her sister climb down from the stage and head toward their table.

"Well, she did quite wonderfully up there, wouldn't you say?" asked Matthew.

"Yes, she did," replied Bell. "I'm proud of her for keeping it together." She turned and looked at Hector who was now standing next to the booth. "Hector, thank you. I think it was very kind of you to put your money out there for Bernie."

"Hey," he said, "don't think anything of it. Besides, you're family to me. Anyway, I better go pay my tab."

"Oh. My. Goodness!" yelled Bernie. "That was intense! I didn't know what to expect, and then as the bids started rolling in, I felt my nerves start to kick in, and I had to focus on the music and pretend I was alone in my bedroom dancing."

"That was smart thinking," said Alex. "You looked great up there, and you did very well."

Bell stood up and pulled her sister into a hug. "We're all proud of you. Not just for getting through this but also for putting this event on. We made a lot of money for charity today."

"Thanks," said Bernie. "I'm lucky to have such a great family backing me. Anyway, I need to hit the restroom before we move on to the second half of this event."

"I'm with ya," said Alex.

Bell watched her siblings walk off toward the restrooms. "Hey Matt, what are you going to do while I'm on my so-called date?"

"Sit at the table next to you and stare uncomfortably at Jordan."

He did his best to put an intimidating and mean look on his face. She supposed it was possible that any person who wasn't privy to his gentle nature might be put off by his angry stare, but to her, he was just a sweet and playful bulldog pup. "Yeah, you might fool him, but I'll probably start laughing," she said in return.

"Not very convincing?" The look on his face was of disappointment. "Well then, I guess I'll hang out at the bar and try to learn a little more about our friend Aiden."

"Oh, yeah, I'm always game for that scenario. I just want to make sure he isn't another Martin or someone who will hurt Bernie. I can tell she doesn't want to allow herself to like him, but Alex did a great job finding a man with similar characteristics to Bradley. I'm still not sure if that's a good thing for my sister, though I know it's been a blessing for the club."

"I'm not going to make any major decisions on what I think until I've had a little more time to get to know him. We haven't been around here as much with all of the work we've had to do at the house. I'll try to look into his background some more, and we can go from there."

"Good deal, officer." Bell leaned in and kissed his cheek. Reaching up, he pulled her in for a kiss on the lips.

"You can't get away that easily," he whispered. As Bell pulled back from their kiss, a loud scream broke the silence, causing a chill to rush through Bell's spine. Paralyzed with fear, her wine glass fell to the floor, shattering into a hundred tiny pieces. Matthew jumped to his feet, climbing over the table to exit the booth. Coming back to the present moment, Bell chased after him as he ran toward the bathrooms. "Who was that?" he asked.

"I— I'm not sure. It could have been Alex or Bernie. They both have high-pitched screams," she said. "But it sounded a lot like Bernie—on the day we lost Bradley."

Barreling into the women's bathroom, they found Alex hugging Bernie, who was slumped in the middle of the blue tile floor. He had one hand over her eyes and pointed at the mirror with the other. Bell and Matthew shifted their gazes and immediately saw what had caused the scream. The entire mirror was covered in what appeared to be blood. There was a severed finger lying in the sink, and someone had used it to wipe away sections of blood in order to create an unsettling message.

Chapter Eight

Bell stared at the mirror in a daze. Her stomach felt sick, and she instantly snapped back to the moment when she had found Bell holding Bradley on the front steps of the police station. Turning, she thrust herself into the first stall and began dry heaving. She hadn't eaten in hours, so there was nothing in her stomach to lose.

She could hear Matthew as if he were far away. "Alex, take Bernie out of the bathroom, and don't let anyone in here. Flag down one of the staff members to get the janitor over here with a sign to show it's out of service, then call the police and ask for Wells. Tell him I'm already here, but we need him right now and to be discreet because we have a huge event going on. Oh, and lock all the doors and station an employee at each entrance. We cannot let anyone leave the club."

"What do I tell people when they ask why they can't leave?"

"You tell them this club has been quarantined, local authorities are on their way, and they will have more information shortly. Tell the staff to be strong and hold their ground."

The door to the stall opened, and she felt a pair of strong hands grab her around the waist and pull her away from the stool. He lifted her with ease into a standing position and carefully turned her to face him. "I need you to hold it together. I know this is a shock to your system, but you're okay, and we're going to handle this promptly."

Bell stared at the dripping mirror. Her entire body shuttered. "You'll be joining Bradley soon," she read out loud. "Look! This is proof that someone is after my sister. Her life's been threatened by someone who's in this building! They were in here while she was in the bathroom! Whoever it is, they're watching her and waiting to make their move!" Bell's head began to pulse. She felt as if she might pass out. She couldn't lose anyone else. She wasn't scared for herself but for Bernie. Her little sister was fragile as it was, and now it was clear she was being targeted. Her body began to tremble as her brain took over, adding in every possible scenario of what was coming next.

"Look at me," commanded Matthew. He grabbed her chin and turned her to face him. "I'm going to be very blunt right now, and I need you to hear this. We're going to turn around and leave this bathroom. We'll act as if nothing happened. I'm going to walk you to the VIP room, and I'm going to grab Alex and Bernie along the way and bring them with us. I will then usher everyone else out of the VIP room, and you are going to lock the door and stay there until I intercom you to let me in. Do you understand what I'm saying? Bell, are you hearing me?"

She nodded her head and then reaching up squeezed his hand to show compliance. She could do this. She would just keep telling herself that. She needed to stay strong for Bernie. Her little sister needed them all to stay strong. She could do this.

"Okay," he said. Leaning in, he kissed her forehead. "Let's go." He squeezed her hand firmly and then, turning, led her out of the bathroom. There was already a sign posted and an employee standing guard. Matthew could see Alex by the bar, so he made a beeline toward him. Stopping briefly, he said, "Follow me," and gave a slight tug on Alex's coat.

Alex nodded at Aiden, who came around the side of the bar and wrapped his arms lovingly around Bernie's shoulders. When Alex was sure Aiden had Bernie and that Bernie would follow, he turned and marched after Bell and Matthew toward the VIP room.

Matthew stopped outside the room. "I'll be right back."

Bell watched him enter the room and then pop his head back out a moment later.

"It's empty. Come on in," he said.

The group filed into the room and sat down on the couches. Bell was still shaking uncontrollably. She couldn't seem to slow her breathing and her heart.

"This is what's going to happen," said Matt. "The detective will come in, and I'm going to allow him to make the announcements to the guests. You stay in here. You're safest in this room at this time. Wells will want to speak to all of you first. Aiden, you have to leave the room. I'm sorry, you're technically a suspect at this time." Turning away, Matthew left to meet the other officers.

"No!" protested Bernie as Aiden stood.

"Yes, Bernadette," said Aiden. "I'm sorry, I can't stay. Your safety is number one, and he's following protocol. Don't worry, they'll clear me soon enough, but I get where he's coming from." He patted her hand. "You seem to be growing quite attached to me." He smiled down at her and then turned and left the room.

Bell watched as a tear ran down Bernie's face. Taking a deep breath, she said, "It's going to be fine. We won't let anyone hurt you." She almost believed her own words.

"I'm not worried about me," she said. "I'm worried about who else might get in the way of this psycho and what they might do about it. Bradley died because of me."

"Martin is in jail because of me and Alex. My guess is, we're all being targeted, unless Martin's previous attacks and the more recent events are unrelated," said Bell. She personally believed it was highly unlikely that the events were unrelated. She could feel it inside, and her gut was never wrong.

"What are we going to do? Are we supposed to hire 24/7 bodyguards?" asked Alex.

"I don't know," replied Bell. She had finally quit shaking. "I guess we have to hear what Detective Wells has to say and go from there."

"Let's think for a minute, who here could be the culprit? Who was around when Martin was out? It could be staff, models—heck, it could be anyone," he said.

"It could be someone we didn't realize was around too," mentioned Bernie. "Martin wouldn't have hired someone who was noticeable on a regular basis, would he?"

"I don't know," said Alex. "Someone who's around all the time would have had us feeling safe and unsuspecting, but someone we didn't know would have likely gone unnoticed. You tell me. Which is the better choice?"

Bell shook her head. "It could be anyone. We know Martin had been speaking to Bernie for six months before their first date. I'm sure he was planning all of this from the start, don't you agree?"

"Yes," agreed Bernie. She sounded broken.

"Who came into our lives around that time or shortly thereafter?" asked Bell.

Alex grabbed a pen and some paper off the coffee table. "I'll make a list."

"Well, let's see," said Bell. "Jordan, Audra, Matthew, Torrence, Lee, Aiden. Those are the people we see the most who are also new in our lives from that point forward. We also spend some of our personal time with them. The other new people are the type that would blend in, so I think we should also add staff to the list and let Detective Wells know who they are. I'm not sure if this is a keep your enemies closer situation or a blend into the surroundings situation."

"It's hard to say," said Alex as he rhythmically tapped his pen against the notepad.

While the siblings silently sat and contemplated their situation, the door to the room opened, and Matthew and Wells walked in.

"Hello everyone," said Wells. "I have good news and some bad. The good news is we now know you're being targeted, so we can proceed with a better understanding of what we're dealing with. The bad news is that it could be anyone in this club. On top of it all, whoever is targeting you has also slashed Bernie's tires."

Bernie threw her hands up in the air. "Well, that's just great!" she shrieked. "What's next? Are they going to burn my house down while I get the tires fixed?"

"Whoa," said Alex, "don't joke about that. We don't need any more fires."

"We're sending officers over to your homes to inspect them before you leave tonight. We'll also have officers stationed outside each house so you can rest easy. We'll catch whoever committed these heinous crimes. I promise. But first, I need to hear from each of you in regard to what happened here this afternoon."

Wells was efficient. He spoke to Bernie, then Alex, next Bell, and lastly Matthew. It took him one hour to get the story from the four witnesses. Once he'd finished making his notes, he gathered everyone inside the club into the showroom and explained to them that an incident had occurred and each person had to be questioned before leaving for the evening. Luckily for them, the club had plenty of free food for those who had donated or participated in the auction and a great band coming in to provide entertainment for that evening. If you had to be stuck somewhere for several hours against your will, the club was the place to be.

The siblings exited the showroom. Matthew and Hector followed closely behind.

"We need to make sure everything is in order and ready to go for dinner," said Bernie. Bell looked at her sister. She could see she was operating in survival mode and was concerned that she might crash and lose it. What if this situation pushed her backward, and she decided to hide out in Alex's guest room again?

Bernie turned toward Bell and glared at her. "Knock it off. You're looking at me as if I'm going to fall apart at any moment."

"Are you?" asked Bell. "You're in survival mode. I can see it. You're acting like nothing happened."

"Um, yeah. I am. I don't have much choice at this point in time. I need to get through this night and make sure the people in the club enjoy themselves despite the incident that took place in the bathroom. How exactly should I be acting? Is it irrational for me to try to push back my feelings just to get through this event? I mean seriously. What am I supposed to do, Bell? Tell me. I'm asking you, what am I supposed to do since you seem to know just how to handle a bloody severed finger death threat?"

"I don't know how to handle this, but it's okay for you to show some emotion." She stood there watching Bernie. Matthew reached out and grabbed her wrist to show her that he was with her.

"This isn't the time to be emotional. If someone is out to get me, I need to be vigilant. I need to keep my wits about me because that's how you survive. I don't want to cower. Frankly, I'm a bit pissed off right now, if you haven't noticed."

Alex stood by and looked at the girls. Bell gave him a nod to try to get him to chime in on his thoughts. She hoped he'd back her, but instead, he shook his head and put his hands out in front of himself.

"You're playing the concerned parent when you need to focus more on being the big sister, Bell. This is a big deal, and I think Bernie knows that. Personally, I agree with her. She needs to get through this evening, and once we're home safely, we can process this further and cry, scream, or rant if we need to," said Alex.

"Believe me, Bell, I'm not ignoring the situation. I thoroughly understand that this is a big, scary deal. I just can't let our guests see me as some broken person who wants to run and hide. The person who did this may still be in the club," said Bernie.

Staring back at her brother and sister, she could feel the wave of sadness coming. Tears began to roll out of her eyes and down her cheeks. "I don't want anything to happen to you," she gasped. Matthew softly brushed her cheeks with a tissue and wrapped her in a hug.

"It's okay, Bell. I'll be fine. I'm a fighter, remember?" Her tone was soft. She took a couple of steps closer to her sister and Matt. "Let's get this evening started, and tonight, why don't we all stay at Alex's."

"Yeah, that sounds like a good idea," said Matthew. "I'll let Wells know that we'll be in the same house tonight." He squeezed Bell, kissed her on the forehead, and walked off to find Wells.

Alex put an arm around each of his sisters. "Come on girls, we have work to do."

"Yeah, we do. I just got a text from the band; they're outside. Alex, will you please go let them in while Bell and I make sure the restaurant is on track for dinner. I think we should also set up wine service early since people are stuck here." She grabbed Bell's hand, pulling her toward the bar. She had to admire Bernie's tenacity at that moment. "Hey, Bell," whispered Bernie, "do you think Aiden is a suspect?"

"I guess he could be," she whispered back. "I think we need some strong evidence to prove his innocence if we want to rule him out."

"Yeah, I guess something definitive is necessary at this point. It's hard to look at things from a law perspective regarding 'innocence until proven' guilty when your life is on the line."

Bell made a frustrated face and nodded in agreement. "I think it's best if you're not alone with him until we're able to come up with some concrete information regarding what's going on and why. I'm starting to get the vibe that the person attacking us might be someone we know fairly well."

"Do you have any specific thoughts on who it might be?"

"No, do you?" Bell could tell Bernie had been thinking about it a lot from the look on her face.

"Maybe?" she replied. "I think it could be Jordan. He showed up around the time that Martin came into my life. He's shown a real desire in the past few months to get into our agency. I just can't help but wonder if it's him."

"Oh, just my luck," said Bell. "He's my wonderful date this evening."

"Ask him questions and see if he gives anything away," said Bernie.

"Like what?"

"I don't know, but be sneaky about it."

"Oh, hey, Jordan, are you friends with Martin? Yeah, just wanted to know if you're a psycho killer sent to drive my family batty. What's that? You're here to see if you can sleep with as many women as possible? Oh, by all means, proceed onward," said Bell sarcastically.

Bernie glared at her sister. "Yeah, that's not quite what I meant, but you get the idea."

"I'm not thrilled to spend any time with him, but I'll see what I can do."

"You know, Lee, Torrence, and Audra all showed up when Martin did as well. What if it's more than one person?"

"Like some sort of gang or Martin club? How many people could that man possibly get to help him? What would their motives be? Why would they still be out to get us? Martin couldn't possibly be paying them to come after us, could he?"

"I don't know. I honestly don't know what to think about any of this," said Bernie. "Let's table it for now."

Sighing deeply, Bell agreed. "We've had enough setbacks today. I think we'd better take care of business before an angry mob forms."

Bell walked up to the bar and asked Aiden for two glasses of merlot. He grabbed a bottle and was about to pour when she stopped him. "Aiden, would you mind opening a fresh bottle? I like that particular wine so much more when it's first uncorked." She wasn't taking any chances. Martin was sneaky, and this person seemed to be even more so, considering they hadn't given their existence away during Martin and Bernie's marriage.

"Sure thing," he replied. He made a sad attempt at a smile as he uncorked the bottle and poured two healthy glasses. Setting the bottle back down, he replaced the cork and handed the glasses to each sister. "Do you want me to pour the rest of the bottle now, and you can take the glasses with you to share with others, or what would you like me to do with the rest of it?"

"Pour them out," said Bernie. "We'll give them to Matthew, Alex, and Hector."

Grabbing the bottle, he poured out three more glasses and placed them on a tray. "Enjoy."

"Oh, also, will you please have the crew set up the wine service and begin serving guests early. I want everyone to relax a little and not stress too much about this investigation since they're kind of trapped here," said Bernie.

He nodded in understanding. "I'll get on that right away. Happy guests spend more money anyway." He gave her a grin.

"Here's to faking it until it feels real," said Bernie, clanking her glass against Bell's.

Rolling her eyes, Bell said, "Let the date party begin."

The second half of the event went on almost as if nothing had happened. Detective Wells had several officers helping him interview guests. The bathroom in the bar was shut down and being analyzed for evidence, but luckily, the club had several other restrooms available. Bell noticed every so often that one of the dates would be interrupted, and an officer would lead someone away from their table to be questioned, but each person usually returned quickly and was able to continue on with their evening, smiles and all. She assumed the free beverages were a huge help in the matter at hand.

Dinner had been served, and the band began to play. Bell stared at Jordan while he went on about his modeling career and his childhood, and blah, blah, blah. Luckily, he didn't notice she was altogether disinterested. She wanted to help Bernie by asking some questions but couldn't get a word in edgewise.

He was vain, and even though this date should have been a way for him to get to know her and the company more, he wasn't taking advantage of that aspect. She made sure to tell the waitress, Emily, to keep the wine coming. She could only hope that either Jordan would drink too much and stop yammering on, or she would drink too much and be rendered incoherent. She knew that in reality, neither of those things would happen, nor would it be good for her to be blackout drunk in her family's club. The situation didn't seem to have a winning side.

"So that was the fifth show I did while I was in high school," said Jordan. He ran his fingers over his nearly bald head. His hair was white blond and buzzed short.

"Very interesting," she said without fully knowing what she was responding to. Staring back at him, she had to admit, his hair looked soft, and she liked how velvety it felt when running her fingers over a man's short, fine hair. When Bell had first met

Matthew, his hair had been very short, but now it was non-existent. He was wearing it clean-shaven, and she couldn't keep her hands off. It felt so good it sent shivers through her every time she ran her fingers over his head. He recognized that it was a turn-on for her, so he vowed to keep it clean if it meant making her happy. She smiled, recalling how he'd said those words. He cared about her happiness, which was a nice change of pace from her past relationships.

"You like that?" asked Jordan with a smile.

Aw heck, she had no idea what he was talking about because she'd completely zoned out. "Sure," she replied. Oh, how she hoped that was the right response. Jordan jumped to his feet, and in two long strides, he was standing over her. He reached down, placed his hands on her shoulders, and began dancing seductively in front of her. It had definitely been the wrong response.

He instantly noticed the wide-eyed look on her face. "What's wrong?" he asked with a laugh. "You don't like this?"

"Well, I am your employer," she replied snappily, hoping it would cause him to back off. But it didn't.

"Oh, it's okay, you can relax. I'm not worried about you taking advantage of me. We're just having fun. Besides, I kind of miss being a dancer," he stated, then grinned seductively at her.

"What is everyone else going to think? Not to mention the fact that I'm in a relationship with Matthew, and he's somewhere in the club. You need to stop." But Jordan did not stop. He kept on grinning, and before she realized what was happening, he was tearing off his button-down shirt and wearing nothing but his suit pants and a black bow tie. Had he planned this ahead of time? She couldn't help but notice his perfectly chiseled abs. He was ridiculously fit but a horrible clod of a man. "Seriously," she pleaded, "you need to stop!" she stated sternly while trying to push him away. Like a giant boulder, he didn't budge. "Jordan, this is wildly inappropriate." She was feeling very uncomfortable. Reaching up, she did the only thing she could think of and slapped him firmly across the face. Oh, how she hoped no one else was watching. Talk about embarrassing.

"Ouch," he said in a playful tone. "I know you're enjoying this. I can see your eyes and how you've been staring at me all night," he said coolly.

"I mean it, Jordan!" Her eyes had darkened, and she was glaring back at him.

"WHAT are you doing?" demanded Bernie's angry voice.

Jordan removed his hands and stepped back. "Oh, well, I was just showing Bell my moves from college, back when I was a dancer," he said innocently. Bell knew Bernie wouldn't be fooled by that.

"Put your clothes back on this instant! This is not a male review night. And you!" she shouted at Bell, "What were you thinking!"

Bell stood up and rushed Bernie ten feet away from the table while Jordan pulled his shirt back on. "He wouldn't stop," she rebuked. "I asked him more than once. I even slapped him across the face, and he thought it was a game."

Bernie tapped her foot as she contemplated Bell's statement. "He was given the rules of the date. He absolutely must be removed." Shaking her head, she said, "This looks beyond bad. You need to fire him. We cannot condone this sort of behavior inside any of the businesses."

"He hasn't been questioned yet by me or the police. I couldn't get him to stop blabbing long enough to ask any questions. Sorry, Bern."

"Well then, I'll make sure he's next," said her sister. She watched as Bernie turned and marched over to Jordan. "You're out of here the second they finish speaking to you about the incident tonight," she declared loudly. "I'm not putting up with your crap." If anyone liked Jordan less than Bell, it was Bernie, and now that he was a suspect, she was clearly showing she had no time for him.

"What? What did I do?" he asked as if he had no idea.

"You know what you did," she replied sharply. "You made my sister uncomfortable and acted inappropriately during a black-tie affair. You're out. There are rules at these events, and you were made aware from the beginning what those rules were." She turned and marched back over to Bell. Her jaw was set, causing her mouth to create a pencil-thin line. Her eyes looked as though they could light on fire with how intense her stare was.

"Thank you," whispered Bell as Bernie walked past. Reaching out, she gave her a low five and followed her out of the room.

"Thompson," called Bernie as they entered the hall, "will you please question Jordan next? I want him out of here. He just acted very inappropriately during his date with my sister, and he's not welcome here anymore."

"Sure thing, Bernadette," replied Thompson. "By the way, we still haven't had our chat. Let's do that sometime soon, okay?"

Bernie nodded. "I haven't forgotten; I look forward to it," she replied, turning back toward Bell.

"How did your date go?" asked Bell.

"Great up until now. Now I have to go tell Hector that you have to fire Jordan due to his boneheaded move in there."

"Yup, you can definitely be the one to tell Hector that."

"Tell me what?" asked Hector as he came around the corner with Alex.

"That Jordan is being let go," replied Bernie.

"What? Why?" asked Alex.

"He just made a huge display out of giving Bell an unwanted lap dance. He took his shirt off and everything."

"I asked him several times to stop. I slapped him, and he thought I was playing."

"Dang," said Hector. "That's not cool."

"No, it's not cool." You could feel the heat in Bernie's voice. "I won't be putting up with that sort of thing in this club during such an important event, especially when he's altogether disregarding Bell's request to stop. She's his boss, for heaven's sake."

"Can't you just reprimand him?" asked Hector with pleading in his eyes.

"Why are you so bent on him being a part of Price & Fitz?" asked Bell. "Is there something you need to share with us?"

Hector pinched the bridge of his nose between his pointer finger and thumb, then exhaling, said, "He's my cousin. I hate telling people because of how he acts. I know he needs to grow up and knock off the ridiculousness. He doesn't need money. His parents thought I could influence him to do better. A job was the only thing I could think of to help him take some form of responsibility in life. I made an agreement with my aunt and uncle to get him a job where I could keep close tabs on him. Your modeling agency is known for producing poised and well-adjusted models. I thought getting him into Price & Fitz might help him become a better person."

"He's like the whitest guy ever," said Bernie. "He has red hair and blue eyes. How are you two related?"

"My auntie married his father, and then his father passed away, so she adopted him and raised him as her own. His mother died in childbirth. He never knew any other mother. He's a pain in the butt, but he's like my brother."

"Hector, what the heck, why didn't you tell me?" asked Alex. He looked as if he'd been kicked.

"I don't like to tell people because I don't want them to think he's getting special treatment."

"But he is getting special treatment," stated Bell. "This whole time, I thought Alex was the one pitching him to me."

"Yes, but people don't know that. I had to have Alex pitch him to you, or he would have never made it in."

"So, what do you want me to do with this information?" asked Bell.

"Can't you just put him on probation or some sort of suspension for a while?" asked Alex.

"You two are going to owe me big time," said Bell. "He should be booted for his antics tonight. Not to mention, I still wonder if he isn't Martin's missing partner. How well do you know your cousin?"

"Pretty well," replied Hector. "He's not your guy."

"How do you know?" asked Alex.

"I just know," snapped Hector.

"Wow, okay," said Alex. "Wanna take it down a notch?""Well, you're accusing my cousin of murder. I think I have a right to be a little upset. He's still family."

"We aren't accusing, just asking. We thought we could trust Martin as well," replied Bernie.

"He's not involved with Martin. Let it go," said Hector. The irritation was still present in his voice, and he was scowling at Alex.

Bell watched as Alex reached for Hector's hand, and Hector pulled away.

"I'm going back to the table," said Hector. Turning on his heel, he stomped off in the opposite direction.

"That didn't go well," said Bell. "I hope he'll be okay."

"He'll be fine after a bit," said Alex. "He just needs a moment. In ten minutes, he'll be back to his lovely self again."

"Wow, must be nice," said Bernie. Pointing at her sister, she said, "We get in an argument, and we might not speak for a month."

"That better never happen again," replied Alex. "It's just wrong for family to hold a grudge for that long. What if something had happened to one of you during that time? How guilty would you feel?"

The girls looked at each other and frowned. Bell realized that Alex was right, and she hoped she and Bernie never fought like that again.

"Alex, how is your evening with Eloise going?" asked Bernie. She was grinning with delight.

"Oh man, don't get me started on her. She keeps going on about how one night with her can make any man straight. She seems to think this is some sort of game where she can change the outcome with persuasion and pouty red lips. She keeps trying to touch me, and I keep inching farther away from her. Everyone in the room can see how uninterested I am, except her."

"Geez, maybe we should set her up with Jordan," laughed Bell.

"That's not a bad idea," replied Bernie. "Eloise and Jordan would make a great couple, I think."

"They might be too much alike," said Alex. "They're both so vain. They think the opposite sex lives to worship them."

Bell shook her head in agreement. "Very true, and neither one wants to shut up and let the other person speak."

"Is it time to go home yet?" asked Bernie. "I'm tired of this day, and I've got zero energy left."

"Just a few more hours." Alex laughed.

"I agree with you, Bernie. I want to go home, too." She reached up and unfastened the clip holding her long strawberry blonde hair in an updo. Running her fingers through her hair, she smoothed and brushed it out. It cascaded in ringlets down the middle of her back. "Where's Matthew?" she asked her siblings.

"Last I saw him, he was in the game room watching a soccer match and having a glass of wine. He said something about horrible girlfriends and lap dances."

"He did not!" gasped Bell.

"No, he didn't." Alex snickered.

"Jerk," said Bell. "Last thing I need is for him to be mad about that."

"How could he be? Jordan was in the wrong," said Bernie.

"I'm going to check in and see if he's ready to leave. I don't have to stay, do I?" she asked Bernie.

"No, you can go, but we won't be leaving for a while yet," she replied.

"I need to get some things from the house before I come over tonight. Let me go talk to Matt, and I'll get back to you on what our plan is." She worried the discussion would be awkward. He'd undoubtedly wonder why she'd cut her date short. She hoped he would understand the awful predicament Jordan had put her in.

Wandering off down the hall, she passed a very irritated-looking Eloise and couldn't help but smile a little.

Backtracking slightly, Eloise flagged Bell down. "What's with that brother of yours anyway?" she asked snottily. "Any man would kill to be with me."

"He's gay," replied Bell. "That's not something you just turn on and off. He's not bisexual. He doesn't feel anything toward women. You have absolutely no appeal to him. No offense." Her tone was cold. She tried to be nice to Eloise normally, but tonight, she was in no mood for her games.

"Whatever. He just doesn't know how great it could be," she said, sauntering down the hall toward Alex. Bell shook her head and continued on her quest.

Matthew was right where Alex said he'd be, sitting at the bar in the game room. She walked up behind him and tapped him on the shoulder. "Hi handsome, how's your night going?"

He smiled at her. Reaching out, he placed his hand on the back of her neck and pulled her in for a kiss. "Better now," he replied, looking into her eyes. "Like perfect pools of water," he mused. "I could stare into your eyes all night long."

"That's sweet, Romeo, but I'm thinking about heading home. What would you like to do?"

"Why are you leaving so soon? Where's Jordan?" A look of concern filled his eyes. "Did something happen?"

"Yeah, you could say that. Jordan is a total jerk, and I want him out of my agency." She pouted. "He made an advance on me. Tried to give me a strip dance. I asked him to stop several times. I actually slapped him across the face because he wouldn't let go of me, and he thought I was playing some coy little game. He didn't stop until Bernie showed up and screamed at him."

"Wow, that's not cool. Do you want to press charges?" asked Matthew in a serious tone.

"No. I just want to go home and forget about him. I'm so sorry," she said. She could see the anger flash in his eyes. Matthew so rarely lost his temper.

"Is he still here? I swear, I'll give him a severe tongue lashing," he said through gritted teeth.

"Whoa, whoa, let's not lose it over that jerk. Thompson will interview him and send him on his way." She reached out and firmly squeezed Matthew's hand. She noted that her manicure was once again a wreck from her nerves. Daddy would have given her that scolding look and told her to knock that off.

"Okay, let's go home, sweetie. We can grab some clothes and head over to Alex's house. Maybe watch a movie and forget about Jordan."

She smiled at him. "I love you. You always know just what I need."

"That's why we work so well together." Hopping up from the bar stool, he nodded goodbye to the bartender and grabbed Bell's hand. She was happy to follow him. Nearing the front entrance, she saw Bernie still standing off to the side, talking to Alex.

"Hey, we're going to grab some clothing and head over to your house, Alex."

"Okay, Thompson finished talking to Jordan and escorted him to his car. He said the finger in the bathroom wasn't a finger at all. It was a finger cot covered in blood. The person who wrote on the mirror must have used it to keep their hands clean."

"Thank goodness," said Bernie. "I was worried as to where the finger had come from. That's at least a little better."

"It wasn't even blood," said Matthew. Some food mixture. Probably corn syrup."

"It was still terrifying," said Bell.

"I know, sweetheart. It's okay. We'll get to the bottom of it," said Matthew.

"You should head out," said Alex. "Thompson's waiting by his cruiser to escort you two home and then to Alex's. Marx will be joining him tonight to watch over us."

"Sounds good," said Matthew. "Alex, we'll message when we get to your place."

"Alright man, be safe," replied Alex as he bumped his fist into Matthew's.

"See you soon," said Bernie. "I have to stick around at least another hour, or until some of the guests, such as Eloise, head out."

"Ugh," said Alex, "Eloise, Eloise, Eloise." He rolled his eyes at Bell, and she couldn't help but giggle at his frustration. "I'll work on annoying her so she decides to leave sooner." He raised an eyebrow at his own mischievousness.

"Be careful, Alex. You never know how Eloise might react. She could begin to want you even more," said Bernie. She gave him an exaggerated yuck face. Alex stifled his laughter at the ridiculous expression and waved Bernie off.

"Don't you have work to do?" he asked.

"Yeah, I suppose. Well, see you two later," she called over her shoulder.

"Ciao," said Bell with a wave. She was excited to get out of the club and into the sanctity of Alex's house, where she could wrap herself in the safety of Matt's arms.

Thompson followed closely behind Matt and Bell as they headed for home. They made a quick pit stop at the station to pick up

Marx, who looked as if he'd just rolled out of bed. He stood on the curb, tucking in his shirt. Bell watched him crawl into the cruiser and fasten his jaw-length hair in place with a band. Straightening up, he then tossed his hat atop his head. Once he was situated in Thompson's car, Matthew pulled away from the curb and headed toward their home.

"I didn't know you were allowed to have longer hair in the department," she commented.

"He's not technically, but as long as it doesn't get much longer than that and he keeps it pulled back, the chief's ignoring it. Marx has been going through a rough time lately, and they're being a little lax with him. He hasn't been on his game as of late, which is why I'm not sure I feel comfortable with him as our backup. His wife left him for his sister, and while investigating a robbery a couple of months back, he was shot in the shoulder. It's a crummy draw, but I would feel better if the chief gave him leave until he gets his act together."

"Dang, that's not cool. Why in the heck are they letting him work?"

"The chief is trying to decide if he's stable and whether or not he can be alone. They gave him two weeks of observation, and if he doesn't pull out of this so he can again be on his own, they're planning to get him further help. I would've preferred they put him at a desk during his evaluation period."

"His wife left him for his sister? Talk about icing on the cake. Did he know his wife was into women?"

"Well, it used to be his brother until four months ago. It's taken some major adjusting within his family."

"What?" Bell gaped at him. "Does that really happen?"

"Apparently. It's one thing to get a sex change, but then to take your brother's girl in the process. That's just cold."

"Great, now I feel sorry for him."

"Everyone feels sorry for him. I hope the chief is right and that he just needs a little time and understanding from people. Luckily, Thompson is on detail with Marx, or I'd put my foot down and ask him to be replaced. We should be cautious and focus our concern on your family and the situation we're currently dealing with."

Pulling into the driveway, Matt waited and let the officers get out first. They did a quick perimeter check and then motioned that it was safe to exit the car. Bell unlocked the front door, and Marx and Thompson proceeded inside. The couple stood in the entryway while the officers methodically checked each room in the house. Once they were given the clear, Matthew and Bell headed to their room to pack clothing for the next few days. Neither spoke. They just grabbed what they needed and headed back to the car.

Upon arriving at Alex's house, they repeated the whole process over. The house appeared untampered with, and the officers returned to their cruiser, where they would spend the night. Bell felt a lot better knowing they were stationed outside and that they would be watching for Bernie and Alex to arrive.

"I want to put our things in the bedroom and change into something comfier," she called over her shoulder.

Matt smiled and sauntered up behind her. Placing his hands around her waist, he pulled her tightly against his body and kissed her neck. "I'll join you," he whispered in her ear.

"I don't know if this is necessarily the time for a playful romp," she replied

"Why not?" he asked, grabbing her hand and spinning her around. "Don't you want to play with me?" He grabbed the overnight bag from her other arm and threw it over his shoulder.

"Well, you are quite charming," she blushed, trying to hide her smile. Her body was already filling with excitement. "I don't know. It's been such a weird day."

"What don't you know?" He spun her again and began dancing her down the hallway. Stopping, he ripped off his shirt and pressed her against the wall outside their bedroom door. He threw the bag off his shoulder, around the corner and into the room. Grabbing her wrists in one big hand, he firmly raised her arms above her head and began kissing her neck.

"If I can get into this?" she said as if it were a question that no longer needed answering. She felt the desire rising up inside her. No matter what happened in life, this man acted like a rock, making her feel safe, sexy, and like she was the only woman in his world.

"Do you want to table this?" he asked as he lovingly nipped at her ear.

"No! Don't stop," she demanded.

"Okay." He laughed, scooping her up and carrying her into the bedroom.

"Never a dull moment with you, I see, Mr. McKinney."

"Heck no!" he hollered, kicking the door shut behind them.

At nine-thirty, Bernie and Alex came bursting through the front door. Matt and Bell were curled up on the couch watching a movie, tired from their bedroom romp.

"Alex, I didn't take it off!" shouted Bernie. She sounded frantic.

"Take what off?" asked Bell.

"Bradley's necklace. It's missing," replied Alex.

"Did you retrace her steps at the club and ask the staff if anyone turned it in?" asked Matthew.

"Yes, we did all of that." Alex sounded exasperated. "I don't know what else to tell you, Bernadette. We've exhausted our options unless you want me to call back every guest and question whether or not they may have taken your necklace."

"No!" she snapped and then stomped off down the hall. A moment later, Bell heard her sister's bedroom door slam shut.

"Great," said Bell, "just what we need at this moment. Did they at least get her tires fixed?"

"Nope," replied Alex. "They didn't have her tires in stock, so they have to be ordered. Andre will be driving her around the remainder of the week unless she wants to take the Porsche, but she hasn't touched it since Dad passed away. She can't stand the fact that Martin was in love with that car or that Dad was so quick to hand it over to him.

"Is it in your garage? I guess I didn't even realize it made it through the fire at their house," said Bell.

"Yeah, it was parked outside by the greenhouse, so it wasn't damaged. I had Hector put it in my garage, hoping she might come around at some point. Technically, Martin's name is still on it, but I'm sure the judge will award it to Bernie along with a speedy divorce."

"For sure," chimed Matthew.

Bell nodded her agreement. "Anyway, the necklace will turn up. We can send an email tomorrow in case any of the guests found it and took it home with them. No one in their right mind would keep something of hers with the knowledge of what she's been through."

Chapter Nine

It had been two beautiful days of nothing extreme happening. Bell and her siblings spent Sunday and Monday relaxing at Alex's house. Matthew and Hector came and went depending on their work schedules. They played pool, watched some movies, cooked a lot of great food, and sat around a fire drinking wine. The entire group welcomed the reprieve from the craziness of Saturday. It was a staycation that, unfortunately, was coming to an end.

Alex and Bernie were participating in Bernie's first therapy session, Matthew was working, and Bell was at her house cleaning. She wanted to get the house in order before the frantic energy of the following Friday's runway show set in. She felt pretty good about her achievements thus far. It was only ten in the morning, and she had managed to sweep and vacuum all floors, clean all of the bathrooms, and complete two loads of laundry. Smoothing the final crease out of her and Matthew's bed, she took a moment to appreciate the tidiness of their room. As she went to fluff the throw pillows, she was auditorily attacked by the incessant ringing of the doorbell in the next room. Her entire body tightened. Mariska had chosen a trumpet to announce visitors. She and Matthew hadn't found time to fix the obnoxious ringer. Bell added the task to her mental to-do list.

Hurrying toward the sound, she stopped long enough to check the peephole. A young woman holding a bouquet of flowers stood on the other side, chomping on a large wad of gum. She had earbuds haphazardly swung over her shoulder, and her hair was blowing freely in the wind. Bell pulled open the door.

"Hi. Delivery for Bell Price," she said.

"I'm Bell. May I ask who they're from?"

"You may," she replied, shoving the bouquet into Bell's hands. "But I don't have an answer for you because I haven't seen the card. I just deliver them. Have a nice day," she murmured, scurrying off down the drive. Bell watched as she blew a large bubble and it popped all over her face.

"Thanks," yelled Bell as the girl peeled back the gum and disappeared into her delivery van. A moment later, she peeled out of the driveway, leaving tire tracks in her wake. "Seriously?" Bell let out a deep sigh. Turning to the flowers, she said, "Hm, you're awfully pretty. Who sent you?" she smiled as she walked toward the kitchen. Removing the card from its holder, she opened it and read:

> Bell,
>
> I'm going to make you scream.
> We'll play soon.
>
> Sincerely,
> Your Cunning Adversary

She threw the card on the table and marched into the kitchen. Grabbing her phone, she punched in Jordan's number. It rang twice before he picked up. She was so angry she wanted to scream.

"Hello?" he asked as if he'd been sleeping.

"You have some nerve!" she bellowed. "I can't believe you would even make contact with me after Saturday's fiasco. You should be ashamed. I want nothing to do with you, and if I have it my way, you'll never work for my agency again!"

"Bell, what are you talking about?" There was a definite sense of confusion in Jordan's voice.

"The flowers and the disgusting note you sent," she stated venomously.

"I didn't send you flowers or a note," he replied defensively. "I got the message loud and clear that you want me to back off. I promise I won't make another move unless you initiate it."

"Are you being serious right now?" she asked.

"Yes, Bell. I didn't send you any flowers. I drank too much on Saturday night, and I'm horrible at reading social cues when I'm drunk. I'm an asshole. I know I made a mistake, and I'm truly sorry for that. I never meant to make you uncomfortable, and while I have had feelings for you for quite some time, how I acted was incredibly disrespectful. And, if I'm being honest, frankly, Matthew scares the crap out of me, so I definitely don't want to get in his way. I promise, unless you reach out to me, I'll leave you alone."

"Why does he scare you?" she was caught off guard by his comment. She didn't know anyone who found Matthew to be scary.

"He's way too calm. I feel he might be one of those people who could go off at any time."

"I think he exhibits great patience with everything in life. I've never seen him lose his cool," she replied.

"Whatever you say."

"I'm sorry I jumped to conclusions and yelled at you. Thank you for your apology. I'll get back to you concerning your job," she said and hung up. She had no idea what was happening, and the mystery bouquet was absolutely freaking her.

If it wasn't Jordan, then who sent it? Was it a threat or some weird admirer? She was perplexed by the situation and unsure what her next move should be. She proceeded back to the bedroom to continue with her cleaning.

Moving around the room, she put away laundry and mused over how lucky she was to have such a neat and orderly man. Matt never left things lying on the floor. He always cleaned up after himself. She was the messy one. She tended to walk into the room at bedtime and toss her clothes in a pile on the floor. The only thing out of place on Matt's side of the bed was a flashlight that she'd left on the nightstand when they were going through closets and getting rid of her mother's unnecessary belongings. The electricity had been off briefly due to a mix-up regarding the bill.

Grabbing the flashlight, she opened the top drawer of the nightstand with her free hand. Adjusting some books to make room for the flashlight, something silver caught her eye. She tossed the books aside and peered inside. A chill ran down her spine, and her body began to go numb. There, in the bottom of the drawer, were several unexpected items. She was frozen to the spot, staring incomprehensibly at what should not have been.

The first item that had caught her eye was unmistakably the missing cross necklace that Bradley had left to Bernadette. Next to the cross was a bracelet with the name Linz written across a sterling silver plate, a sapphire ring that had belonged to her mother, and one of her father's favorite golf balls. She felt panicky. "No!" she cried aloud. "This can't be! There's no way this can be!" She knew not to touch the items, but part of her wanted to. She was torn. Hide them and believe there was no way Matthew was involved or turn him in. She didn't know what to do, and she wasn't sure her legs would allow her to stand. Was it possible he had deceived them all in an attempt to cover his involvement with Martin? She didn't want to believe it, but what if she was wrong?

She sat staring and contemplating for twenty minutes. Tears streaked her face. The items were, without a doubt, keepsakes of her deceased parents and friends. She couldn't fathom Matthew being the killer, but how could she take a chance when Martin had fooled her sister and father so well.

Pushing herself off the ground, she swallowed her pride and found the strength to march out of the room, out the front door, and up to Thompson's car stationed at the end of the driveway. Smiling, he rolled down his window. "What's up, Bell?"

"I need you to come inside and look at something," she said cautiously. His gray eyes filled with concern.

"Okay," he replied, stepping out of his vehicle. "Lead the way."

He followed closely behind her as she walked back into the house. Instead of heading for the bedroom, she brought him into the kitchen, where she had left the flowers. The card was lying on the counter. "These just arrived, as I'm sure you probably know. Take a look at the card. It's very strange."

Peering down at the counter, he took in the words on the card. "Do you have any idea who sent this?"

"No. I thought it was from Jordan, so I called him. He swears he didn't do this. He even apologized for his behavior Saturday night. Beyond that, I haven't a clue."

"This could mean any number of things." Thompson's eyes darkened as he analyzed the card. "I don't like this at all. I'm concerned it's from the same person who slashed your sister's tires and put the blood note in the bathroom. I think I'd better call it in and get forensics over here."

"Just wait." She put a hand up in the air to motion for him to follow her. "I haven't shown you the more disturbing discovery."

He looked at her with confusion. "There's more?"

"Unfortunately, yes." He followed her into the bedroom and over to the nightstand. "Look," she said, pointing. "That necklace was Bradley's, the ring was my mother's, the ball my father's, and the bracelet was our model friend, Linz's. How did these get here?" Standing with her hands on her hips, she stared back at him. Her face filled with sadness. She shook her head in disbelief as a tear trickled down her cheek.

Thompson let out an exasperated sigh and shook his head. "This isn't good. It's Matt's nightstand?"

"Yeah. He—he can't be involved. He just can't," she said, her hands now trembling.

"Bell, look at me," said Thompson. Reaching out, he tipped her head up so that she was looking at him. "I've sworn an oath to protect and serve, and if I let this go, I'm not doing my job, and I'm definitely not helping to find my son's killer. Matthew needs to be brought in for questioning. If his prints are on any of the items, he'll be arrested. Your family's safety is top priority. I'm sorry."

She collapsed to the floor, adrenaline coursing through her body, causing her head to lighten. It was impossible to control anything as the world appeared to crash down around her. Like

Alice, it felt like she was falling down a long dark hole with no end in sight.

Thompson bent down in front of her. "Bell! Can you hear me? You're going to be okay." She nodded her understanding. "I'm calling Wells, and then I'm calling your brother. You're going back to his house until this is sorted. Hopefully, Matt isn't involved, but we have to follow protocol."

"I don't want to hide every time something happens," she mumbled.

"You aren't hiding. You're making it easier for us to protect you."

"Doesn't that also make it easier for this psycho stalker to keep an eye on us?"

"Yes, but I can guarantee we're going to bump up the patrol around your neighborhood because we want to figure this out as badly as you do. I really hope Matt's not a part of this, but he's known Martin for many years. This could have been Martin's backup plan all along. Come on," he said, grabbing her hand. "Let me help you to your feet."

"That doesn't make sense," said Bell. "Why did he help us capture Martin if he was his partner? And he obviously didn't shoot Bradley."

"I don't know, Bell. I don't have the answers. I'm sure there's more to all of this than what we're seeing. Go take a seat in the living room. I'll call Alex."

Bell walked out of the bedroom and took a seat on the sofa. Pulling the down throw from the back of the couch, she tucked it around her. Matthew's involvement was a difficult concept to grasp. He wasn't Bradley's killer because the killer had fired the shots while Matthew was with her. His involvement would mean at least three people were working with Martin unless the shooting and other attacks were unrelated. Her mind was spinning out of control.

"Bernie!" called Alex. His sister had fallen asleep on the couch. "Wake up! We have a situation."

"Huh? What situation?" she replied groggily.

"Matthew's been taken in for questioning."

"What? Why?" demanded his sister as she rubbed her eyes.

"Bell found items belonging to Mom, Dad, Bradley, and Linz in his nightstand drawer. They're testing the items for prints as we speak. Bell's a mess. She's terrified of Matthew, but at the same time, she has no idea how he could be involved. Thompson said he's going to bring her over here shortly."

"What the freak? Do you think Matt could possibly be involved?"

"No," he said abruptly. "I think someone is setting him up and trying to make us question our trust. Not only that, but if any of us were to believe Matt is guilty, it would obviously create a rift in our relationship."

"Well, they're doing a great job of that. I don't know what I believe. He was Martin's college roommate. Maybe he is involved?"

Alex looked at his sister. She was sitting with her head in her hands. Her long red hair was all over the place. He realized this information would shake her. If Matt was bad, then who could they trust? "I mean it, Bernie. I don't think Matt took your necklace or any of those other items. We have got to stick together on this."

"From what I recall, Linz's bracelet was in police custody. It would take someone on the inside to get it out, wouldn't it? That alone points the finger at Matthew."

"Not if it had been released to her family. Someone could have stolen it, just like your necklace."

"That's true, but who and why?" Bernie shuttered. "Not to mention, how creepy. The person was close enough to take it off me without my realizing it."

"Obviously, I don't know the answers, but I feel some people we know aren't smart enough to put a plan like this together. Very few of them would be smart enough. Who has the motive? What are the questions we need to answer?" Alex looked at Bernie, who had a look of desperation on her face. "I think we need to get the story directly from Matthew."

She shook her head in agreement. "It could be a while before they let us see him."

"True," he replied, "but I think it's worth a trip down to the station to find out."

An hour after the phone call, Thompson showed up with Bell. She trudged into the house and dropped her duffel on the floor. Dramatically, she flung herself onto the chaise lounge. Thompson went back outside to do a perimeter check.

"Hello to you too," said Alex, who was sitting on the far side of the couch. He threw a pillow at her, knocking her in the shoulder.

"I'm so not in the mood right now," she replied. "My boyfriend is probably going to jail."

"Yeah, probably," said Bernie, who had just walked into the room. She took a seat on the couch next to Alex. "Gee, you know how to pick them." She laughed.

"Did you just make a dark and twisted joke?" asked Alex. "Are you feeling okay?"

Bernie laughed. "This is just par for the course, I'd say."

"Yup," said Bell. "Laugh it up. At least it's not you this time, right?"

"Oh, stop it, Belinda," said Bernie. "I'm pretty sure this affects us all, and I wouldn't wish for you to go through the same scenario I experienced with Martin."

"Don't call me Belinda. I hate that," she said through gritted teeth.

"Then don't act like a brat," snapped Bernie.

"You're both acting like bratty children," chimed Alex. "We need to take a moment and calm down. Fighting with one another won't fix anything, and it won't help us figure out a plan regarding what should happen next. I say we take five minutes and just sit quietly. After the five minutes are up, we can discuss our feelings and how we'll deal with this."

"Fine, whatever," said Bell. She proceeded to lean back and stare up at the ceiling. She was in an awful mood, and she definitely brought the frustration with her when she walked into the house. She knew her siblings didn't deserve her snotty behavior, but Bernie's reaction was not helpful.

She couldn't stand it when people called her Belinda, and her sister understood that. When she was in middle school, she met a boy named Ian, and she developed feelings for him. She and Ian passed notes back and forth between each other for weeks. They were a couple, which back then meant they spent time together on school grounds and not much more.

Outside of school, Bell met another boy named Christopher. She'd known him for years; he had been her first real crush. Her friend Ellie was aware that she had a crush on Christopher, and one day, while she was on the phone with Christopher, he told her he had feelings for Bell, too. Thinking she was helping the situation, Ellie set up a movie date for Bell with Christopher and called and told Ian that Bell no longer wanted to be his girlfriend.

At first, Bell was thrilled about Christopher because she had liked him for a couple of years, but it didn't take long for guilt to set in. She felt horrible about what Ellie had done to Ian. She really liked Ian a lot. Bell immediately decided to break it off with Christopher, and she wrote a note detailing her feelings and everything she liked about Ian in the hopes that he would take her back. The following day, she dropped the note into Ian's locker.

Bell, never in a million years, could have guessed how cruel sixth-grade boys could be. By the time lunch was over, her note had been photocopied and was all over the school. Classmates were chanting Belinda and standing in front of her, reading her own private words out loud. She was beyond mortified. She wanted to switch schools. She wanted to die. The letter continued circulating for weeks, and many tears were shed because of innocent puppy love and stupid mistakes.

"Bell," said Bernie. "What are you thinking about?"

"The letter," she replied.

The look on her sister's face instantly became apologetic. "Oh, no, not the letter. I'm sorry. I shouldn't have called you that."

"You still think about it after all these years?" asked Alex.

She was once again biting her nails. "Yeah."

"Why? Didn't you confront him about it when you were seniors in high school?" asked Bernie.

"Yes, I did."

"You don't feel any better?"

"When I confronted him, he said he didn't even remember doing that to me. In the end, he grew into a pretty decent person, and I forgave him, but that feeling still surfaces every now and then. I don't think anything more embarrassing could have happened. Amongst the things I said in that letter, I called him jazzy, and I can still hear kids picking on me for that. I was just trying to be silly and sweet."

"Okay, I won't call you Belinda anymore," said Bernie. "Or at least I will try not to."

"Who does that?" asked Alex. "I can't fathom thinking it would be okay to copy a private letter and hand it out all over school."

"Kids can be cruel," said Bernie.

"Anyway, I reflect on it, and I can feel empathy for those who have been bullied. I'm not actually angry anymore, but I just can't stand the sound of my formal name after that whole incident."

"Okay, so back to the present situation," said Alex. "What are your thoughts?"

Bernie shook her head. "I'm on the fence. I want to believe he didn't do anything. My gut says he didn't, but after being deceived by Martin, I don't exactly consider myself a great judge of character anymore."

"I'm kind of with you, Bernie," said Bell. "I trusted him, and I know he didn't shoot Bradley because he was with us when it happened, but how do you explain the necklace and Linz's bracelet?"

"I think we need to ask him some questions and see how he responds," said Alex.

"Hold on, my phone's buzzing," said Bell while pulling her cell from her pocket. "It's Wells. I'll put it on speaker. Hello?"

"Hi, Bell. Wells here. Sorry to be the bearer of bad news, but I'm calling to let you know that we've arrested Matthew. His prints are all over the items you found."

Hanging her head, she said, "Great."

"I'll do everything I can to find all the pieces and figure this out. He's one of our own, so he deserves the benefit of the doubt, but we can't let him loose and take any chances until we've proven, without a doubt, that he's not involved. You understand?"

"Yes, I understand. You have to do what you have to do to uphold the law. Keep me posted."

"Trust me, if I find any proof that he's innocent, you'll be the first to know, after him, of course."

"Thanks," she said and hung up the phone.

"Man-oh-man, that's not good," said Alex.

A somber look had appeared on Bernie's face. "Nope, it's not good at all."

Bell pushed herself up and walked out of the room. She shut herself into her bedroom and crawled into bed. Pulling the covers up over her head, she just wanted to fall asleep and wake to find that this had all been a bad dream, but she knew that wouldn't happen. Giant diamonds were not floating in the air that night.

"We shouldn't be doing this," said Bernie. "She's going to be so mad that we went without her. Thompson is already blowing up my phone, wondering where we went. The fact that he's Bradley's father makes this feel even worse."

"Thompson will be fine. He's doing his job, and we're going to the station. It's not like we're disappearing into some nightclub," said Alex. "We're literally going to one of the safest places around."

"He could get in trouble for losing us. The last thing I want to do is put a strain on him and the job he's supposed to be doing," replied Bernie.

"He's going to be fine. He can't help that we deceived him. Geez, that doesn't sound great when I say it out loud, but in all seriousness, we need to do this."

"Okay then, let's make it quick." Bernie was feeling agitated. She didn't want to return to the station after what they'd been through the day Bradley was shot. She nervously wrung her hands while waiting for Andre to park the limo. They had snuck out the back of the house and met him a block over in order to escape Thompson. She felt lousy thinking about it, but Alex was right; they needed to hear Matt's side of the story from his own mouth.

"Come on, let's go." Alex reached for her hand to pull her out of the backseat. Her anxiety was flaring, and she began to wonder if she'd be able to walk up the stairs to the station. She noticed an iron wreath with a cross hung on the railing in memory of Bradley. The image made her feel worse. Alex must have recognized what was happening because he linked his arm through hers and pulled her close for extra support.

"You're okay. Nothing is going to happen. We're taking this one step at a time, and I am staying right here by your side."

They approached the steps, and she stopped walking. She could see the plaque on the cross, which read, *In Loving Memory of Bradley Cordine*. A tear escaped from the corner of her eye.

"You can do this. One step up," he said, placing his foot on the first.

"One step up," she repeated as she did the same, her body trembling.

"Now another."

Unexpectedly, she felt her adrenaline kick in, and she was overcome with the urgent need to get indoors. "Okay, we need to go," she said, barreling up the stairs and nearly dragging her brother. Alex recalibrated and stuck by her until they reached the top and pushed through the doorway.

"All right," he said as they stopped momentarily. "I guess that's one way to do it." He smiled back at her. "That wasn't so bad, was it?"

"Yeah, it was bad, but here we are. Please give me back your arm." The adrenaline had turned her legs to jelly, and she felt a tad unstable.

"No problem." Stepping off down the hall, they nearly collided with Wells.

"What are you two doing here? Where's your escort?" he demanded.

"We took my limo. Please don't punish Thompson. He had no idea we were going to sneak out the back. We have no intentions of stopping anywhere else but here this evening."

"Not good, my friend," replied Wells. "You need to be careful, especially when Bernie's the one being called out, and you've taken her away from her detail."

"We want to see Matthew," stated Bernie. "We need to hear his end of the story."

"The only way I'm allowing that is if I'm in there with you, and that's providing he's okay speaking to you without an attorney present."

"Okay, deal," said Alex. He held out his hand, but Wells walked away, rolling his eyes and shaking his head.

The siblings followed him down the hall to the room where Matthew was being held. Turning to them, he said, "Wait out here," and then disappeared into the room. A moment later, he popped his head out and motioned for them to enter. "You can take a seat," he said.

"Hi, Matt," said Bernie. "How are you holding up?"

"Well, you know, it's like staying at the Hilton. I can't complain," he replied with a sheepish grin. "Why are you here?"

"We want to hear your side of the story if you're willing to share it," said Bernie. He looked awful. They had surely put him through the wringer.

"Guys, you know I didn't do this. I would never hurt Bell. I love her. I don't know how those items appeared in that drawer. I firmly believe someone is setting me up. How's Bell doing?"

"She's a mess," replied Alex. "She locked herself in her room. She doesn't even know we left."

"Tell her I'm beyond sorry she's been given any reason to doubt me. I'm sure after all you went through with Martin, you're wondering if it's possible that I'm not who I say I am, but I assure you, I'm no Martin Day. I believe in justice and doing the right thing. I've always believed in being on the proper side of the law. If I had anything to hide, I wouldn't be speaking to you right now."

"How can we know you're telling the truth?"

"I have no proof, only my word at this time. I wish I could give you more. You know I didn't kill Bradley. I'm hoping you know somewhere inside that I could never hurt the people I love. You've become my family."

The look on his face was genuine, and Bernie had never seen him react violently. It was rare that his voice ever waivered from its normal low and even tone. He was a patient and kind person. She couldn't imagine there was anything improper about Matthew. She believed her sister had found a real man who wouldn't hurt anyone unless that person was trying to hurt himself or someone he loved. "I believe you," she replied.

"Me too," said Alex.

Wells stood at the back of the room, taking everything in. "I have so much I want to say, but I'm not allowed at this point. You two should go. Matthew will be moved to a holding cell for the night. We'll find out about a hearing in the morning. Hopefully, he'll be released on bail."

"Okay," said Alex. "Night, Matt. You're in our thoughts."

"Bye," said Bernie. "Stay strong."

"Tell Bell that I love her, please. And make sure you don't trust anyone at this point. Whoever the killer is, he's still out there, and most likely, it's someone you know."

"We'll send your love, and we'll definitely be cautious around our friends and coworkers," said Alex. He grabbed Bernie's arm and led her out of the room. "First, we must deal with some stairs."

Bernie had already begun trembling again. "Fun," she replied. "I feel like a toddler."

Chapter Ten

The week had flown by, and it was already Friday. Matthew was still stuck in a cell. Bell was stressed to the max, and her nails were taking the brunt of her anxiety, as usual. She had replaced them twice since Tuesday. Bernie joked that Bell was dual-handedly keeping the salon in business. She was not amused with her sister's comment and was trying desperately to replace her nail-biting habit with anything else.

Bell still didn't know what to think about the situation with Matthew, though her brother and sister seemed to believe he was innocent. She couldn't get past the concept of how the mysterious items had gotten into his nightstand drawer. There had been no signs of breaking and entering while they had been away, and she didn't know of anyone else besides her siblings who had a key.

"Hurry up, Bell," called Bernie. "We're going to be late, and it is extremely tacky to show up late to your own show. Especially when we own the place."

"I'm hurrying!" she yelled back. She couldn't believe her sister had settled on a dress before she had.

"Bell?" asked Alex. "Where are you?" He had walked into her bedroom, which was now covered in clothing, shoes, and handbags. With Matthew in jail, she had decided to move back into Alex's house temporarily, and she held no qualms about making herself feel right at home.

"I'm in the closet."

"Well," he laughed, "I guess I'm not the only person who's struggled with that."

"Ha-ha, you're hilarious," she replied.

"Whatcha doing?" he asked, popping his head inside the closet.

"Changing clothes for the umpteenth time. I can't seem to decide on an outfit for tonight. I want to wear one of the current pieces, but none of them feel right."

Bernie appeared in the doorway next to Alex. "Here," she said, handing Bell a pink champagne-colored dress. "This will look amazing on you."

Bell took the dress from her sister and looked it over. Gasping, she said, "This is the newest Clairrianne DuBois. How is this possible?"

"She wanted me to wear one of her dresses tonight, but I think the dress will look much better on you. I'm wearing one of her older pieces. The new is much more in line with the 1920s theme rising again this year."

"Yes, I see what you mean. It's very flapper-like. Thanks, Bern. This makes my night." She smiled.

"No problem. I'm just glad I found something you like, and we can get this show on the road."

Bell pushed her siblings out of the closet so she could change. She was ecstatic to be wearing one of Clairrianne's dresses. She was one of the major up-and-comers, and her work was exquisite. Actresses were requesting her, which projected great things for the future.

Bell slid the dress on and delighted in finding it fit perfectly. It was a sheer dress adorned with beautiful lace applique and crystal accents. It cut off four inches above her knees and had an asymmetrical slit that curved upward, showing just a little more of her left leg than her right. Along with the dress, she had short matching gloves and rose gold stiletto heels. It was a modern take on a retro theme, and she knew the crowds would take notice.

Stepping out of the closet, she watched her sister's lips curve into a smile. Alex nodded his approval. She grinned in ecstasy.

"I found you a handbag," said Alex, holding out a rose gold Louis Vuitton clutch that matched her stilettos. "A special gift for one of my favorite sisters."

"Here," said Bernie. She handed Bell a pair of dangling rose gold diamond earrings. "Tiffany thinks you should wear these." She winked. "Oh, and happy birthday, sis."

"Well, I think Tiffany is right. Dang, what did I do to deserve these?" asked Bell.

"You got older." Bernie laughed. "Glad it's you and not me," she teased as she wrinkled up her face and stuck her tongue out like a five-year-old. "After the show tonight, let's celebrate your thirtieth birthday!"

"Woah, not funny. I'm only turning twenty-eight. If this was my thirtieth, we'd be out having a serious celebration, not working."

"Bernie, quit picking on your sister," said Alex. "She can't help that she's getting old." He laughed. "Come on, ladies; this is the first Price & Fitz clothing line to hit the runway since our parents passing. Let's show them we're stronger than ever, and Price & Fitz is here to stay!"

Three hours later, the siblings were seated in the showroom, sipping cocktails and mingling with guests. The show had been a success, and lots of people were excited about the new line that Price & Fitz was introducing.

"Bell, lovely show this evening. I hear happy birthday is in order," said the ever-smug voice of Emmy Lou Baker.

Bell stared at her. She was dressed in a simple black flapper dress, as were many of the other attendees. Bell bit back the anger that was threatening to eject from her mouth. Just the sight of Emmy made her want to spit acid. "I'm surprised you have a kind word in you, Emmy," she replied. She knew she shouldn't have said it but couldn't help herself. "You seem to take pride in regularly attacking me, so tell me, what did you not like this evening?"

"Oh, Bell, you know it's just business and not personal. I loved this evening's show. You have a lot of great designers on board, and I can see this line being very successful. By the way, darling, that dress is absolutely gorgeous on you," she purred.

"Thanks. I'm glad you enjoyed the show." The anger had deflated, and she had nothing else to say to Emmy.

"Emmy, why don't you go over there and meet Clairrianne DuBois? That's who made the dresses Bell and I are wearing tonight," said Bernie. "She's pretty amazing."

"Yes, I think I will do just that. Well, toodles. Enjoy the rest of your night." She had a fake smile plastered across her face as she walked away.

Bell erupted the second she was out of earshot. "That woman is so vile! Where does she come off walking up here and telling me happy birthday after all the articles she's written in the last year where I took a sound beating? This isn't business, it's war!"

Luckily, Aiden walked up and put a quick end to her rant. She shouldn't let Emmy ruin her night; she wasn't worth it.

"Miss Bell, a charming dress you have on this evening. You look divine," he admired as he placed a chocolate torte on the table. It had twenty-eight candles lit around its perimeter. Her siblings and Aiden sang Happy Birthday, and all the nearby guests joined in. At the end of the song, she blew out the candles, and the room erupted into applause. Her wish was simply for Matthew to be declared innocent.

Aiden turned to Bernie and smiled at her. "You also look gorgeous this evening." Picking up her hand, he held it gently. "When are you going to let me take you on a date, Miss Price?"

"Maybe never," she replied, pulling her hand away. She began rubbing one of the cloth napkins between her pointer finger and thumb, which she did when she was nervous.

"Ouch," he said and leaned in a little closer to her. "Why is that?"

"I'm your boss, for starters." Despite her turning him down, Bell could see a small smile playing on her lips. She could tell her sister liked Aiden, but she could imagine that she was worried she didn't know him well enough. Who could blame her, considering all that had happened with her deranged ex?

"That is a very true statement." He frowned. "With that, I shall leave you to your drinks and return to my duties." He gave a slight bow, straightened his grey tux jacket, and strutted confidently back to the bar, where a young blonde in an overly short flapper dress instantly monopolized his attention.

Bell watched her sister, who was staring across the room at Aiden. "I'm not certain he isn't involved in this whole messed up ordeal," said Bernie.

"Is that why you're playing this game with him?" she replied.

"I can't let myself get close to him until I know for sure he isn't another player in this sick and twisted game."

"Lord, help us. I'm just praying Matthew's not a part of it at this point." She watched as Alex raised his glass into the air.

"Here's to you, Bell. May this birthday be safe and fun for everyone involved, and may the police find answers and put the nightmare that is our lives back in order quickly before anything else negative happens."

"Cheers," said Bernie as the three siblings clanked their glasses together.

"Dang it!" exclaimed Bell. Her drink had sloshed over and onto her dress. "So much for my Clairrianne DuBois."

"Oh, it's fine," replied Alex. "Just run into the VIP room and grab one of the fabric wipes. That will take it right out, and no one will be the wiser."

"Okay. Bernie, hand me that napkin you're attacking, please. I don't want anyone to see this, least of all Clairrianne."

Bernadette handed over the napkin. Standing, Bell turned toward the VIP room. "I'll be right back, and then maybe we can corral our friends over here to eat some of this torte."

"Sounds like a plan," said Alex. "Hurry back."

Bell fast walked the entire way to the VIP room. She didn't want any guests, especially Clairrianne, to stop her for fear they would realize she was hiding a spill. She managed to beeline into the room just as Emmy Lou came around the corner.

"That was close," she said to herself. Making her way to the back of the room, she opened the wardrobe and looked up to see the fabric wipes sitting on the shelf. Reaching up, a sudden chill ran down her spine, and the next thing she knew, a black-gloved hand was clamping firmly over her mouth. The assailant forced her forward, pressing her firmly into the wardrobe door. She tried to scream, but the glove muffled the sound. Unable to see, adrenaline shot through her body as thoughts of what might happen next raced through her mind.

Over the struggle, she heard the door to the room open, and her attacker shoved her hard in the opposite direction.

"Hey, Bell—Woah! What the—" She heard Aiden shout as she crashed into and somersaulted over the back of the sofa. She heard something hit the floor nearby as the perpetrator dashed out the door. Aiden was immediately at her side, grabbing her elbow and pulling her upright. "Are you okay?" he asked, his voice full of concern.

"I don't know. Am I still intact?" She felt dizzy. "Did you get a look at whoever that was?"

"No. Everything happened too fast. They caught me completely off guard and body-checked me as I was coming through the door."

"Will you take a look around," requested Bell. "I heard something hit the floor."

Aiden got down on his hands and knees and, almost immediately, popped back up. "This is not good," he blurted as he held up what appeared to be some sort of small needle.

Bell looked at the object in his hand, and her mouth gaped open for a second as she realized it was meant for her. Sitting down on the sofa, a hundred different thoughts flooded her mind. Did they intend to kill her, drug her, or knock her out so they could take her? Or were they trying to get her blood? "What do you think their intentions were?" she whispered.

"Are you sure you're alright? They didn't hurt you or get a chance to stick you with this?"

"I don't think you gave them a chance." She brushed herself off and stood. "I came in here for a fabric wipe," she sighed and returned to the cabinet to get what she had come for. Her body was still shaking. Tearing it open, she pulled the wipe out and proceeded to clean up the spots on her dress. "I know I should be more concerned about the attack, but if people see this mess, it's just going to be one more stressful embarrassment, and I don't need that." Her hands shook as she worked on the dress. She didn't know any other way to react at that moment. She was merely attempting to keep calm, and this was the only way she knew how.

"Hey," he said, "I'm not judging, but I think you should sit back down. You seem like you're in shock."

She was in shock. Beads of perspiration were threatening to roll down her forehead, and she couldn't seem to slow her pounding heart. Lightheadedness set in as adrenaline continued to course through her body, and she worried she might pass out. Turning slowly, she crept back to the sofa and took a seat. Aiden followed her. Grabbing her wrist, he counted briefly and then appeared to scan the rest of her body for damages. When he finished his assessment, he fished his phone out of his pocket and dialed a number.

"Hey, it's Aiden. I think you'd better come inside. Bell was just attacked in the VIP suite by someone in a mask. The person dropped some kind of small needle." He paused to listen and then proceeded on. "She's thoroughly shook, but I think she'll be okay. I don't see anything to suggest the perp stuck her with anything. They fled the scene when I entered the room. I have no idea if they're still in the club." Another pause. "Yes, I can do that. Thanks."

"Marx and Thompson are checking the perimeter to see if there's anyone suspicious about it, then they'll come inside and take a look around as well. They asked that I stay here with you until they're finished scouting the area."

"Okay," she replied as she exhaled.

"That was a crummy birthday present," said Aiden.

"Yeah, I'd say." She looked up at him. Trying to calm herself, she decided to change the subject to something a bit happier. While not the most appropriate topic, she shouldn't think of anything to say but, "You're utterly smitten with my sister, aren't you?"

"It's awfully obvious, isn't it." He smiled. "She's smart, beautiful, and witty. She works hard and seems to know what she wants out of life. I appreciate that. Too many people have no idea where they're going or what they're doing with their lives, but she's got it together. Even with current and past events, she's doing quite well."

"Yeah, she's pretty amazing. Not every woman born into a family like ours would have gone after a law degree when they were already set for life." Bell smiled with admiration toward her sister. Despite their mother's ridiculousness, she had turned into an amazing young woman. "It's a wonder how she turned out the way she did."

"Why's that?" asked Aiden.

"Our mother wasn't a great role model. She taught us how to be models but didn't push us to be anything more than someone's arm candy. She felt we should rely on our looks and land rich men to care for us, but neither my sister nor I wanted to go down that road. Sure, she taught us about the family business, but I honestly think it was only because we asked about it. Bernie and I have always strived to be our own people and do what makes us happy, no matter how much work is involved. Our father was the one who promoted the values we each adopted."

"Your father must have been a wonderful man."

"He was. He always told us we could do whatever we wanted. He never pressured any of his kids, including Alex, to take over the family business. We were always given a choice when it came to our futures. I suppose that freedom allowed us to grow a fondness for the family businesses."

"When things aren't forced, it's much easier," he said with a sincere smile.

"What about you? What was it like growing up in your family?"

"Dad was a drunk. He used to throw beer bottles at us kids." Aiden pointed to the scars on his face. "That's how I got these. He was abusive. Ironically, he doesn't have a bit of Irish in his genes." He laughed. "He also wasn't my real father. I don't know who my real father was, but I do know that he died sometime before my birth. When I was eighteen and finally able to leave for college, Mom and Dad were killed in a drunk driving accident."

"Your father was driving, I take it?" asked Bell.

"No. That's the crazy end of the deal. The person at fault wasn't my father but the other driver in the collision."

Bell's eyebrows furrowed as she stared back at him. "Dang. I didn't expect you to say that."

"Yeah, nor did I. I always assumed my crazy drunk father would be the one to drink himself to death, not that some other crazy drunk would be the one to kill him off instead."

"That has to be some form of karma, don't you think?"

"I do." The look on his face was somber. "Life is funny, isn't it?"

"Right now, it's not so funny," she said quietly. "I feel like my world defines insanity. Bernie has had it even worse. Most of the things that have happened over the past year have happened directly to her, and now this killer is threatening her life. Has she told you anything about Martin, or have you heard the stories?"

He waited a moment before answering. "No, she's told me nothing of her past."

Bell didn't think he was lying outright, but she didn't believe his answer either. "Is there something you aren't telling me?" Her tone was slightly more accusatory than she'd intended.

"Nope," he replied. She didn't believe him, but she didn't know what he could possibly be hiding or why he wouldn't admit to knowing something about her family's past.

"That response doesn't make me feel confident that you're telling me the truth. Should I be concerned?"

"Nope."

"Seriously?" she asked. Her tone had raised an octave.

"Listen," he said, "you don't have to worry. Trust that I have your best interest at heart. People talk; maybe I've heard rumors.

I'm not going to judge anything until I hear it from you or your siblings firsthand. That's all I'm saying."

"Oh, well, okay then. I guess I feel a little better about your response, but trust is something that's become increasingly difficult for my family. Without trust, you won't get too far with any of us."

"Don't read into it. If I wanted to harm you, I would have already."

"Gee, that makes me feel even better." She laughed. "I mean, what's stopping you?"

"I'm not a psychopath!" he chortled.

"Oh, is that all? What else ya got?"

Grinning, he raised one eyebrow and said, "I'm a great juggler. Does that make me seem more trustworthy?"

"Ha! Not at all," said Bell. Rolling her eyes, she shook her head at his response. "I guess it's a start, but you'll need to prove this juggling talent at a later date." She didn't know what to think about Aiden. He had an interesting sense of humor, but knew how to throw out all the stops while working in the club. Smooth in the spotlight, but awkward in a one-on-one. *So odd,* she thought.

"Hey, Aiden, Bell," called Marx. "How are you two holding up in here? Any changes since we spoke?"

"No, nothing's changed," replied Aiden. "We're just waiting for you to take our statements."

"Did you get a good look at the guy? Height, weight, anything?" he asked.

"No," said Bell. "He grabbed me from behind, and when he realized we weren't alone bolted. He pushed me, so I didn't get a look at him."

"He was wearing a face mask," said Aiden. "Honestly, I thought it was a dude, but it could have been a woman. They were about 5'8", 5'9", I'd say. Thin and muscular. Not sure that says much. They could have been wearing heeled shoes, and so many thin muscular models are running around here tonight. No idea what the purpose of grabbing Bell was. Could have been a kidnapping or worse. Who can say? This syringe is the only thing we found."

Bell frowned at him. "That's disturbing. Whatever their intention, it wasn't good."

"Yes, it is, young lady," replied Thompson as he trailed Marx into the room. "This is why you have us following you around."

"I can see where you're coming from, but at the same time, you following us around didn't stop this person from attempting whatever they were trying to do tonight," she said. "That makes them quite ballsy, doesn't it?" Staring back at the officers, she watched Marx remove his hat. He pulled the hair band from his hair and regathered the stray strands. Knotting it back up, he twisted the band and replaced his hat.

Looking at Bell, he puffed out his cheeks in frustration. "I know it seems like we're not doing anything, but we are. This will end soon," he said with confidence. He turned away from her and began looking around the room. Thompson took the opposite end as they combed it for any missed evidence.

"I know you're trying. Thank you," she said as Alex and Bernie walked into the room.

"What's going on?" asked Alex. "Why didn't you come back? Did something happen?"

Bernie stopped between her sister and Aiden. "We saw Thompson and Marx enter the club and thought we should come check on you."

"Someone attacked her," said Aiden. "Luckily, I walked in as it was happening."

"Do you have any idea who?" asked Alex.

"No," replied Bell. "I don't know who it was. I guess the question is, who has been present during all of these situations?"

"Let's see. Eloise, Emmy Lou Baker, Lee, and Jordan," said Bernie.

"Also, Flora, Max, and Torrence," noted Alex. "Who else?"

"That's just it," said Bell, "several people have been at these events because they're regulars or staff. Flora and Max are the only people who started at the club around the time that Martin came along, but several of the staff fit as far as being in the vicinity during all of these attacks."

"Well then," said Marx, walking back over to the group, "I think we'd better look into that list a little more."

"Do you think Linz really died from a heart attack, or should we be looking specifically at people present during our trip as well?" asked Bernie.

"As of right now, we have no reason to believe Linz's passing had to do with foul play. She was overtly underweight and had a history of not eating, so while I can appreciate where you're coming from, it just doesn't fit without more evidence."

Bell couldn't imagine that the person causing this could be any of the people they named. She still wasn't sure Aiden didn't have something to do with the situation. After all, he was the most recent addition to the club, and he had shown up right when everything had begun. She decided she would keep an eye on him. Matthew, of course, was another question she needed an answer to. *What if Matthew and Aiden are both involved in this whole fiasco? How deep could it run?* The panicked thoughts played through her mind while she pretended to listen to Marx and her siblings.

"Right, Bell?" asked Bernie.

"What? Sorry, I guess I was zoning," she replied.

"I said we would appreciate it if they could get us further information on Matthew and his situation. I asked if they had found anything to rule him out as a suspect and if will he be released on bail?"

"Oh, yeah, more information would be welcomed," she agreed.

"Well," said Thompson, "we can't rule anyone out as of yet." *How long has he been standing next to me,* thought Bell? Thompson looked at her. She understood how he had ended up with the deep worry lines that ran across his forehead. "We'll comb the property once more and go back to our posts. I'll send the needle to the lab to find out what it is. As soon as I have answers, I'll let you know. Call if you need anything."

"Thanks," said Alex. "We appreciate you being here."

"No problem," said Marx. "This is our job." The officers turned and left the room.

"Okay, family, I think whatever we do from here on out, we need to keep a closer eye on our friends and colleagues and note if anything suspicious happens," said Bernie.

Alex nodded. "I agree with that. If anyone sees anything funny, even if they aren't sure whether it's important, we should let each other know, as well as Thompson or Marx. You never know when something could be important."

"Okay, let's check in with each other at least twice a day from here on out," said Bell.

"Agreed," said Bernie and Alex in unison.

"Bell, it's still your birthday. What would you like to do now?" asked Bernie.

"I don't know," she replied. "I'm not feeling too celebratory. Matt's not here, and now this loony appears to be after me."

"We can go home," said Alex. His look was full of understanding. "This hasn't been an easy week for you. Shall we grab your birthday torte and go?"

"Yeah, let's go home," she replied. "I'd feel safer."

"Okay, I'll go get the torte, and we can head out."

Alex pushed open the door to let his sisters out into the club and then wandered off to package up the birthday treat. Jordan, Lee, and Torrence were waiting patiently on the other side. Bell considered each of them. She couldn't imagine any of her models showing a violent side. Torrence had a horrible temper, but she was this cute tiny blonde that everyone adored. Bell couldn't picture her holding a gun or any sort of deadly object other than the foul words that burst forth from her mouth every now and then. Of course, she couldn't imagine Lee being a danger to anyone, either. She didn't know what to think about Jordan. She couldn't stand him. But he was a clueless jerk, and she didn't know if he was smart enough to pull off such heinous crimes.

Walking up to Bell, Lee reached out and grabbed her hand, giving it a squeeze. "You look beautiful," she admired while continuing to hold her hand. "You also look a bit uneasy. Did something happen?" she asked.

"Yeah, someone attacked me, which is why we were in the VIP room for so long. We had to wait for Thompson and Marx to do their sweeps."

"Oh no! Are you okay? Do you need a hug?" Lee didn't give her a chance to answer; she just wrapped her arms around her and pulled her close. "I'm here if you need to talk," she said with sincerity.

"Lee, you can let go. I'm okay, really," squeaked Bell from under the crushing force of Lee's arms. The girl was strong. Another fine attribute.

Lee frowned apologetically at her. "Are you sure you're okay? I'm sorry, maybe you aren't the hugging type. I shouldn't have done that." She stepped back slightly, assessing the situation.

"No, it's fine. I just want to get out of here," Bell replied.

"When is this going to stop?" asked Bernie to no one in particular.

"You have been under a lot of stress lately," said Lee. "You know, I'm trained in massage. I can help you ease some of that tension if you'd like." She was smiling warmly, and Bell knew she meant well.

She smiled back. "Thanks, Lee, perhaps later in the week."

"Okay, just let me know," she replied. Reaching out, she squeezed Bell's wrist.

Bell noticed Bernie watching her with one eyebrow raised in curiosity. Lee had turned away and was refocusing her attention on Torrence and Jordan, who were debating whether or not they would be going out dancing that evening or heading home and calling it a night. Bell shook her head dismissively at Bernie. Bernie tried to stifle a laugh, and Bell shot her an icy look in return just as Alex rejoined them. Looking around, he noticed the weird exchange between his sisters.

"I called Andre, and he's outside waiting. What am I missing?" he asked.

Bernie pulled him closer and lowered her voice. "Oh, you know, it's a girl thing," she said with a giggle.

"What? Why are you telling me then?" Alex asked with a frown.

She winked at him and reiterated, "*Girl thing*."

"Like my sort of girl thing?" he questioned.

"Now you're getting it," she said, slapping him on the shoulder.

"*Shut it!*" hissed Bell. "There's nothing going on."

"Does she know that?" asked Bernie with another muffled giggle. Alex had placed his hand over her mouth and was nearly dying as he tried to keep a straight face.

"Seriously. You two are awful," snapped Bell.

"Nah, we just love you so much!" yelled Bernie. The rest of the models turned to look at her.

Bell shot her another dirty look. "Let's get out of here already." She turned and rushed for the door. Alex and Bernie nearly had to run to catch up with her.

"Hey!" called Lee, "What's the hurry?" to which the siblings, Bell included, burst out laughing.

"We need to get out of here," replied Alex. "This night has been much too eventful, and we feel we're better off retiring to the house for the remainder of the evening."

"That's unfortunate," replied Lee. "I was hoping we would get to go dancing," she pouted.

"Sorry. Raincheck," said Bernie.

Exiting the club, they found Thompson waiting outside Andre's limo. "I'm sorry to have to do this, but your family is to return to the house. After tonight's attack, I've been instructed to keep you under strict supervision."

"Don't worry, that's precisely our plan," said Bell.

"Perfect. You're to remain at Alex's house until further notice," said Thompson as he opened the door to the limo.

Bell was the first to climb in. Scooting across the seat, she noticed a floral birthday card. Grabbing it, she flipped it open and read out loud:

> "Happy birthday, Bell.
> Enjoy it while you can.
> Your time is coming to an end."

"Everyone, back out of the limo, now!" yelled Thompson. He pulled his gun from its holster and scanned their surroundings. "We'll have to give you a ride back to the house. This vehicle is no longer deemed safe."

Bell was crouched on the curb with her head in her hands. "Does this ever end?" she asked. The frustration in her voice was clear.

"Yeah," replied Bernie, "when one of us dies."

"Don't say that!" Alex's tone was angry. "We aren't giving up, and we're sticking together. Don't ever say that again!" he snapped. Bell began to cry. Sobs racked her body. Alex wrapped his arms around her. "Shh. It's okay, sweetie. It's going to be okay. I shouldn't have yelled, and Bernie shouldn't have said that," he said with a scowl. When he looked up, quiet as she was, Bernie also had tears flowing from her eyes. "Come here," he said, waving her over.

"I'm sorry," she sniffled. "This is just too much. I was feeling so good, and now I'm back to feeling consistently on edge. I'm sorry, Bell." She crouched down and hugged Bell from behind. It's your birthday. This should have been a good day," she said with another sniffle.

Thompson waved at Marx, who was parked nearby in his cruiser. He pulled the car into the parking spot nearest the door.

"Get in," said Thompson. "Marx will take you home. Remember, if anything else happens—"

"We know. We'll tell you right away," said Bell as she wiped the tears from her eyes. She knew, in her heart, that it would only be a matter of time before something else happened. The question was, what would that something be?

Chapter Eleven

Martin Day spent what seemed like unending hours contemplating his situation. Most of his anger and hatred was directed toward the entire Price family, but a special fire was burning for Bernie. He couldn't wrap his mind around how a stupid piece of arm candy managed to cheat him out of the future for which he'd worked so hard. He'd done everything he could to mold her into a perfectly obedient wife, and somehow, it hadn't stuck. She'd turned on him despite all he'd done for her.

His partner was not in agreement as to the source of the problem. Bell Price was the one who had acquired the voice recording of Martin. She was the reason he was behind bars, and it was that recording that would be the final nail in his metaphorical coffin. There was no one else to place the blame on. Without the recording, Martin would have gone free. Hell would have to freeze over before Bell Price would be let off the hook for her life-altering retaliation toward Martin.

Martin had minimal time, but he picked up the phone and dialed. Everything he said had to be meticulously planned to keep his partner safe and hidden. They made sure to always use code names. The UIA had served them well and taught them everything they needed to know about deception.

"Fox," answered his partner. The number from the jail would have been recognizable, and the timing lined up. No need to wonder who was on the other end.

"It's Briar," said Martin. His partner's full name was Fox Whisper, and his had been Briar Rose. A silly name for a man, but his trainer had said it was because he was handsome but deadly. He accepted it because he'd been given no choice. From that day forward, when the situation didn't require a full name, he went by Briar.

"How are you holding up?" asked Fox.

"Swell," said Martin. "I love it here."

"I'm so sorry. I know it's awful. I wish I could get you out. I'm working on a plan, but I don't know how long it'll take. A lot of components need to fall into place."

"That's fine. What else is new regarding our little game?"

"Did I tell you that Matthew's in jail? He's their prime suspect. They believe he might be your partner."

"That'll never stick, but nice work." He smiled at his partner's tenacity.

"I know, but I thought you'd appreciate it after everything he put you through."

"Trust me, I'm enjoying that tidbit very much. You've made my day."

"We're getting close to the end. Just a few more moves until checkmate." Fox laughed.

"What day do you think the game will end?"

"Friday."

"That's less than a week out. Are you sure you've got all your moves lined up?" he asked.

"Undoubtedly. I've got every move on the board mapped out, and it's going to end Friday."

"That's wonderful news," said Martin excitedly.

"I wish I could see the look on your face when everything finally falls into place."

"I know, but that's not possible at this time. One day, we'll celebrate," said Martin. "I look forward to that day."

"Me too. Business isn't as exciting without you here."

"Be careful, Fox."

"Don't sweat it, Briar. You know how good I am."

"I know, but still. Be careful."

The line went dead, and Martin was again left alone with his thoughts. The next inmate was approaching the phone, so he moved out of the way and began the trek back to his cell. He wished he could be out there with Fox, conning people and taking their money. They'd become so good at running their scams. How he lusted for the thrill of hunting down his next victim and getting them to fall helplessly for his charms.

It was the ultimate game of cat and mouse, and he enjoyed every moment, from the hunt to the sex to taking everything away at the end. If someone died in the process, it was all the more exciting to him. He was stronger and smarter. This was survival of the fittest, and he was the winner. Despite his current state, he would find a way to finish the game and come out on top with Fox's help.

Fox had not been his partner in the UIA, but they had run into each other while in training and were reintroduced during a mission when he was twenty-one. They quickly established a connection and discovered they worked well together. After two years of running missions for the UIA, they decided to go into business on the side. Money was the name of the game, and they found they were very good at manipulating people. Martin was the face, and Fox ran everything behind the scenes.

Soon after beginning their side venture, the duo concluded that their futures were bigger than the UIA and needed a way out. They had already been given a future assignment where they would again work together. With careful planning, Fox created what appeared to be an unavoidable disaster, which included some very real grenades, lots of gunfire, and the death of each of their partners. Martin and Fox then proceeded to put on the best Post Traumatic Shows they could muster, and the agency deemed them unfit for duty. They were discharged and sent out into the real world with strong recommendations for therapy.

Once finished with the UIA, Martin continued his education. He'd lived with the same roommate all through school, Matthew McKinney. Matt had been a lot of fun in the beginning, but eventually, he'd gotten in the way of one of Martin's schemes. He had put feelers out on several occasions to see if Matthew could possibly be the type to join him and Fox, but he wasn't. Matt was just too righteous, and he believed in abiding by the law.

Before he realized it, his college years had come to an end. In one final heinous act, he had stolen Matt's girlfriend's honor, her twin sister's heart, and their unsuspecting family's money. He then skipped town with Fox, but not before Matthew landed one sound blow, providing Martin with his first black eye. Matthew had flown into a rage when he found out Martin had taken liberties with his girlfriend. His heart was broken, and he'd instantly become dead weight to Martin.

Arriving back at his cell, he thought about Matt and how he was also sitting in jail somewhere. It was so ironic. His incarceration, no matter how temporary, was payment enough for the black eye he'd provided all those years earlier. He knew Matt would get out, but at least he'd made everyone around him question his knighthood. No one would ever forget that. Matt would be left alone to overthink his situation, and perhaps it would eat at him knowing he was unable to protect anyone while sitting in his own cage. Martin was tickled pink just thinking about it.

"Matt," called Tony, "You're getting out."

"What? Who's paying the bail?"

"We all know you're too proud to ask for help, but we couldn't let you sit here when none of us think you belong in jail. Wells called your father, and he paid your bail."

"What?! You did not call my father. Please tell me you didn't. I'd rather stay in here," he stated firmly. The look on his face was fierce. "You have no idea what you've done. My father's help always comes at a cost, and it's never to be paid in currency."

"Dang, Matt, you needed to get out. Your father should be present at times like this. That's what parents are for," he insisted, holding his arms up for emphasis. "Besides, that man has more money than he knows what to do with."

"Just because he has a ton of money doesn't mean I want it, or his help. Now he knows where I live. He's going to come for me."

"Well, we'll worry about that when it happens," said Tony offhandedly. "For now, I'm not going to feel bad for you. You're getting out. Let's go collect your things and send you home to that beautiful girlfriend of yours."

"Yeah, if she still wants me," he huffed. His ego was feeling a little bruised. Never in his wildest dreams could he have imagined being accused of any crime, or that someone would call his father to bail him out of jail. He was always enforcing the law, and here he was on the opposite side of the bars. He believed Martin was the one to blame. The whole situation reeked of him.

"Listen, I don't have all day. Are you going to come out of there or not?" The irritation was quite apparent in Tony's voice. "Never in my years did I think I'd have to beg an inmate to leave."

"I'm not your average inmate, I guess!" snapped Matt.

"Woah, McKinney, relax! We believe you're innocent, don't worry. I'm sure you'll be cleared of this whole thing."

"Yeah, well, that can't happen soon enough."

"Just keep your wits about you and stay sharp," said Tony, "you can't afford to lose it now, especially if someone's gunning for you."

He was right. He had to keep it together. Hopping off the cot, he headed for the door. He was glad to put the cell behind him even if he didn't know what awaited him outside.

"Hey, McKinney, you know the rules. Don't leave town," Tony yelled after him.

It was Monday evening, and Bell was back at her house cleaning and gathering different clothes for the week to come when a knock sounded at the front door. She rushed toward it and looked through the peephole. Frowning, she turned the handle.

"What are you doing here?" she demanded.

Jordan looked at her questioningly. "You invited me," he replied. "You asked me over for dinner." He pushed the door open, letting himself into the house. Bell could smell whiskey on his breath.

"I did not invite you over," she said sternly. "Have you been drinking?"

"Come on, Bell, I'm so tired of these games you play." He reached out a hand and brushed back the stray hair hanging from the bun atop her head. She took a step backward. "You don't need to pretend you dislike me, especially when we're alone. Let's just have an enjoyable evening. It's not like we're committed to anyone else."

"Speak for yourself," she glared at him. "I'm still in a relationship with Matthew."

"He's in jail, Bell. Possibly for killing your family and friends. Doesn't that count against him?" he asked. There was a hint of kindness and understanding in his voice. "Besides, you're the one who said you didn't want to be alone tonight."

"There's no proof that he's to blame—What do you mean I said I didn't want to be alone?" she asked heatedly.

Jordan reached out and grabbed her hand. Lifting it, he placed it lightly over his heart. He was warm, and she could feel his heart beating. "I care about you. Can't we just spend this evening together and see where it goes? Don't be afraid of your feelings."

She yanked her hand away. "You said I invited you here. How did I invite you?" she demanded.

"You sent me an email. I have it right here," he said, shaking his phone.

"I want to see it."

"Okay, sure." He scrolled through his phone and handed it to her once he found what he was looking for.

Skimming it over, she noted the person who had sent this was throwing themselves at Jordan, and she knew without hesitation she wouldn't have done that even in her wildest dreams.

"I definitely didn't send this to you." She was completely taken aback.

"You're kidding, right?"

"Jordan, this didn't come from me. I would never say any of those things to you."

"Well, if you didn't send it, then who did?"

"I have no idea."

"Come on, Bell," he coaxed as he advanced on her, "are you sure you didn't write this?" Reaching out, he grabbed her arm and yanked her toward him until their bodies touched. Before she could stop him, his lips were crushing into hers, and she was screaming, "No!"

Bell's hand flew back, and with a quick sweep, she landed her fist against his cheek, sending him reeling backward. "I would never!" she screamed. He tasted like whiskey, and she instantly felt ill. "Jordan, you're drunk, and you need to leave!"

Anger filled Jordan's eyes. Stepping toward her, he raised his hand to strike back. Before he could land the blow, someone else grabbed his arm in midair.

"I don't think so, buddy," snapped Matthew. "You need to get out of here right now before I lose my temper. She doesn't want you, and she's made it clear."

Bell stared wide-eyed at both men. Jordan looked stunned. He turned swiftly and bolted for the door, passing by a confused Marx on his way out.

"What just happened?" asked Marx.

"He's assaulting my girl," said Matthew through gritted teeth. "And he's drunk. You should probably call for backup before he kills himself or someone else."

"I'm on it," replied Marx as he reached for his radio.

Bell launched herself into the air, wrapping her arms around Matt's neck. "Thank God you came in when you did," she sobbed. "Someone was in my email. They sent him a message asking him to come over and saying how wrong I've been about my feelings and that he's the person I need. They told him to meet me for dinner and that I couldn't stand to be alone and without him any longer. I would never in a million years say that. I hope you believe me, Matthew."

"My sweetheart, I know. I don't believe you want him. Not for a single second."

Pausing for a moment, she looked him suspiciously in the eye. "How are you out? Have you been cleared?"

"No. I haven't been cleared yet, but they let me out on bail."

Bell let go and slowly pushed herself away from him. "Who got you out?"

"My father," replied Matt.

Bell's happiness dissolved as she slowly backed away from Matt. "Marx, escort Matthew out of the house, please. He can return after I leave. I won't stay in the same place with him until I know his name has been cleared."

"Bell, you know me," said Matt, his voice full of hurt.

"I think I know you, but Bernie thought she knew Martin."

"I'm not Martin. I love you, genuinely. I could never hurt you."

"I want to believe you, but I can't let my guard down. I can't be with you until this mess is straightened out. I'm sorry, Matthew. If you won't leave, I will." She walked back to her bedroom, grabbed a bag, tossed several items inside, and then hurried back toward the door. "I hope they clear you soon. I miss you, and it's quite unbearable, but I'm refusing to be the victim. Please understand.

As much as I love you and want to believe you, I have to think of me first in this situation."

He looked like she had stabbed him with a dagger, but she wouldn't budge, not right now, not with how crazy her world had become. "Marx, you can follow me to Alex's," she said.

"I'm right behind you, Bell." He nodded apologetically toward Matthew and followed her out.

Chapter Twelve

It was now Wednesday, and Bell was feeling restless. She paced back and forth in front of the picture window in Alex's living room. Her nails had been reduced to short, ragged nubs, and she needed something strong to calm her nerves. She walked into the kitchen and grabbed a bottle of scotch from the top shelf of the pantry. Alex kept the scotch around because of their father, but he rarely touched the stuff himself. Alan had a taste for the finer things in life when it came to food and drink, but in moderation, unlike their mother. He liked a nice glass of Oban 18 year, especially when their mother was leaning on his last nerve.

Bell grabbed a crystal lowball and poured herself two fingers of scotch, and then, walking over to the freezer, she opened it to find the whiskey stones. She tossed two into the glass and headed back toward the living room. She watched the mailman, Kirk, working his way from the east end of the street, going from house to house. She'd been stuck inside Alex's house so much lately that she had gotten to know his mailman, who also played poker with her brother and his buddies.

Kirk was a middle-aged man with grown children. He hadn't always been in the mail delivery business. He once ran a flower shop, but he retired early as his children became young adults and left them to run affairs. They had the largest shop in Tulsa, catering to all major business events in the area. After a month of sitting around the house, he was bored, and his family encouraged him to find a hobby. He didn't need the money, but he liked the outdoors and exercise, so the mail carrier position was perfect.

Bell caught herself yawning while she watched Kirk. She had barely slept since Monday night, and she couldn't stop thinking about the look on Matthew's face when she'd told him they couldn't be together. He looked betrayed. Her always calm and cool man had been broken by her words. She never thought she'd see such a day, but these were dark and messed up times. She hoped and prayed that the end was near. How much more could they endure? How bad would it have to get before it would stop? There were so many questions with no answers.

Kirk stopped to pet Trigger, the Silver Labrador who belonged to Alex's jokester friend, Tyler. Trigger was a well-behaved dog who wagged his tail with excitement every time he saw the neighborhood mailman coming. Kirk snuck him milk bones regularly, and Tyler pretended not to notice. Giving Trigger one more head pat,

Kirk headed toward the next residence. Trigger tore off across the yard, jumping and snapping happily at a bird, his tail flying in every direction. At barely a year, he was still very much a pup.

Bell turned away from the window and walked back to the kitchen. She had finished her scotch and was feeling much more relaxed. Carefully setting the glass on the island, she walked to the back of the house to look out into the yard. The sun was shining, and the day looked nice. She knew better, though. Things were off. Today, she felt worse than she had days earlier. It had been too quiet since Monday evening.

Turning toward the hall, she opened the door to the den. Her siblings were inside watching a movie. She had tried to join in but couldn't sit still. "How's it going?" she asked.

Bernie snapped her head away from the oversized screen and glared at her sister. "Bell, it's the same as it was twenty minutes ago when you asked. Nothing's changed. We're still watching a movie. Stop pacing; you're making me more nervous."

"Don't you feel it?" she asked. "Something's going to happen."

"You're willing negative energy into motion," replied her brother. "We don't need something to happen unless it's for the positive," he matter-of-factly pointed out to her.

Bell rolled her eyes at her brother and closed the door. She couldn't help it. She felt uncomfortable. There was a chill in the air despite the warm sunshine she could see outside. She walked into the kitchen and grabbed her glass. Picking up the scotch bottle, she was just about to pour herself another drink when she heard the mail slot. Setting the bottle down, she rushed toward the door. Throwing it open, she saw Kirk's surprised face.

"Hey, Kirk, how are you?" she asked.

"It's not—" his words were cut short as he began to choke.

"It's not what? Can I get you some water?" she asked.

His hand flew up to his throat as he struggled to breathe. In the next instant, he was collapsing onto the ground. Letters flew into the air around him and scattered in the wind. Brixton, the officer stationed at the end of their driveway, noticed the commotion and sprang into action.

"Bell, I'm calling for help!" he yelled to her.

"Oh, my God! Alex! Bernie!" she screamed. "I need you! Now!"

She knelt down next to Kirk and rolled him onto his back. Feeling his neck, she couldn't find a pulse. Brixton rushed toward her. "This is not happening," she said loudly. "Come on, Kirk! Don't you dare die on me!" He was turning purple, and he didn't appear to be breathing. She began compressions on his chest, remembering to keep time with one of her favorite Queen songs, *Another One Bites the Dust*. She realized the title was dismal, but she couldn't think of anything else at that moment. Brixton was beside her, feeling for a pulse and shaking his head. Bell leaned in and, tipping Kirk's head back, gave him a couple breaths of air and continued compressions.

"Oh my, God, Kirk!" yelled Alex. He and Bernie stood in the doorway, staring in shock. Alex noticed something odd about the mail scattered across the ground. "Bernie, look at these," he said, holding up an envelope. "They're all the same. Are they all the same?" His sister grabbed an envelope and opened it.

"It says: *You're Next*."

"Son of a—" said Alex as Bell's voice cut in.

"No! No! You don't die!" she screamed as she thudded her fist on Kirk's chest. He wasn't responding. The group could hear sirens coming. Bell was pretty sure Kirk was a goner, but in defiance of her own shaking body, she continued with the compressions.

"I'm concerned, Bell," said Brixton, "you gave him air, and if this is homicide, he could have ingested poison. I think we should be looking into your safety first and foremost."

"I can't worry about that, Brixton!" she screamed hysterically. "This man's dying because of us. This is our fault! He has kids, a family, a happy life. The dog across the street gets excited about seeing him each day. People will miss him!"

"Bell, let me take over," Brixton replied sternly. "You need to step back."

Bell didn't stop. She couldn't stop. She wouldn't stop until she knew no life was left in him.

"Bell, I think he's gone," said Alex. He could barely get the words out.

"No," she said with tears streaming down her face. The ambulance pulled into the driveway, and a moment later, someone was pulling her away from Kirk. The EMTs had taken over. "No!" she screamed. "No!" She tried to advance back into the situation, but Alex grabbed her and, wrapping his arms around her, he picked her up and pulled her backward. He held her as she cried and hyperventilated. Bernie stood next to them and stared blankly as they lifted Kirk onto a gurney and stowed him inside the ambulance.

"You did everything you could," said Brixton. "He's gone. They'll run tests to find out what happened. It looks like a heart attack. Of course, the bag of threats lying here says something entirely different."

"If that was a heart attack, then you all need to start looking into the concept of it being an induced heart attack," fired Bernie. "There's no way that this was natural."

"I agree," said Alex. "Kirk was a good guy, and this is a serious blow for this whole neighborhood. We have blood on our hands."

"No, you don't. You didn't cause this. The person doing this is fully to blame," Brixton patiently replied.

"Yes, but they're doing it because of us. Of course, we feel guilty! This is our own freakin' fault!" Alex rarely raised his voice, but this was one time when he had clearly lost his calm.

"What could you do to change any of this?" asked Brixton.

"I don't know! Maybe leave this psycho a note telling him we give up, come and get us as long as you leave everyone else alone?"

"Sheep for the slaughter," said Bell. "Why not?"

"So much has happened. I just want it to end," lamented Bernie. "Maybe giving up is better than allowing more innocent people to be harmed?"

"Oh my God. I can't believe I'm hearing this," said Brixton. "Your lives are not bargaining chips."

Bernie let out a big sigh. "What's left?"

Brixton stared at the siblings. "Don't give up. This is the home stretch. We're going to get this guy." In support of his statement, two other police cars pulled into the drive. Wells and Thompson got out and marched over to the front porch. Wells looked angry, and Thompson was all keyed up.

"What happened?" asked Wells as he bent down and grabbed an envelope with one of his gloved hands. Discarding the first, he picked up a second and then a third. "They all say the same thing," he stated and then grew quiet for a minute while he appeared to be contemplating the situation. "Well, you've got me. I'm sure this wasn't another heart attack. Do you all have anywhere else you can go that's discreet and away from here for a while? Think about it and let me know," he said as he fired off his thoughts to whoever was listening.

Bell had stopped crying and watched as a couple of men roped off Alex's front yard and combed the scene for any evidence of what may have happened to Kirk. Another good man was gone.

She felt utterly defeated. Giving herself up to put an end to the killer's spree was sounding better by the minute.

Several hours had passed since the incident with Kirk, and the siblings were left alone, sitting in the living room, staring at one another.

"Let's go to the cabin," said Bernie. "It's the perfect place to get away from everything. The house is remote, and there are no neighbors or service people to be dragged into our situation. Most of our friends have no idea where the cabin is. We can either hide in peace or if this person is serious and they're coming for us next, we can take the fight out there. No one else needs to get hurt."

"It's not a bad idea," said Alex. "We can pack things for the weekend, and whatever happens, happens."

"I'm game," said Bell. She wanted nothing more than for the fear and terrorization of her family to end, and at this point, she didn't really care how, as long as it did. "It could be the best way to corner this person. Force them to follow us and make a move to expose themselves. It could work."

Alex shrugged. "Let's hope so. It's life or death at this point."

"What if it's one of our friends or colleagues?" asked Bell.

"Either way, this will prompt them to make a move and hopefully expose themselves," replied Alex.

"Are you both down for this plan? One of us could die if things go wrong. You know that's a chance we'd be taking," said Bernie.

"Let's not die," said Bell. "We go down fighting if it comes to it."

Alex shook his head in frustration. "I'm with you. We can't continue this game any longer. It feels like we're waiting for the worst by staying here."

Okay then, it's decided. We'll leave tomorrow before first light. Alex, why don't you go outside and let Marx know the plan. He can relay it to whoever needs to know. After you talk to him, come back inside, and we'll pack everything we need for the weekend," said Bell.

She watched her brother walk out the door. Turning, she made a beeline for the kitchen. Bernie followed closely behind. Noticing her empty cup on the counter, she grabbed the bottle of Oban, and instead of pouring it into the cup, she took a long pull from the bottle and passed it to her sister, who took a drink in turn. The two silently walked down the hall and retreated to their separate rooms to gather their gear.

By midnight, they had Andre's Range Rover packed to the gills. The limo was still out of commission, so Andre had offered up his personal vehicle. Alex didn't want to bring Andre into the situation, but Andre was like family and refused to be turned away. "I'm here till the end, bro," said Andre. "I'll just drop you off and retreat to the nearest hotel I can find. That way, I'll be ready if you need me to come back."

Alex slapped him on the back. "I'll wire you money for the hotel. You're a good man. I appreciate everything you do for me and my family. Why don't you chill on the sofa until it's time to go? We should all try to get a little sleep."

Andre retired to the sofa, and the siblings went to their separate rooms, but no one slept that night. They decided to head out at four in the morning under the cover of darkness. Thompson and Marx were following in their own unmarked cars. The trip would take two hours, but it would accomplish what Wells had requested. They would have a low-key place to hide out for a few days. Bell hoped the killer took the bait and followed.

Chapter Thirteen

It was Thursday afternoon, and Matthew was camped out at his and Bell's home. The house had a cold feel without her presence. Though his heart ached from the iciness of her words, he understood that nothing would change until the killer was caught. He kept himself busy by jumping into the deep end of the research pool. He couldn't return to his work at the force until his name was cleared. He would have to take matters into his own hands and rely on his background as a private investigator.

While he had no idea who the outside person was or if there was more than one involved, his gut was telling him that everything from Bradley's murder to the placement of the deceased's valuables was related to Martin Day. After racking his brain endlessly for hours, he couldn't see any way around it. He would have to speak to Martin directly and see if he could manipulate him into giving away his plans. The outsider was much too cunning and had left no real evidence in determining who they were.

To accomplish what he wanted, he had to make a deal with Wells. Wells had to agree to allow Matthew to go in and talk to Martin. He needed to know that Matthew wasn't hiding anything and that he wanted to find the answers as much as his precinct did. Wells didn't agree at first, but he always backed Matthew, and after a long discussion, he came around. He'd allow it since Matt was so upfront about his intentions, and because he believed that Matt was an honest and innocent man. He put his job on the line when he pulled the strings to allow him inside. Wells's only stipulation was that Matt would have to agree to wear a wire so they could get further information out of Martin.

Walking into the jail, his throat felt dry, and his stomach knotted. His body ached thinking about the cot he'd slept on while he was being held across town. He wasn't at all worried about the wire but concerned that Martin may not agree to see him. His hope was that Martin's vanity would get the better of him and that the meeting would go off without a hitch.

Vanity won out. Martin greeted him with enthusiasm.

"Hey there, Matt, what's new in your life?" he asked the question as if he was greeting a long-lost buddy. Matthew was fighting the desire to pistol whip him, even though he had neither a pistol nor the proximity to do so.

"I think you know all about my life," he replied curtly.

"I heard you were in jail for a brief stint as of late." He was like a dog with a new bone; he couldn't wipe the smirk from his face. Matt knew he enjoyed that delectable piece of information.

"Yeah, makes me wonder what your hand was in that whole fiasco?" he replied sourly.

"Come on now, Matthew, how could I be any part of that? They've had me locked up for weeks."

"I know you've got someone on the outside, Martin. It's simply a matter of time before they catch your partner. Why don't you tell me who it is?"

"What would be the fun in that?" he asked, and then just as rapidly, he said, "Maybe whatever's going on in your world is totally separate from the past?"

"No, I think you're behind this. The whole thing reeks of Martin Day. I think you have at least one partner. I swear to you that I'll figure out who it is, and when I do, there will be serious consequences," snarled Matt. "Who knows, I might accidentally shoot them. After all, they made the rules when they shot Bradley. Anything goes, right?" His statement was dangerous, and he realized it could get him into trouble. He would have to take extra precautions not to shoot the assailant once he found them.

"You'd never do that, white knight," Martin said, calling his bluff. He knew that he would, but any tiny detail he could get Martin to give away was a benefit to the case.

"Are you sure about that? I might just end your partner. Why give them a chance to get out and create more trouble down the road?" he asked.

"You can say it all you want, but I know you don't have the balls," said Martin. "You're still the same weakling I knew in college. Crying over your girlfriend." He laughed.

"Maybe I'll take a page out of your book," said Matthew. "Maybe I'll torture and beat down your partner until they're broken and bleeding and begging me to stop."

"You'll never get close enough to her to do that!" he bellowed. Matthew had found the proper nerve.

"Oh, so it's a woman?" he asked with surprise. He hadn't expected Martin's partner to be female, especially since he'd primarily chosen women to take advantage of. "Does she realize you believe you're the superior sex?"

"I don't believe that about myself. Besides, she's unlike any woman I've ever known."

"You could have fooled me. Who is she, Martin?"

"If you don't know already, then it'll be too late by the time you figure it out," he said, raising one eyebrow. Martin still thought he had the upper hand, though his face had reddened. "My sister's a smart and tough woman! She'll be gone before you can ever put a stop to her plan!" he roared.

"Your sister?" Matthew's mind was reeling. Could it be Lee? She was darker skinned, though not as dark-skinned as Martin. He couldn't think of anyone else that would come close to fitting the profile unless she was an adopted sister. There was no way to match their features, as Martin had modified his so much that there was no trace of his old face left. Matthew decided to take a stab at it and see how Martin reacted. "Lee's your sister?" asked Matthew. Martin didn't even flinch at his statement.

"I think you know I won't verify that, but I will tell you that you're out of your league. She's a trained killer," he said nonchalantly. "We both were members of the UIA, and there's nothing to stop her when she puts her mind to something. She's going to destroy the Price family, and she's going to enjoy every moment. I'll take great pride in knowing she did all of it for me, and then she'll disappear without a trace, and you'll never see her again," he said, followed by what could only be described as a maniacal laugh.

"Oh! There's that crazy again," he said.

"I'm not crazy. Don't you dare call me crazy!" bellowed Martin. "You hear me, Matthew? I'm a God-damned genius! I'm ten times smarter than you!"

"Enjoy rotting in that cell, ya God damned genius!" Matthew called over his shoulder as he walked away. "Cause they're never gonna let you out."

Meeting Wells outside the jail, he peeled off the wire and handed it to him.

"So, that went fairly well," said Wells.

"Yeah, it did. I can't believe he was willing to give his sister away like that. While he didn't confirm, I believe it's Lee Cartier. She's the closest profile I can think of."

"Are you sure? If that's true, how did we overlook her?" asked Wells.

"I keep asking myself the same thing. She is lighter skinned than Martin. Her accent sounds different. More British. Do we know where she's from?"

"All of the information I have on her says she was living in the UK prior to the US, but I haven't been able to pinpoint her birthplace."

"Yeah, me neither," replied Matt. "Her background is lacking in detail, which makes me think Martin may have been truthful about her involvement in the UIA. They would have whittled her records down to the bare minimum, and then who knows what's factual?"

"I see you've been doing your homework," noted Wells. "Once a P.I., always a P.I., huh?"

"Yeah, it's a hard thing to shake once you've lived the life for as many years as I have."

"Ya got any idea where Lee is right now?"

"Not a clue," said Matt. "I think we need to get over to Alex's house and make them aware of the current situation," he replied.

"That's not possible," said Wells. "They're no longer at the house. I sent them away to a more remote location because too many people around town know where Alex lives. There were too many possible suspects."

"What?! You sent them away? What if the killer is following them?"

"Calm down; I didn't send them alone. Thompson and Marx are on their detail."

"Where are they?" asked Matt.

"They went to the family cabin this morning. I don't know if you've heard, but the mailman was killed outside Alex's house yesterday. He was carrying a bag full of threatening postcards. Each card read the same thing. They've confirmed it was a heart attack, but we believe he was injected with something due to the threatening letters.

"While you were locked up, Bell was attacked on her birthday, and the perp tried to inject her with what we believe to be the same substance. Luckily, Aiden showed up when he did and scared the person away. They dropped this odd little needle, which we now believe to hold some type of Cyanide. We've decided to go back and take another look at Linz and compare notes with what we find from the mailman's autopsy. I suspect they're going to match up perfectly."

"Why didn't anyone tell me Bell was attacked or that this mailman was killed right in front of her? It's bad enough I couldn't be with her on her birthday, but this makes it even worse. She must be a wreck. What on Earth has been going on around here?" he fumed.

"Matt, you aren't married to Bell, and you were listed as a suspect. You know the rules. This isn't hard to understand. Calm yourself down and think logically for a minute." Matt ran his hand over his head and attempted to sort the information he'd just received. He felt like it was his job to protect her, and he was failing miserably.

"Martin said that he and his sister were both members of the UIA. That would explain a lot of his capabilities over the past several years and how he eluded capture for so long. For the most part, he didn't leave evidence. Considering the death his grandfather met, it makes me wonder if he or his partner had a hand in that? At the same time, though, I don't think Martin has resorted to poison. His retaliations seem to lean more toward brute force and planned accidents, so that makes me think his sister is the one who prefers the quieter and more lethal methods of disposal since she's always been the hidden face."

"Now that we have an idea of whom and what we're dealing with, their luck is going to run out."

"What bothers me is how the UIA hasn't taken action," said Matthew. "Wouldn't you think they'd notice their rogue actions over the passing years?"

"I have no idea. They're a whole other animal compared to us." Wells scratched his head while he thought about Matt's comment. "Maybe Martin and his sister are off their radar somehow?"

"Do you know any contacts in the UIA?" He was hopeful that Wells would say yes, but the answer was a letdown.

"No, I don't. The UIA isn't like the CIA. They have their own priorities. The whole purpose is to keep peace amongst the different countries and work to diffuse situations that could cause war. They keep peace at any cost. If they dismissed Martin under positive circumstances, then they may not be keeping tabs on him."

"If that's the case, someone in that agency is a poor judge of character," said Matthew.

"That may very well be," replied Wells. "Anyway, we can speculate all we want, but the truth of the matter is, this is in our backyard right now, and we're being left to deal with it."

Matt pulled out his phone and dialed Alex's number. There was no answer. He scrolled through his contacts and dialed Bernie, but she didn't answer either. "I don't think they get much for cell service at the cabin, if I remember correctly. Bernie once commented about how they have to walk up the hill to get service when they're out there."

Wells nodded, "I'll radio Thompson. We probably should have discussed that aspect further before giving the go-ahead," he commented.

"Let's just go," said Matthew impatiently. "I know how to get there. Bell drove us once so I could see where she spent her childhood summers. I'm pretty sure I remember the way."

"Just slow your roll," replied Wells. "You haven't been cleared yet. You shouldn't even be a part of this. You can't leave town, remember?"

"Come on, Wells, this is a load of crap, and you know it. The longer we wait, the worse this will get."

"I know, Matt, but the law is the law, and right now, I have nothing to prove your innocence. For all I know, you and Martin could have planned that exchange before his arrest."

"I know you don't really believe that," replied Matthew, shaking his head.

"No, but it still doesn't clear your name. I need concrete proof."

"Fine," he said in defeat. "I'll go home and wait. Call me as soon as you have anything."

"I'll see what I can do," replied Wells. "Your car is parked up the block. I had the boys bring it over when we found out you were being released. Keys are under the floormat." Looking down at his phone, he was too busy playing with his GPS to notice the look of stubborn determination on Matthew's face.

"Thanks," said Matt as he headed for his car. There was no way he was going home. The P.I. in him said he needed to act now, or he was going to miss something big.

Opening the back door to his Lexus, he paused to take off his button-down shirt and replaced it with an older black t-shirt. He smiled, thinking about Bell and how she liked to run her hand over his pecs whenever he wore his fitted tees. He missed that girl like crazy and wanted more than anything else to prove his innocence to her.

Shuffling things around the backseat of his car, he noticed a worn pair of work pants. He debated for a moment but quickly moved on. He was already wearing an older pair of jeans, but he decided to replace his loafers with black steel-toed boots. He liked to be prepared for anything, and at this point, he had no idea what he was walking into. After making sure his laces were secure, he reached under the seat and pulled out his backup Glock and a pocket knife. He stowed the knife in his back pocket and placed the Glock in the holster already strapped to his ankle.

Smiling to himself, he climbed into the driver's seat. There was still something thrilling about private investigation. He liked that he was in charge of what he was doing and that anything could happen, though he always dreaded negative results. A small knot always appeared in the pit of his stomach when he feared for someone's life. This moment wasn't any different from any number of occasions he'd dealt with previously.

Reaching up, he grabbed his black sunglasses from the visor and placed them over his eyes. Checking for cars, he pulled away from the curb to begin his trek to the Price family cabin. He realized the trip wasn't short, but he also knew he wouldn't be going the speed limit. He didn't have time for dawdling when the woman he loved might be in trouble.

It had been hours since Bell and her siblings had arrived at the cabin. Since none of them had slept that night, they all decided to get some much-needed rest upon arrival. The cabin had five bedrooms, one of which had two sets of queen-sized bunk beds. Each room had its own ensuite bath. The rooms were rustic, with log-style bed frames and plush down comforters. There was a full-size kitchen with a built-in bar area and a mudroom with a washer and dryer. The cabin had all the amenities of a year-round house and was on the more luxurious end, per their mother's specifications.

The Price family had once frequented their luxury cabin, but as the kids had gotten older, they disappeared to their getaway home less often. Everyone was too busy and preferred to leave the state or the country when they were able to take vacations. Now, the family mostly used the cabin for a weekend getaway once or twice a year with their friends. No one, however, had visited in well over a year, so the entire place needed a decent cleaning, which would have normally been seen to by the caretaker, given proper notice.

Bell was lying in bed, staring at the ceiling. She'd slept for several hours, and now she couldn't get herself to crawl out from under the safe, warm, oversized comforter. Bernie was lying in the bed across from her and Alex up above. They had taken the bunkroom because they all felt safer in the same place. If one person was woken by anything, they would alert the others. Bell felt like she was part of a prairie dog colony. She hoped she wouldn't have to squeak to let her brother and sister know danger was approaching. She laughed to herself while she thought about the prairie dogs.

"What are you giggling about," asked Alex as his head appeared over the side of the upper bunk.

"I was imagining we were prairie dogs and that we would have to squeak to let each other know if danger was approaching."

"My older sister is a weirdo," said Bernie sleepily. She yawned and gave a big stretch as she rolled over to look at Alex and Bell. "Should we get up and do a little cleaning and unpacking?"

"Do we have to?" whined Bell. "I'm so comfy."

"No, we don't have to, but if we don't, things aren't going to get done, and we'll likely starve to death by nightfall," exaggerated Alex. "I'm hungry. Let's clean the kitchen first and then get some grub."

Bernie had already jumped out of bed and was rummaging through her bag for a bandana to tie her hair back. She wrapped her hair and tied a knot at the front of her head. "Let's get to it. Chop, chop," she clapped her hands at Bell and Alex." Alex dropped himself down from the top bunk and walked out of the room.

"Fine," said Bell, "I guess I'll get up." Bernie took a flying leap, landing on all fours next to Bell on the bed. She proceeded to bounce obnoxiously up and down. "I said I'm going!" yelled Bell.

"Not fast enough, sister!" She bounced off the bed and ran out of the room. Considering the craziness, it was nice to see that her family could maintain a sense of humor. She recognized that people without siblings would never understand, but a certain connection allowed them to remain children at heart whenever they were together. They had an unspoken understanding of one another. It was easy to recall the silliness of childhood, even as an adult, when you had siblings with whom you remained close.

Bell climbed out of bed and headed for the kitchen. She was already wearing her favorite ratty sweatpants and her dad's old t-shirt. Though she felt warmer and as happy as possible, given the events of the past twenty-four hours, she still felt a chill that ran deep into her bones. She shuddered as the memories of the past day replayed in her head. Losing Kirk had been surreal. She knew his death would haunt her forever, but she couldn't have stopped it from happening. She could only hope they would catch no one else in the crosshairs.

"Here, Bell." Alex handed her an oversized cup of steaming coffee. "I don't know where these mugs came from, but they're comically large."

Bernie was trying to hold back laughter without success. "They're twenty-four ounces. I bought them and put them here after that Christmas when mom was ranting about all the coffee mugs being too small. I thought it would be funny when she opened the cabinet to find all the eleven-ounce mugs missing and replaced with extra-large ones."

Bell smiled at her sister and the memory of their mom's rant. "She would have loved it."

"That was the last Christmas we all spent together, wasn't it?" asked Alex. "That was, what, three years ago?"

Bernie nodded. "Yeah, it feels like ten years ago. I was shocked she agreed to come on that trip. That was when they decided to give it another shot."

"Yeah, that worked out well," said Bell. She remembered the trip like it had happened yesterday. After a week and a half together at the cabin, their mother and father had gotten into a fight, and she remembered Mom screaming about how their father cared so little that he didn't even notice she was unhappy or cheating. They argued for an hour, and then their mother got into her car and drove off into the night. It was New Year's Eve, and they awoke the next morning to find her gone. Their father was heartbroken yet again because of Mariska.

Interjecting into her thoughts, she heard Alex say, "Despite how it ended, it was a pretty great Christmas."

"Yeah," said Bernie. "It was nice and festive."

"What was your favorite part?" asked Bell. "Mine was watching *Christmas Vacation*, *Holiday Inn*, and *White Christmas* as a family."

"I do love those movies," said Alex.

"I enjoyed decorating the cabin and Christmas trees," said Bernie. She really got into the holiday spirit. Bell wasn't surprised that decorating was her sister's favorite part.

"I enjoyed the elaborate meals we cooked together and the awesome wine pairings," said their foodie brother.

"Yeah, the duck that year was exquisite," noted Bernie.

"Overall, I most enjoyed that we were all together," commented Bell.

"Yeah," said Bernie, pulling her brother and sister in for a hug. "I miss that." Alex and Bell both nodded their agreement.

Their hug came to a close as a knock sounded at the door. "Do you think that's Marx or Thompson?" asked Bernie. She headed for the door and slowly began to open it because there wasn't a peephole. "What are you guys doing here?" Opening the door all the way so her siblings could see who she was speaking to, she waved to Thompson, who was escorting the unexpected guests into the cabin.

"Hi, Bell," said Lee. Torrence, who was standing with her, gave a wave in her direction.

"Yeah, what brings you here, and how did you find us?" asked Alex.

A look of confusion crossed Torrence's face. "You invited us for a weekend getaway."

"What? No, how did I invite you?" asked Alex.

"You emailed us," she replied.

"Yeah," said Lee. She pulled her phone from her purse and walked toward Alex. "Here," she said, handing him the phone. Bell could tell Lee was slightly concerned as she watched Alex read the email.

"Yeah, that definitely looks like an invitation, but I didn't send it to you."

Torrence's expression changed to that of confusion. "Who sent it then?"

"I don't know, but I would guess the same person who sent Jordan the date invitation from me," said Bell.

Alex was shaking his head. "This just gets creepier and creepier. This person is hacking into our accounts. What all do they know about us?"

Thompson's mouth puckered, and he shook his head. "Not to scare you, but it's more along the lines of, what don't they know?"

Torrence had the usual look of confusion on her face. "Wait, what's going on? We weren't invited here this weekend?" she asked.

"No, sorry," said Alex.

"Does that mean we drove here for nothing?" pouted Torrence.

"No," said Bell, "you can stay."

"Bell!" exclaimed Bernie. "Are you sure that's a good idea considering our current situation?"

"What situation?" asked Torrence.

"You aren't that dumb, are you?" asked Bernie. "We're being targeted by someone. The same person who killed Bradley, Linz, and yesterday, Alex's postman."

"Bernie!" exclaimed Bell. "Be respectful." Torrence was glaring at her sister. The two had never bonded over anything, but they were usually civil with one another. Clearly, the stress was causing her sister to lash out.

Lee frowned. "I can't believe someone would kill your postman just to get to you. Seriously? That seems a little far-fetched, don't you think?"

"Sounds like a psychopath," said Torrence, "something straight outta the movies."

"Yeah, except that it's our lives," replied Bernie, irritated.

"I say we let them stay. No reason we can't try to enjoy the weekend," said Bell. "Alex, why don't you choose a room for each of them and let them get settled."

"Okay, you two, follow me." He set off down the hall with Torrence and Lee in tow.

Bell waved Thompson and Bernie in closer and, lowering her voice, said, "I think it's better to keep our enemies close. Since we don't know exactly who the killer is, but they obviously know where we are, let's play along and hope this person exposes themselves at some point so we can end this."

"I'm not so sure that's a good idea. What if someone tries to poison you or inject you with a needle while you're sleeping?" asked Thompson.

"All three of us will stay in the bunk room. You and Marx can stand guard in the house so that we aren't attacked in our sleep. We'll be fine," replied Bell.

"Okay, you just call out if you need anything. We'll be checking in frequently, and we will definitely be staying in the cabin tonight to stand watch either way."

"Sounds like a plan," said Bernie, though she didn't sound overly convinced.

Thompson paused for a moment. "Bernadette, I know we've had little chance to talk, but know that I came to Bradley's funeral. I paid my respects and slipped out after the service. You all were so busy talking to guests that I knew it wasn't the time for new introductions, considering the length and background of the story. I'm sorry I couldn't have been more help with the arrangements. I took a while to come to grips with things. Bradley had only just come into my life. Our time was too short, and the loss was heartbreaking."

"Even if you had made yourself known sooner, I wasn't in a functioning state until after the funeral. I'm glad you could be there. It would have meant a lot to Bradley."

"Thanks. I know things have been crazy, but once they settle down, we'll have to grab a cup of coffee and share stories."

"You've got a deal," replied Bernie.

Thompson turned to leave the cabin, and a second knock sounded at the door. He opened it, and yet another surprise presented itself. Standing on the porch were Aiden, Hector, and Audra.

"Let me guess," said Bernie, "You all received an email invite as well?"

"Wow, Bernie, you sound so happy to see us," replied Hector.

"It's not that," said Bell, "we are happy to see you, but we didn't send the invitation. Someone has hacked our emails, and they want you to be here for whatever reason."

"That's a little scary," said Hector.

"It sounds like a recipe for trouble. We should go," replied Audra. "I don't want to be here. This doesn't seem safe."

"Or we can stay and see what happens," replied Aiden. "I'm not afraid of any ghosts. Especially ones that have flesh," he laughed.

"Do you have some sort of death wish? Haven't you noticed the bad things that have been happening to this family?" asked Hector. "I would go, but I can't leave Alex. You should go, both of you."

"I'm staying," said Aiden. "I care about this family, and if I can help, I will."

Audra had backed herself out the door. "Aren't you the heroic sort," she said with disgust. "I'm out, sorry. Tell Alex I apologize." She stepped off the porch and jogged toward her car.

"We don't blame you," called Bernie. "We'd leave too if we could."

"Love you, glad you understand," she called over her shoulder.

"What's going on?" asked Alex as he walked back into the room with Lee and Torrence. "Hector? You received an email, too? I don't want you involved in this," he said with concern. "You need to leave."

"Yes, I received an email, and no, I'm not leaving. You know I want to be here for you no matter what." Turning toward the girls, he said, "Lee and Torrence, if you ladies want to leave, it might be in your best interest." The look on his face was serious. Bell wondered if there was any possibility that the killer could be him or Aiden. The whole situation was maddening. No one ever wanted to accuse someone they thought to be a friend of anything bad. But, if it wasn't one of their friends, who was it?

"No, I'm staying," said Lee. She reached out and put her hand on Bell's shoulder. "I want to be supportive of your family."

"Trust me," said Bernie, "if you leave, we won't think any less of you."

Bell looked at each of their friends. Most likely, the killer would stay due to ulterior motives. She found herself praying they would all leave, but they all wanted to help. It was most likely one of them, which made her feel betrayed on a deepening level.

Torrence shrugged. "I made the decision to stay when I put my belongings in your guest room. No harsh words from your sister will scare me away from you in your moment of need." She glared back at Bernie.

"Thanks, Tor. I appreciate you wanting to support us," replied Bell.

"Let's get this day started and make some breakfast," said Bernie. "I'm starving." She walked into the kitchen and took the eggs and bacon out of the cooler. "Alex, why don't you whip up your awesome cinnamon chocolate chip pancakes."

"Will do," replied her brother as he joined her in the kitchen.

Several hours passed. The group enjoyed a nice brunch and then spent the afternoon cleaning and organizing the cabin. Bernie was making her father's famous veggie lasagna, cheese-stuffed meatballs, and spaghetti with garlic bread. Dinner would be an Italian feast, and Bell was excited to be eating Bernie's cooking. The therapist had mentioned that things such as cooking could be a great release for Bernie, and that would help her deal with some of the stress in her life.

Watching her sister work, Bell grabbed a bottle of wine from the rack. "You think this is any good?" she held out the bottle for her sister to see.

"Yeah, that pinot noir should be awesome. Definitely pour it into my glass," she said with enthusiasm.

Grabbing a corkscrew, she popped the cork out of the bottle, poured a nice healthy serving for her sister, and then a small amount for herself. She didn't want to go overboard when she didn't know their company's intentions. Looking toward the living room, she called out, "Would anyone else like a glass of wine?" The friends were gathered around the coffee table where they were intently working at putting together a large jigsaw puzzle.

"Hector and I would love some," said Alex.

"Me too," replied Lee.

"I'm good," said Aiden. "I could use more food before I start drinking wine."

"I'm going to pass for now," stated Torrence. "Although, I would take a vodka and soda water if you have it."

"Spoken like a true model," commented Bernie under her breath.

"Bern," said Bell, "knock it off. What's your deal with her anyway?"

Bernie turned toward her and heatedly said, "She's a stereotype, Bell. She's precisely what's wrong with the modeling world. She walks around with a stick up her butt, even though she's a shorty. She pretends she's better than others. She's rude and dumb, and she's most likely bulimic or something. On top of that, my gut says not to trust her."

"Okay then," said Bell. "You don't like her."

"Nope, I don't like her, but I'll try to curb my lack of enthusiasm and play nice."

Bell was feeling a little exasperated with her sister's newly admitted distaste. "I guess that's all I can hope for. "Cheers," she said, clanking glasses with Bernie who was scowling at the living room.

Bell poured three glasses of wine and set to making the vodka and soda water. Alex and Hector retrieved the beverages and delivered them.

"Aiden, would you like something else to drink?" called Bernie.

"No, thanks," he replied.

An hour and a half later, everyone was again seated at the table, enjoying the awesome meal Bernie had prepared.

"Bern, you're a great cook," said Aiden, cutting into his fourth meatball.

"You have a healthy appetite, boyfriend," commented Hector as he playfully punched Aiden in the shoulder.

"Well, I haven't eaten much today, so I have lots of extra room for food right now." He laughed.

"You know it doesn't work like that, right?" asked Alex.

"What? It doesn't?" questioned Aiden, his voice exaggerated.

"Nope. Your stomach is the same size either way. As a matter of fact, contrary to popular belief, and from what I understand, stomachs don't even shrink," noted Alex.

"Wow, that is interesting," said Torrence. "I thought for sure my avoiding food was causing my stomach to shrink. It feels like it holds less."

"That's probably just your appetite resetting," replied Alex.

"Very interesting," said Aiden. "So, I should have stopped two meatballs ago, huh?"

"Nah, man, eat as much as you like." Hector smiled back at him.

"I agree. It's hard to stop when the food's so awesome," replied Alex.

Bernadette was grinning from ear to ear. "Thanks, guys."

After the dishes were done and everything was cleaned up, the crew decided to play poker. The siblings continued with their decision to keep a close eye on the group, and what better way than to engage everyone in a game together. Alex located the poker set, and he and Hector began divvying up the chips.

Lee and Aiden were strong Poker players and definitely gave the Price family a run for their money. Bernie put the biggest fight. During one hand, she and Aiden went head-to-head, bidding each other up. In the end, Bernie won the hand with four jacks.

"That girl is as sly as a fox." Aiden winked at Bernie. Torrence snorted at the comment and shook her head slightly. She looked angry. Bell didn't understand the issues between her sister and Tor, but they absolutely needed to get over it if they were going to continue working together.

The night proceeded on. The friends laughed and joked, and the siblings pretended to enjoy themselves, though each was on their guard. Bell began to doubt that anything negative would happen, and part of her wanted nothing more than for her friends to be innocent. She was happy that everyone seemed to be having fun.

At seven, the officers came inside and posted out at separate ends of the house, keeping an eye on things. Marx was on the phone with his ex and could be heard screaming into the receiver at one point. Thompson dropped what he was doing and went to deal with the situation. The group heard Thompson tell Marx to stop, but the rest of the conversation was muted. Five minutes later, Thompson returned to the front of the house.

Fifteen minutes after the officers had come inside, dark clouds rolled in, and the weather turned hazardous. A torrential downpour was slamming the cabin's tin roof, and thunder rattled the wine glasses hanging in the kitchen. It had been a while since Bell had heard such a storm. Alex dealt the next hand, and the lights went out.

"Oh man," said Bernie. "Whenever this happens, we lose power for hours at a time."

"That's not good," replied Aiden. "Do you have a backup generator?"

Alex shook his head. "No, but we have two lanterns in the garage, although I think the propane might be in the shed at the back of the lot."

"Where's the breaker box?" asked Thompson. "I think I should take a look at it to make sure it really is the storm and not someone tampering with the lights."

"It's in the garage," stated Bell.

"I'll take care of that," opted Marx, who had appeared in the room with his flashlight. He and Thompson promptly headed out the door to the adjoining garage.

"I have a battery-operated lantern in my car," said Lee. "I can go grab it quick."

"Bernie, help me get the candles," said Alex.

"I'll open another bottle of wine," said Bell. She didn't know what else to do at that moment.

"I think we're out," replied Hector.

"Oh, okay, we have more in the cellar," she replied.

"This place has a cellar?" asked Hector.

Bell nodded at him. "Kind of. It's pretty small and meant mostly for fruit, but we also store wine down there."

"Do you want any help?" asked Hector.

"Nah, I should be okay; I have to go outside to get to it, and there's no point in both of us getting wet," she insisted as she got up.

"I'd love to see what other wine options you have if you don't mind my tagging along," said Torrence.

"Okay, sure," she agreed, heading toward the front door. "Just a warning, you're going to get wet. The cellar is located on the side of the house."

"No biggie," replied Torrence, "I brought extra clothes."

Chapter Fourteen

Outside the cabin, Matthew had just pulled into the driveway. He was shocked to see Lee outside in the rain. She was rummaging through the back of her car. He pulled up next to her and cut the engine. Before exiting his vehicle, he reached down and grabbed the Glock from his ankle. He wasn't going to take any chances.

"Hey," he called out over the roar of the storm.

Not hearing his car in the loud rain, Lee was startled and slammed her head into the trunk. "You scared me half to death!" she yelled.

"Interesting!" he hollered back as he pointed the gun at her.

"Why is that interesting?" she demanded loudly.

"Because I know who you are, and I would think you'd be a little more guarded."

Lee whipped around to face Matthew. Squinting through the rain, she advanced on him, apparently not noticing the gun. "What was that?" she asked as she stood before him. She was close enough to touch the Glock. "Why are you pointing a gun at me?"

"I said, I know who you are."

"You do?" her voice remained even and steady. "Yes. You're Martin's sister. I should have figured this out much sooner, but the only picture I'd ever seen of you was from when you were roughly four years old."

"You don't know what you're talking about," she stated sincerely.

"So, you're not Martin's sister?"

"Yes, I am Martin's sister, but I'm not an active part of Martin's life. I had a huge falling out with him years ago, which is why you never saw me around." Pausing for a moment, she reached up and pushed her rain-drenched bangs out of her eyes. "You were Martin's roommate. You two were thicker than thieves in college, so it stands to reason that maybe you would be the person most likely to help him carry out all of his crazy schemes."

"Bull!" yelled Matt. "You and I both know you're the one who killed Bradley and all those other innocent victims. You were a part of the UIA along with Martin. While you had been apart for years, you reconnected and decided to join forces. I spoke to him earlier today, and he was more than willing to tell me how his sister was going to take care of everything for him."

"You're lying!" Leaping forward, she dropped down and kicked his legs out from under him. Matthew fell to the ground, cracking his head on his own bumper. The gun flew into the air, landing on the ground a short distance from him. Lee paused momentarily to assess, but Matt didn't move. He had blacked out from the hit to his head.

Hurrying, she grabbed some bungee cords from her trunk and bound Matthew's wrists and ankles together. Once satisfied with her knots, she grabbed the gun and the lantern and bolted for the house just as Bell and Torrence appeared in the front yard.

Bell waved at Lee. "Hey! Where's the lantern?"

"I have it right here!" Lee screamed over a loud crack of thunder. "Do you want it right now?"

"Yeah, I'm trying to get wine out of the cellar. Silly me, I didn't think about the fact that I would need light down there as well." Looking past Lee, she noticed a car that looked a lot like Matthew's. "Is Matt here?" she asked as Lee closed the distance between them.

"Yeah, but no need to worry, he's unconscious."

"What do you mean *no need to worry*? Why is he unconscious?" asked Bell.

"He pulled a gun on me. I think he's lost his mind. We need to get Marx and Thompson out here. I secured him with bungee cords from my trunk," she replied.

"Why would he pull a gun on you?" asked Torrence.

"It's a long story."

Torrence frowned at her. "Hm, you think maybe it's because he knows you're Martin's sister?"

"What?" Bell stepped back from both women and stared accusingly at Lee. "What is she talking about?"

"How do you know that?" asked Lee. "I haven't told anyone that information. I didn't want anyone to know."

Bell was now visibly shaking. She pointed her finger at Lee. "You stay away from me. You're as sick and twisted as Martin. Why? What happened in your family that would cause you to become so unbelievably deranged?" she asked as a fearful tear ran down her cheek.

"Bell, I'm not the killer. I didn't do any of this."

"Really?" asked Torrence. "You seem the most likely suspect."

"How long have you known that she's Martin's sister?" snapped Bell.

"I didn't know for sure, but I suspected. She just confirmed it," replied Torrence.

"I'm not the killer, Bell. You have to believe me. Martin and I had a falling out years ago. I found out he was taking advantage of women, and I wanted nothing to do with him."

"Who, other than Martin's sister, would have a reason to back him and protect him?" asked Torrence. "She and Martin were part of the same organization even."

Realization flashed across Lee's face. "So, help me," said Lee. She raised the gun and pointed it at Torrence. "You're getting on my last nerve, bimbo. Bell, you have to believe me when I say I would never hurt you. I absolutely adore you. If I'm to blame, how does she even know Martin had a sister?"

"Oh, my God, this is not happening," said Bell. "I don't know what to think about either of you." She backed herself farther away from Lee, but Lee advanced toward her and Torrence. Lee had a murderous look on her face.

"I should shoot you," said Lee. "You don't deserve to live."

"Fine," said Bell, "take your revenge and shoot me, but please, leave my family alone. They've been through enough. Bernie, especially, has been through enough." She noticed Lee was looking at her with confusion. Torrence, taking advantage of the distraction, leaped at Martin's sister with the ferocity of a lion. The two women fell to the ground. The gun flew into the air and landed five feet away from them. Bell stared in horror as Torrence overtook Lee and was on top of her, landing one swift blow after another while Lee tried to block. Bell couldn't stop staring at the spectacle. She'd never seen two women fighting so viciously. They looked like trained killers.

Shifting her weight, Lee managed to trap one of Torrence's legs, forcing her off to the side. Before Torrence could retaliate, Lee swung her leg around and clocked Torrence in the side of the head, sending her toppling over onto her left side. Turning around, Lee began to scurry for the gun, but realizing what was happening, Bell grabbed Lee's legs, giving Torrence enough time to pull herself together and get to the gun first.

"Funny how these things play out," said Torrence, pointing the gun toward Lee. "I don't think anyone will be hurt if I shoot you. I'd probably be doing a lot of people a favor."

"Please don't," said Bell. "She should go to trial just like her brother."

"I'm so sorry," said Lee. "I feel like I've let you down. She's not talking to me. She's talking to you, Bell." Bell let go of Lee's legs, and her words began to sink in.

Torrence laughed as she moved closer.

"You seriously aren't the killer?" Bell asked.

Lee shook her head no.

"She's just a sad pawn. She doesn't have a brilliant mind like her brother, but I do," replied Torrence. "It was you that got Martin arrested. If it hadn't been for you, he'd still be free, but that tape," she hissed. "That tape was the missing piece to the puzzle. It's entirely your fault in the end. Bernie could never be as guilty as you, and for that, you'll be executed, and it's going to feel fantastic!" she squealed as she released the safety on the gun.

Bell was frozen in place. Every second felt like an hour. She heard Lee exhale as if she'd been holding her breath, and then she heard a whooshing sound. She watched as the vengeful look on Torrence's face went blank, and her body fell toward the ground. It seemed like forever before she landed with a sickening thud. Behind Torrence, in the distance, she could see Aiden lowering his firearm and Matthew taking off at a sprint in her direction. In the next moment, she found herself wrapped tightly in Lee's arms. She couldn't move her body even if she wanted to. Shock and bewilderment had taken control.

"It's okay," soothed Lee. "I've got you. You're safe now."

Chapter Fifteen

Fifteen minutes after the shot was fired, the entire group gathered in the living room while Thompson and Marx secured the crime scene and waited for the ambulance and forensics team to arrive.

"I meant what I said. I care about you, but I would have taken even stronger precautions if I'd realized sooner that Torrence was Martin's partner and not Matthew," said Lee. "For that, I'm sorry."

Finding her words, Bell spoke. "Will you please explain all of this to me? I feel like this is some weird dream I'm unable to wake up from."

"Have you heard of the UIA?" asked Aiden.

"Yeah, briefly," she replied. "Is it like the CIA?"

"There are some similarities, but not the same. The United Intelligence Agency," stated Bernie. Bell was surprised her sister had heard of it. "There are sectors in every country, and they're supposed to work unbiasedly to maintain peace across the world."

"So, all of this started with the UIA," said Aiden. "Martin, Torrence, Lee, and I were all part of the agency. Lee, here, was brought on when she was 17 after her brother had already been a member for a year."

"I was on a very destructive path in life, and my parents were both dead. My uncle didn't know how to handle me anymore, so knowing that my grandfather's good friend had found Martin a place in the UIA, he reached out to that same friend, who was more than willing to help. The UIA was the best thing that ever happened to me because they provided me with worldly knowledge, made me an upstanding citizen, and taught me how to fight and defend myself, all while making the world a better place."

"You're Martin's sister?" asked Bernie.

"Unfortunately, yes," replied Lee. "But I'm nothing like Martin. When I was young, I wanted so badly to be with him and my grandfather in America. My family was poor, and there were few opportunities for women in my village. I realized at a young age that I wanted something different. When the UIA took me in, I was sent on different retreats in the US, and I visited my brother. I quickly realized that something was very wrong with him. He was greedy and cared more about money and recognition than he did about family or changing the world. At first, I wanted to trust him, but there were always things in his history that didn't add up. Many deaths from heart attacks lay in his wake, and when my grandfather died of such, it was the last straw.

"I confronted Martin at the funeral, and while he didn't admit to doing it, he didn't deny it either. I realized he was connected to the mysterious deaths, and that same day, I told him I wanted nothing more to do with him. I left and never looked back until I heard he'd been honorably discharged from the UIA for post-traumatic stress. Martin is a sociopath. I never for one second believed there was anything honorable about the events that led up to his discharge, but my superiors had no reason to believe differently at the time."

"How does Torrence fit into this whole picture?" asked Alex.

"Torrence is known in the agency as Fox Whisper. She was involved in the event that led to Martin's honorable discharge and her own. While we knew her name, neither Lee nor I had ever worked with her and couldn't access photographs. The UIA is very secretive and tries to keep its staff off of all imaging software for their own safety, and that information is not released unless it is proven that the agent has gone rogue and is a threat to society. In her case, it was never proven until now," said Aiden.

"So, you're also a member of the UIA?" asked Bernie.

"Yes, I'm actually Lee's partner," replied Aiden.

"So, how did you end up here?" asked Bell.

"After my falling out with Martin, I still kept tabs on him. When other people started disappearing in his wake, I decided to take a sabbatical from the agency to do my own research. I wanted to figure out Martin's motives and to collect evidence to build a case against him for the UIA," said Lee. "I, as you already know, ended up in your family's agency around the same time Martin came into your lives. Martin, at times, does some pretty stupid things, but for the most part, he has covered his tracks quite thoroughly. I think when things hit the fan with Bernie, he started to get careless. He was thoroughly confused by the fact that she would not conform to what he wanted, which drove him mad."

"Aiden, why did you come?" asked Bernie.

"I grew concerned when Lee didn't return after a few months. I wanted to find out what she was up to. When I realized she was investigating her brother, I confronted her. I refused to leave, knowing that she would most likely need backup. At the time, neither of us had any idea of Torrence's involvement."

"It took a lot of work to remain hidden from Martin in regard to the agency, but he never found out I was modeling. Aiden helped notify me of his whereabouts so we wouldn't cross paths."

Aiden smiled at Bernie. "After Bradley's death, Lee and I decided together that my involvement at the club would be helpful to the whole family, though I admit there were things that got past me. Torrence was exceptionally good at covering her tracks inside and outside the UIA. She worked hard to make it look like Matthew was Martin's partner, but one thing gave her away today, and I knew at that moment that she was the one we were looking for."

"What was that?" asked Matthew.

"While we were playing poker, I made a comment to Bernie about being as sly as a fox. Because Torrence's code name was Fox Whisper, I figured that comparing Martin's wife to a fox might provoke a response from the actual Fox Whisper if that person was present, which it did. Her expression quickly changed to that of rage. I had suspected from the beginning that Fox Whisper was a woman Martin was involved with on an intimate level, but Lee was kind of stuck on the concept of you being Martin's partner since the two of you were college roommates."

"Can you blame me?" asked Lee. "It made sense."

"Oh!" exclaimed Bell. "Now I see why she hated you so much," she said to Bernie.

"Ew," replied Bernie. "I was sharing him with her?"

"Yeah, sorry kid," said Aiden.

"Wow, it's just crazy how much more was happening in the background of this whole ordeal," said Alex. "Hopefully this is the end, and we can finally stop looking over our shoulder every step we take."

Aiden nodded in understanding. "Well, Lee and I have a little agreement, and the agency is mostly onboard, though we still have a few details to iron out. We've decided to stay around a while longer to take care of the massive amount of paperwork that this situation has generated and to make sure we're certain there are no other players or loose ends to be tied up."

"Yeah, we figure it's the least we can do," said Lee, "considering it took so long for us to catch up with Martin and Torrence." Turning to Bernie and Bell, "I'm so sorry that my brother made your lives a living nightmare. If I could fix it all for you, I would."

"Thanks, Lee," said Bell. "We understand that you can't control who your family is and that you were trying to do the right thing."

"You're such a wonderful and kind person," said Lee. "I realize now that Matthew could never hurt you and that he was just misunderstood like me." She smiled at Matt. "No hard feelings?"

"No hard feelings," he replied and flashed her a smile.

"So," said Thompson, "Who's ready to go back to the station to sort all of this out?"

"Ya know," said Alex with a laugh, "I don't think that's ever going to be something that anyone is ready to do."

"It's gonna be another long night," said Bernie, shaking her head in resignation.

"Yeah," said Bell, "but this time, we get to move on with our lives, which definitely deserves a toast." The group raised their recently filled glasses. "To new beginnings," said Bell.

"To new beginnings!" they all shouted in unison.

About the Author

T.K. Ambers lives in Wisconsin with her husband and two cats, Bellatrix and Kit. Her perfect day would be spent lakeside, where she would swim, play games, and then wind down with a bonfire, s'mores, and stories told by family and friends.

www.facebook.com/HappilyWriting
https://tkambers.wixsite.com/author
www.instagram.com/tk_loves_books

Always remember, the best gift you can give an author is a review on Amazon.com.

Acknowledgements

Thank you to my family & friends for their continued support.

To my editor, Kate Seger, and all the wonderful authors who have written the stories I've fallen in love with over the years. You have helped to mold me into the author I am today. I am thankful to have found you.

Made in the USA
Monee, IL
04 March 2024